PRAISE FOR CHRISTO

"Christopher Golden's storytelling is spellbinding. His novels capture the charming mystique that permeates New England, to which he adds a shuddering dose of the occult."

—*Boston Magazine*

"A new book by Christopher Golden means only one thing: the reader is in for a treat. His books are rich with texture and character, always inventive, and totally addictive."

—**Charles de Lint**

"Christopher Golden is one of the most hard-working, smartest, and most talented writers of his generation. Everything he writes glows with imagination."

—**Peter Straub**

"In *Baltimore*, Golden's popular style is impeccable, and horror comics creator Mignola's copious illustrations confirm the tale's dark atmosphere throughout, from no-man's-land to the old inn to the houses and graveyards where the vampire is encountered. A new classic of vampire literature."

—*Booklist*

"Christopher Golden is an imaginative and prodigious talent who never lets genre boundaries hold him back."

—**Douglas Clegg**

CHRISTOPHER GOLDEN

TELL MY SORROWS TO THE STONES

ChiZine Publications

FIRST EDITION

978-1-77148-153-3

Distributed in Canada by
HarperCollins Canada Ltd.
1995 Markham Road
Scarborough, ON M1B 5M8
Toll Free: 1-800-387-0117
e-mail: hcorder@harpercollins.com

Distributed in the U.S. by
Diamond Book Distributors
1966 Greenspring Drive
Timonium, MD 21093
Phone: 1-410-560-7100 x826
e-mail: books@diamondbookdistributors.com

Library and Archives Canada Cataloguing in Publication

Golden, Christopher
    Tell my sorrows to the stones / Christopher Golden.

Short stories.
Issued also in electronic format.
ISBN 978-1-77148-153-3

    I. Title.

PS3557.O35825T44 2013   813'.54   C2013-900801-2

CHIZINE PUBLICATIONS
Toronto, Canada
www.chizinepub.com
info@chizinepub.com

Edited by Brett Alexander Savory
Copyedited and proofread by Michael Matheson

 Canada Council   Conseil des Arts
for the Arts   du Canada

We acknowledge the support of the Canada Council for the Arts which last year invested $20.1 million in writing and publishing throughout Canada.

Published with the generous assistance of the Ontario Arts Council.

CHRISTOPHER GOLDEN

TELL MY SORROWS TO THE STONES

"Therefore I tell my sorrows to the stones;
Who, though they cannot answer my distress,
Yet in some sort they are better than the tribunes,
For that they will not intercept my tale:
When I do weep, they humbly at my feet
Receive my tears and seem to weep with me."

—William Shakespeare, *Titus Andronicus*

I once wrote a love note to my wife that began with the words "Every song is about you." That isn't true of my stories, of course—don't get the wrong idea—but when it comes time to dedicate my books, I always think of Connie first. A collection of short stories is like the strange history of a period in a writer's life, but she has been there since before my writing life even began, and so every piece of my authorial history is also our history. And thus, this one is—

For Connie.
Always.

CONTENTS

A BOX OF CHOCOLATES
AN INTRODUCTION BY CHERIE PRIEST

Christopher Golden is a twisted, sneaky, shape-shifting wizard, and if you didn't know that already then you'd best learn it now—before you start reading *Tell My Sorrows to the Stones*. Because whatever you're expecting, this isn't it.

Unless, of course, you're expecting an assortment of deliciously evil vignettes. In that case, you're right on target—so dig in. But if you're not quite familiar with the wizard in question, or if you just can't decide if this is the collection for you, then let me ask you this: Would you like to be kept awake at night, turning a story over and over in your mouth, tasting it long after you've put the book aside because goddammit, it just isn't finished with you yet?

Well then. Welcome aboard.

These stories are terribly wonderful, each and every one. They'll rev your engine, break your heart, and stop it, too. They'll worry you, walk with you, and make you wonder how much is true and how much is merely a small spell, cast with mischief and malice. They'll leave you second-guessing your eyes and ears, double-checking the lights and shadows. You'll listen for that sound again, and jump when you hear it . . . or swallow hard when you don't, in case it wasn't your imagination and you're not alone after all.

Which is not to say that all these stories are all the same, or even necessarily alike.

No, this is a mighty fine grab-bag with a full range of genres and tricks on display. One hesitates to resort to the old chestnut about "something for everyone"—really, one should be smacked for even considering it—so let us say instead that there's something for everyone with a creepy little dark spot somewhere at the bottom of the soul. Or possibly a horny spot. Some of these are pretty hot. (And kind of messed up.)

So pick your poison. In this assembly you'll find legends both urban and rural, the kind that lead drunk teenagers onto train tracks—or keep smarter locals away. You'll meet monsters from around the world and unnervingly close to home. Here there be demons and demigods who make bargains you'll regret for a lifetime, however long that turns out to be.

And oh, you'll find some ghosts. The ghosts are my favourites.

Keep your eyes open for the lost miner and the cowboy, and don't skip the gothic tales with the family trees that twist and bend, and maybe break when no one's looking. The dead are everywhere, and they aren't always friendly.

In short, this is one sexy stack of screwed-up stories and you should absolutely read the shit out of it. But maybe turn on the lights first. Make sure no one's looking over your shoulder. Fix a drink. Settle in.

And *enjoy*.

—Cherie Priest

ALL ABOARD

That dreadful autumn, Sarah Cooper woke nearly every night in the small hours of the morning and lay in the dark, back toward her husband, the memory of their dead son filling the space between them.

During the day the tension did not weigh so heavily. Sarah and Paul wandered the house only dimly aware of one another, ghosts haunting their own marriage. Resentment and blame hung in the air like static building before a thunderstorm. Sarah knew that she ought to try to comfort her husband, but Paul did not seek her out, nor did she look for solace in his arms. Cruel and capricious happenstance had taken Jonah from them—a bacterial infection, a spiked fever, an ambulance too slow to arrive—but they had to hold someone responsible, and each found fault with the other, and guilt in the mirror.

They couldn't stay in this house much longer. Sarah would never survive it. Fifty-seven Brook Street existed now as a museum of sorrow. Jonah had bounced on the sofa, bumped his head on the coffee table, marched his walker across the kitchen tiles as a baby, and slept in his parents' bed almost as many nights as his own. The toys had all been packed away, but his room remained with its books and stuffed polar bear and the dinosaur border that ran along the top of the bedroom walls. Sarah kept that door closed, but could not bring herself to take down the pictures in the living room and the downstairs hall and from the bureau in her bedroom. Her hairbrush had brushed Jonah's hair. His Spider-Man cup hid at the back of a kitchen cabinet, waiting to be remembered; waiting to remind her.

How did Paul stand it? Sarah didn't know. They avoided the conversation most of the time. That seemed even worse because it felt like they were trying to pretend Jonah had never been there—

that they did not grieve. But Paul made an effort to talk around the absence of their son, just as he usually avoided meeting her eyes.

By October, they spoke only when absolutely necessary.

When Sarah found the fuzzy Scooby-Doo costume she had bought Jonah over the summer, unable to resist even though Halloween had been months away, she crushed it against her chest and wept into the costume, brown fabric soaking up her tears. Then she put it into a box of Jonah's things that she planned to donate to the Salvation Army. She never mentioned it to Paul, and as Halloween approached, he never asked.

In the second week of October, she woke in the night with only the glow of a distant streetlamp filtering through the window. It must have been two or three o'clock in the morning. After so many weeks of such awakenings, she knew sleep would not be in any hurry to return so she lay and listened to Paul's rhythmic breathing.

The gulf between them had grown over the weeks since Jonah's death, expanding a little at bedtime every night. They hadn't had sex in all that time, though there had been times in the small hours of the morning when she had needed so badly to be held, to be touched, to be loved. But night after night they lay back to back, shoulder and neck muscles bunched with tension and expectation, and they edged further away, widening the gap between them.

A glow of moonlight draped across the shadows of their bedroom and the gauzy curtains billowed with the crisp autumn breeze. Sarah lay on her side and stared at the windows, at the curtains, and at nothing. The windows rattled with powerful gusts—the weather changing, winter drawing nearer—and she heard the skittering of dry leaves across the driveway and the front walk.

Then, off in the distance, the lonely whistle of a train.

Sarah had heard the sound every night for nearly two weeks. At first it had been barely audible, so that she had trouble determining its origin. Each night it seemed to become louder, though of course the train tracks couldn't be any nearer. In all the years she had lived in Dunston, she could not recall ever having heard the sound before, never mind seen a train. It must, she told herself, only run late at night when the town slept, when only insomniacs and grieving mothers might hear it.

She listened as the whistle faded and felt a terrible longing, wished she were on board that train, bound for destinations unknown.

When her tears came, she let them slide down to dampen her pillow. Her husband did not stir, but Sarah was not surprised. Paul had long since stopped being stirred by her tears, even in the light of day.

She slid nearer the edge of the bed and watched the moonlight and the billowing curtains and listened to the shush of the autumn leaves blowing across the lawn. In time, sleep would claim her again, tears drying on her face.

Sarah would hear the whistle of the train in her dreams, where she held her tiny son in her arms and rocked him, singing him softly to sleep on the way to his own extinguished dreams.

The new offices of Sterling Software had been built just at the edge of town, near a narrow metal bridge across the Kenyon River. Window glass winked in the morning light as Sarah drove over the bridge, her travel mug rattling in the cup holder on the dash, spurting up a dollop of coffee.

The Kenyon River meandered southward under the bridge. In the spring it roared, but in autumn it remained a gentle whisper. She followed the road northeast on the other side, coming around a corner, all the while keeping the Sterling building in sight. It stood at the top of a hill that had been transformed into a mini-industrial park, complete with a Comfort Inn and a TGI Friday's restaurant. Sarah barely saw any of those buildings. In truth, she barely saw the road or the rich, harvest-hued foliage of the trees around her. Her focus was on driving to work, and she could do that with her mind on autopilot.

The dashboard clock read 9:12. Late again, and she felt badly about it. A tremor of discontent passed through her. Exhausted, she'd rushed to get ready, and the mirror had reflected both her tiredness—in the dark crescents beneath her eyes—and her haphazard attempt at fixing her hair and putting on makeup. *Get your life together, Sarah. You're dropping the ball.* But the advice sounded hollow. She couldn't convince herself that any of it mattered. Work. Sleep. Face. Life.

The car jittered over train tracks, causing her coffee to burble again.

Sarah frowned and tapped the brake, slowing down and glancing in her rearview mirror. She'd been over those tracks twice a day every day for more than a year, ever since Sterling had moved to the new location. There were no railroad crossing signs, no flashing lights, nothing.

Another few minutes won't matter.

She put the car in reverse and backed up, checking to make sure no other cars were approaching. At the tracks she braked again, pausing to peer both ways along the line. Grass grew up between the wooden ties. The rails themselves were dark with rust. In either direction the tracks curved away into trees and undergrowth that had begun to encroach over the years.

Sarah shook her head. No trains on this line. Not for years.

As she drove on, she could not help but glance at the mirror. The memory of the whistle from the late night train lingered, and led her to thoughts of Jonah and her dreams.

No. Work.

If she thought about Jonah, she would be useless at work. They had been more than kind, had offered her as much time as she needed to mourn. When Sarah had announced, after six weeks, that she was ready to return to her receptionist position, the office manager—Ellie Poole—had asked if she was *really ready*. Sarah had thought it a foolish question. How could she ever be ready to go to work, to put her loss behind her?

But at home all that awaited her was the museum of sorrow, the constant reminders. Her co-workers' sympathy made work little better, but at least she could find distraction there.

Sarah found a parking spot near the front of the building and climbed out. Dropping her keys, she swore as she bent to retrieve them, then slammed the door. With her purse over her shoulder and her coffee in hand, she hurried up the walk to the front doors. Inside the glass and chrome lobby, Martin stood at his security post, one ear bud of his iPod in place and the other hanging loose. When he looked up and saw her, his face blossomed into a warm smile. The young guard seemed to be the only one at Sterling who could be genuinely happy to see her without his warmth devolving into pity.

"Morning, Sarah."

"Hi, Martin."

Behind the reception desk, a secretary named Laura Rossi gave her a grim look. Ellie had obviously shanghaied her to substitute until Sarah showed up, and the wide-bottomed, curly-haired woman did not bother trying to hide her displeasure. Sarah was almost glad that Laura didn't tiptoe around her.

"Let me guess—car trouble?"

"I'm sorry, Laura. The last time, I swear."

The woman got up from the reception desk and sighed, rolling her eyes, but she waved the apology away as though Sarah's tardiness was no big deal.

"It's fine. Martin's good company."

Martin grinned broadly. "I was serenading her."

Sarah managed a thin smile. Martin liked to sing, but softly, mostly to himself. She never minded, but she suspected that someone as generally uptight as Laura would be driven near madness by the man's musical mutterings.

The phone began to ring. Laura shot it a dark look, then turned her back and went through the door into the main offices. Sarah hurried over and picked up.

"Sterling Software. Can you hold, please?" She put on her

headset, then took the caller off hold and transferred him to the northeastern sales manager.

"Some people can't seem to figure out how to use an electronic directory," Martin said.

Sarah nodded, but broke into a yawn.

"Don't do that," Martin protested, yawning in reply. "It's contagious. No fair."

"Sorry, just didn't get nearly enough sleep last night."

"Pretty much every night, isn't it?"

His face and voice were kind. The question wasn't an intrusion. Martin never intruded on her grief. If she didn't want to answer, he would not mind. But Sarah found him warm and easy to talk to.

"I fall asleep all right," she said, pushing her hair away from her face to meet his gaze. "But I wake up in the middle of the night and then it takes me an hour or so to drift off again. It's weird what you hear at night, though, y'know?"

Martin removed the ear-bud and held the cord in his hand. "I do. The quietest noise seems much louder in the middle of the night."

"Yes!" Sarah said. "During the day I can't even hear the clock ticking, but at night it's so loud. And now I hear the train every night. I almost listen for it."

The security guard gave a soft laugh and a shake of his head. "Now you're just fooling with me. That's not nice, Sarah."

She stared at him. "What do you mean?"

"Come on. The Three-Eighteen? I'm not falling for that old story. Didn't believe it when my grandmother told it, either."

A tractor trailer growled as it pulled into the parking lot and continued around past the building, headed for the loading dock in back. It distracted them both for a moment. When Sarah looked back at Martin, he was studying her curiously. She sat forward in her chair.

"What's the Three-Eighteen?"

His eyes became narrow slits in his dark face a moment and then widened with sudden realization. "You didn't grow up around here, did you? I forget sometimes."

Sarah shook her head. "Nope. My family comes from upstate New York. I moved here with my father when I was thirteen."

"Right, right. You've told me. Sorry. He worked at the mill, right?"

"Worked and died there," she said. "So what's this train thing?"

"Just a local ghost story. Most towns have a house all the kids think is haunted and I'm guessing we do, too. But the story that always gave me the creeps was about the Three-Eighteen. My grandmother used to talk about it and the counselors at camp used to tell it around the fire, along with the ones about Hatchet Mary and the Hook and that kind of thing."

Sarah frowned. "So, it's a ghost train?"

"That's the story. Passes by every night at 3:18 A.M. 'Carrying the ghosts of the ones folks can't let go of,' my Gram used to say. And it's only those folks, and people near dying themselves, who can . . ."

The words trailed off.

Breathless, Sarah stared at him. "Who can what?"

Martin gave her a sheepish grin. "Who can hear it. That's how all those old stories go, y'know? Supposed to creep us all out. That way if you hear a train whistle after dark or something that even sounds like one, you're supposed to think it's the Three-Eighteen come to collect you."

She dropped her gaze and stared at the marble tile beneath her chair.

"Sarah?"

His voice made her flinch. She looked up. "I hear the whistle every night."

Martin laughed and came over to her desk. He splayed one strong hand on the counter where people laid out their ID to be allowed inside.

"Sarah, come on. It's just a story. Whatever you're hearing, it's something else. Got to be some late night road work, smoke venting from the damn sneaker factory or something. But it's not a train, and it sure as hell ain't the Three-Eighteen."

She took a long breath and let it out with a small, self-deprecating laugh. Of course Martin was right. Sarah felt nauseous just thinking about the few moments she'd spent seriously considering the campfire tale as truth. Every town had local folklore.

"You okay?" Martin prodded. His wide eyes were full of concern. "I shouldn't even have mentioned it, but you brought up the train whistle and I just figured you were teasing me. This isn't the kind of thing you ought to be thinking about."

"I'm okay," she promised. How to explain the numbness inside and the gulf between herself and her husband? How to explain that the word 'okay' had entirely lost its meaning for her. Paul had always liked grim novels about the destruction of human society or the ecosystem or worse; he called it post-apocalyptic fiction. But Sarah was living a post-apocalyptic life. People who hadn't been through it couldn't possibly understand.

"You sure? It's only that you never seem like you're all here, if you don't mind my saying. Ellie Poole's been bitching about you coming in late and, well, looking kind of run down."

Sarah couldn't believe it. Ellie, who'd been so nice, was sniping behind her back after what she'd been through?

"Bitch," she whispered, glancing around at the doors that led into the main offices, just in case the bitch in question might walk in and overhear her. "Am I in trouble, Martin?"

"Not that I've heard. I'd have told you. But that could change."

Sarah nodded. Of course it could change. The second Ellie figured that Sarah had had enough time to mourn Jonah's death that she couldn't file a wrongful termination law suit, the witch would come gunning for her.

With a sigh, Sarah sipped from her cooling coffee. "Guess this is the last late morning for me."

A Mercedes slid through the parking lot and into a space. Martin put the single ear bud back in place. He and Sarah both watched as a man stepped out of the Mercedes and started for the front door.

"Y'know, if sleep's the issue, you oughta get your doc to prescribe something," Martin said. "I took that one with the butterfly once. You know, the one in the TV ad. Worked like a charm."

Sarah straightened her top and smoothed her skirt, trying to look as professional as she could in spite of her state of mind. As the dark-suited man from the Mercedes opened the door, she glanced at Martin.

"I tried pills. They just make me more tired in the morning," she said.

Then she smiled at the visitor. "Good morning, sir. How can I help you?"

The man spoke and she barely listened, her thoughts still on Martin's suggestion. Sleeping pills would have been such a blessing, a respite from restless nights. But the few times she had taken them, they had interfered with her dreaming. And her dreams were the only time she could be with Jonah.

Nothing mattered more than that, including her job. Ellie Poole could go to Hell.

"Have you ever heard of the Three-Eighteen?"

Paul looked up from his plate—he'd made them a risotto that had once been a favourite for both of them, but now tasted bland to Sarah. Everything tasted bland to her now.

"You mean that old story about the ghost train?"

"Yes."

He shrugged. Even his indifference had sharp edges, cutting her with disdain. "Sure. When I was a kid we'd all talk about it. Go out to the tracks. One time I camped out down there all night with Jimmy Pryce—remember Jimmy?"

Sarah shook her head. She didn't. Paul was two years older than she was. She'd only been in high school with him for his senior year and then he'd graduated. But he'd lost touch with most of his old friends over the years. Whoever this Jimmy Pryce was, he hadn't sent them a card or flowers when Jonah died. The parade of faces at the funeral were a blur to her—she couldn't remember who had been there or not—but the cards and flowers she recalled perfectly.

"No? Jimmy thought you were pretty hot when you transferred in from New York." He smiled, and perhaps for a moment there was a glimmer of hope and life in his eyes, of happier times. It dimmed, as it always would, forever after.

"Anyway, we camped out down by the tracks one night. Spent the whole time scaring the crap out of each other with flashlights and telling ghost stories. When you're a kid you believe that stuff, deep down, even though you've gotta act like you're too mature to believe it, and too tough to be scared by it."

Sarah pretended to smile; a kind of peace offering. Then she went back to the flavourless risotto with Paul studying her closely. Their conversations had been infrequent in the past few weeks, and often tense. They talked around and above things and never addressed what lurked below.

Jonah would never hear the story of the Three-Eighteen. He would never camp out by the train tracks and tell ghost stories, never go trick-or-treating or have a friend like Jimmy Pryce, whose antics he would look back on fondly when fatherhood and dreaded maturity came along and the hard climb toward forty had begun.

Forty. At thirty-two, Sarah felt ancient. Sometimes she thought about what it would be like to be truly old and abandoned, stashed in some nursing home, all her passions diminished or taken away, waiting for it all to end. Waiting to die. This didn't feel much different.

"Why do you ask?"

The tone of the question, the awkwardness in his voice, put a chill between them. It should've had the opposite effect. Here he was, trying to have a civil conversation about something more than the weather or perfunctory work-related trivia, but it felt so forced that Sarah only tensed up further.

"No reason. I heard someone talking about it today and was surprised I'd never heard it before."

"You were fifteen by the time you moved here. Probably too old for ghost stories."

Again she forced a smile.

Paul took another bite of risotto and they descended into the sort of funereal silence to which they had become hideously accustomed.

Jonah had had his father's eyes.

Sarah managed a few more bites and then endured several minutes more at the table before allowing herself to rise and bring her dish to the sink. "I'll clean up later. I've been wanting a bath all day."

She'd been taking a great many baths of late. Paul had remarked on it only once, two weeks earlier, and she had told him tersely that she needed the alone time. He'd had no response for that. Once she might have confided in him, told him what she really did during those long evening baths with the radio playing up on the shelf— that sometimes she touched herself and tried to remember what it was like to be alive and in love and full of lust, and sometimes she used the edge of a razor blade or her tiny scissors to scratch and lightly cut her flesh, trying to discover if she had the courage to cut deeper and let herself bleed.

Either way, whether searching for passion or pain, she cried. With the water hot and steam rising, sometimes she even pretended that there were no tears.

Her eyes snapped open and she inhaled sharply. Something had woken her, tonight. It took a moment for her mind to make sense of the thumping bass coming from a car passing by at the end of the street. God, that was loud. Some kind of post-modern blues-funk like Amy Winehouse, and it wasn't drifting off the way it should have been. The car had stopped for some reason.

Rubbing her eyes, Sarah slipped from beneath the covers and went to the window. She pulled the curtain aside and tried to peer out into the dark toward the end of the street. Not much breeze, but the night pulsed with the beat of that song. There came a laugh, the slam of a door, and then the car roared away. Some kind of mischief going on down there—the kind of thing she and Paul might have gotten up to, once upon a time.

Paul had left the window open wide and Sarah backed away and hugged herself tightly, shuddering. Even without a breeze, the night was cold. The weather had shifted again, but New England was always like that.

With a frown, she realized she had been unconsciously rubbing the bandage on her forearm. She had gotten a bit carried away with the scissors in the bathtub tonight. *That's one way to look at it*, she thought, sleep still clouding her mind. Her arm ached where she'd cut it, and she hoped it had not become infected. If Paul noticed, that would be difficult to explain. Of course that was an enormous 'if.' He barely saw her any more. She might as well be made of glass—a window where a woman used to be.

The clock ticked loudly on the nightstand. Once they had kept a baby monitor there and the sound of Jonah turning restlessly had kept her alert. But now there was only the clock and the soft breathing of the automaton who had taken the place of her husband.

Sarah watched Paul sleeping. He had mastered the emotionless mask that he wore during the day, but could not control his unconscious mind. His features were tight with sorrow and consternation. His dreams brought him the nightmares he spent the days attempting to evade.

Beyond him, the clock on the nightstand read 2:13 A.M. Sarah blinked and stared at it and the display clicked over to 2:14. She turned toward the window. The gauzy curtain seemed like a veil, now, but though she could not see as far as the Kenyon River from here, she did not want to look out across the town toward the river.

She climbed back into bed, sliding deep beneath the covers. On her side, she pressed her eyes closed and slid one hand under her pillow, an exaggerated pantomime, as though she could fool her body into thinking it was capable of falling right back to sleep. But experience had taught her better.

For fifteen or twenty minutes she lay there, stubbornly persistent. When she surrendered to the inevitability of her insomnia, she opened her eyes at last and glanced around at the moonlit glow of her bedroom. Paul breathed softly beside her.

Sarah wanted to scream. If only her sleeplessness could have been made incarnate, turned into something she could kick and punch and claw. But it could not be fought. Especially tonight. Just as she had been pretending that it would be possible to simply fall back to sleep, she had also avoided acknowledging the conversation she and Martin had had in the foyer of Sterling Software that morning.

Again, she glanced at the clock: 2:37, and Paul still sleeping, so peacefully.

Sarah slid from bed and grabbed her blue jeans, pulled them on. She'd been sleeping in a light blue t-shirt she sometimes wore to the gym and didn't bother with a bra, just pulling a fuzzy red sweater on over it. With another glance at Paul, she took a pair of socks from the drawer in her nightstand and went quietly downstairs.

She paused only once, while tying her sneakers, to wonder what exactly she hoped to accomplish. Her chest tightened with anticipation, a kind of giddy excitement that might have been hysteria. Then she went out the front door and pulled it quietly closed behind her. Her own car was parked inside the garage and the automatic door opener made a lot of noise, so she took Paul's Cherokee.

As she pulled out of the driveway, her hands were trembling. She didn't click the headlights on until she reached the end of the street and turned onto the main road. The dashboard lights cast an industrial gloom inside the car and the radio played low as she drove away from home, following the same course she took on her way to work.

The clock on the dash read 2:49.

Sarah hit the gas and the car lurched forward, speeding up. She couldn't be late.

She travelled as though she were a dream, gliding through the sleeping town in the small hours when night seemed darkest. Nothing else moved but the wind. In that surreal landscape, anything seemed possible.

At 3:11, her headlights picked out the old bridge over the Kenyon River. Sarah slowed as the car shuddered across the bridge, black water rushing past below. When she hit the pavement on the far side, she turned left and gunned it, tires squealing. All through the drive she'd managed a kind of zen calm, complete with steady breathing and quick but even pulse. The sound of the tires broke her focus. Her face flushed with heat and she felt her heart pounding in her chest as she sped along the road that curved beside the river.

Without a railroad crossing sign or any other warning, she came up on the abandoned tracks too fast to stop. She rocketed over the tracks before hitting the brakes and skidding to a halt on the shoulder of the road.

3:14.

Sarah killed the engine and just sat there for a few seconds, hands on the steering wheel, listening to the car cool and tick and settle. If she gripped the wheel hard enough, her hands wouldn't shake. She felt her throat closing and her eyes brimming and she bit down on her lip.

Go home. Stupid girl. There's nothing for you out here.

Of course there wasn't. Why had she really come here? What did she expect, racing across town in the middle of the night, chasing ghosts? *You're losing it, kid,* she thought, grinning in the dark enclosure of the car. *Just losing it.*

But that was bullshit, too. She'd lost it the day Jonah died, and never gotten it back. Trying to pretend otherwise had been her sole occupation ever since.

With a shaky laugh she took the keys from the ignition and popped the door. The night wind gusted, whipping her hair across her face, crisp with the rich scent of autumn. From somewhere there came the smell of a wood-burning stove, carried on the breeze, and it made her realize that she was not the only one awake tonight. Not alone in the dark.

She slipped the keys into her pocket and shut the car door, then started walking toward the tracks. How many minutes left? Just a couple. Sarah stepped onto the tracks and looked in both directions. The moonlight only dispersed so many shadows, but enough to see that nothing about the tracks had changed. They were overgrown and unused, nearly buried in some places.

Closing her eyes, she raised her arms, imagining the 3:18 coming. Would it pass right through her, or run her down? Or might it, instead, pick her up and carry her away? Her eyes snapped open and she crumbled inward, wrapping her arms around herself. With a deep breath, she stepped off of the tracks, beginning to rub her thumb across the bandage on her wrist where she'd cut too deeply. Last night she'd almost been brave enough to join Jonah.

A long minute passed, and then another. Sarah glanced back and forth along the tracks, and then put her face in her hands, aware of how seriously she had deluded herself . . . of just how lost she had become.

Then she heard the whistle. It came softly a first, a distant, mournful cry. She caught her breath. It was the same sound she had heard night after night as she lay in bed, unable to sleep. Sarah pulled her hands away from her face. Still barely able to breathe, she turned to the left, staring along the tracks.

The whistle sounded again, moving closer, so much louder. Louder than she'd ever heard it.

"Oh my God," she whispered, shaking.

Unblinking, she stared along those tracks, but there was no sign of any train. She stood just at the edge, where the metal rail was sunk into the pavement. The whistle came again, this time so close that she winced at the sound. She could see nothing, but now she could hear the chugging of the train.

Mouth agape, Sarah took a step back.

The whistle blew, and the scream was so loud she covered her ears. Then the wind struck her, the hot blast of air displaced by the passing locomotive. Eyes wide, she stared at the place where it ought to have been, but saw only the road on the other side of the tracks and the trees on the river bank beyond.

And maybe something else. The night air seemed to ripple, to have texture, just a hint of substance. Sarah glimpsed a face through a window. She blinked and other faces flashed by in the zoetrope flicker of passenger car windows. They streaked across the darkness in the space of seconds. Still there was no train, nothing but the night and echoes and the chuff and clank of a machine she could not see.

One of the faces was Jonah's.

A blink, only. There and gone in the fraction of a moment. The strength of her hope and grief could have summoned his image. But Sarah knew. She'd seen him.

"My baby," she said. And then she cried. "My baby!"

She fell to her knees beside the tracks as the wind from the passing train diminished and then subsided entirely, and the whistle grew distant. After a while she crawled forward and put her fingers on the old rail. The metal was so cold. Sarah lay down there in the road for a while, body across the tracks. A car might have come and run her down. The thought occurred to her, but she thought that wouldn't have been so bad.

Sometime before four o'clock, she staggered back to the Jeep. Paul let her sleep in. By the time Sarah rolled out of bed on Saturday, it was after ten o'clock. She took her time showering and getting dressed, then went downstairs and had a glass of orange juice. It had been a dreamless sleep, and when she'd woken it had taken her a minute or so for the mist to clear from her mind. When the events of the previous night came back to her, Sarah felt herself suffused with a profound contentment. Her soul had been empty for so long, but now it began to fill up again.

Jonah was gone from this house—from the world, even. But he was not out of reach.

The front door was open. Sarah went out onto the steps and saw Paul raking leaves in jeans and a New England Patriots sweatshirt. He looked so much like the old Paul, the one who'd loved her before he started hating himself. If only she could have stepped down onto the grass and by doing so enter the time before Jonah, when he would have welcomed an embrace on the lawn, when Paul had been playful and his eyes bright with possibility.

"Good morning," she said.

Her husband looked up. For a moment he smiled as though he'd forgotten all the loss and resentment, but then she saw it draw like a veil across his face. The illusion shattered.

"Morning, sleepy head," he said. Sarah appreciated the effort to be cordial. "You must've been up all night."

"Pretty much. After I woke up, around two, I couldn't get back to sleep until it started to get light."

He leaned on his rake, real concern in his eyes. "Honey, I'm sorry. You sure you don't want to start taking those pills?"

Sarah smiled. "It's Saturday. No law against sleeping in. Listen, I was thinking I'd make some chicken salad with the leftovers from last night. Some onions and celery. Sound good for lunch?"

"Yeah," Paul replied, still studying her. "Sounds great."

She still loved him, and she pitied him, and she hated him, just a little. Sarah did not really blame Paul for what happened to Jonah—that had been nobody's fault. But she wished that they could have found solace in each other. If only he could find some kind of peace in himself, he could stop pretending his heart had not been torn apart. He could have held her and cried, let her feel it was all right to cry with him.

But that time was past.

After lunch, she told Paul she had some errands to run, and went to the cemetery. The leaves eddied on the breeze and rustled in whispers along the grass, red and yellow and orange. She parked her car on a narrow, paved path that separated the modern part of the cemetery from the earliest graves, which dated back to before the Civil War.

Sarah got out of the car and shut the door. Quiet and peaceful, the cemetery seemed beautiful to her. The sky hung bright blue above the rolling lawns and the trees full of autumn colours. Some of the crypts were marble and others granite, while a handful of the older graves were marked by statues of angels.

She took a deep breath and started across the lawn. Tree roots bulged under the soil like raised veins. Sarah brushed a hand against an old oak as she passed. On her way to Jonah's grave she made a small detour, stopping by the granite block that marked her parents' resting place. Her mother had been killed in a car accident when Sarah was very young, leaving her father to raise her. He'd been her whole world, until Jonah came along.

The family name—her maiden name—was engraved on the front in large letters. KOSKOV. On the back, both of her parents were listed, with their dates of birth and death.

Eli Josef Koskov

Teresa Annalise Koskov

Sarah ran her fingers across the engraved letters. "Hi, Daddy." She kissed the tips of her fingers and touched them to his first name.

Three rows farther along she came to another. The cut of the stone differed, and instead of granite it had been fashioned of a blue-tinted marble. This one said COOPER. Sarah didn't walk around to the back. She had stared too long, too often, at the letters that spelled out her son's name.

She sat on the grass just to one side of the grave and sang to him the songs she had always soothed him with when he had trouble falling asleep. Billy Joel's "Lullaby." Harry Connick's "Recipe for Love." Melissa Etheridge's "Baby, You Can Sleep While I Drive."

Sarah had visited Jonah without her husband many times. But that afternoon was the first time she did not cry.

After dinner—a chicken cacciatore Paul had put together while she was out—Sarah cleaned the house. It started with the dishes, but afterward she could not stop herself. Compelled to continue, she moved into the living room and dining room, then upstairs into the bedroom to wash the bathrooms and put away a week's worth of laundry that had lingered, folded, in baskets. Paul watched television on the sofa the whole time, calling to her every half hour or so to come and sit with him, to relax.

Sarah couldn't relax. She could barely stand still.

At bedtime, she slid beneath the sheets, bathed in the blue, flickering light of the television. Paul liked to have the news on while he fell asleep. He took comfort in the chatter, the monotonous drone of the voices. Sarah tried to tune them out. The news held no interest for her; it was nothing but a parade of tragedy. When Paul touched her hip, she thought he might want to make love. The idea startled her; it had been so long. But he only looked into her eyes.

"You all right?"

The question made her want to laugh and scream in equal proportion. Hadn't they both agreed that it was the most foolish question anyone ever asked someone who'd suffered a terrible loss? Of course she wasn't all right.

"Just tired," she said.

"Hope you get some real sleep tonight."

"Me, too."

But his eyelids were heavy. Already, Paul was drifting off, and Sarah didn't know if he'd even heard her.

As soon as he had slipped into a deep enough sleep, she got up again. The clock on the nightstand read 11:49. Pulling the covers up to make sure he wouldn't feel any draft, she left the bedroom. For an hour or so, she sat in Jonah's bed, surrounded by his things, holding a plush raccoon that had been his favourite—it had come with the name Sticky Fingers, but Jonah had mispronounced it as "Tikki," and afterward they had never referred to it any other way. She held Tikki close, rubbing it under her chin.

Sometime before one o'clock she went back into her room and changed into jeans and a sweatshirt. She'd never taken off her socks. After a visit to the bathroom, she carried Tikki downstairs and turned on the television, volume down so low she could barely hear it. Not that it mattered—she'd put on Cartoon Network and it was the visuals, not the sounds, that comforted her. Jonah loved any cartoon, no matter how old or how lame the animation. They had often curled up together and Sarah had stolen catnaps while Jonah watched. Tonight, Tikki watched with her, but there was no chance of Sarah falling asleep.

At two o'clock she set Tikki on the coffee table and turned off the TV. She laced up her sneakers and went out to the driveway. She'd left her own car out of the garage this afternoon. It didn't seem fair, somehow, to take Paul's Cherokee.

The razor cut deep. Blood slid out over the palms of her hands, filling the lines first and then dripping from her fingers. In the chilly October night, the cuts felt like burns, yet she shuddered as she dropped the razor to the tracks.

Sarah grimaced, a strange satisfaction filling her. She let her arms dangle at her sides as she knelt on a wooden railroad tie, right in the middle of the tracks. She had half an hour or so before the 3:18 was due, so she had chosen a spot away from the road. On the off chance that a car came by, she didn't want to get run over. What terrible irony that would have been.

She let her head loll back and she stared at the stars. If she closed her eyes, she thought she might have been able to fall asleep. What lovely irony. It felt as if she'd been holding her breath ever since

Jonah's death, and tonight, at last, she could exhale.

So she waited, and she bled. As the minutes ticked past she began to grow colder, not just on her skin but down deep in her bones. Her eyes fluttered.

It might have been that she closed them for a while.

The whistle startled her. Sarah blinked and caught her breath, staring along the tracks, searching for some sign of the train. That mournful cry came again, much closer than she would have thought. A terrible ache filled her and she felt weak from the loss of blood. Her body's instinct was to rise, to get out of the way, but that sluggishness gave her a moment to consider, and instead she stayed just where she was, content to wait in the path of the 3:18.

She stared down the tracks, narrowing her eyes. A light had appeared in the darkness. The more she focused, the more distinct it became, until Sarah realized that tonight, circumstances had changed.

The 3:18 was coming, and she could see it. The shape of the train hurtled toward her, just a hint of steam blurring the night above the engine. The sound filled the night, then—the whistle, the clank of metal, the chuffing effort of the furnace.

She smiled and her eyes moistened with tears.

The noise grew and the train hurtled closer, a phantom engine, only an intangible silhouette. But it was real. She had not imagined the whistle or the wind, and she swore to herself that she had not imagined Jonah.

Elated, she held her hands up as though to embrace the 3:18. What would happen when it struck her, or passed through her, Sarah could not be sure. But she knew what she wanted, what she had prayed for as she opened up her wrists. The cuts had started to scab but raising her hands tore them open again and trickles of blood ran down the insides of her arms.

She thought of what it had felt like to hold Jonah against her, to rock him to sleep, to watch him at peace.

Her breathing came in short gasps. She closed her eyes and

threw her arms out wider.

The train hissed loudly and a blast of cold air struck her, blowing back her hair. She heard the screech of its brakes and opened her eyes to find the enormous locomotive slowing to a halt. With a kind of gasp, it came to a stop twenty feet away. Sarah stared at the 3:18. In the darkness it looked almost real, but she could see right through it.

An icy ripple went through her. A ghost. So close.

But then the truth of what was happening rushed in and she felt the smile blossom on her face, so wide that it hurt. Weak as she was, she staggered to her feet. She slipped in her own blood and nearly fell, but she ran for the train.

"Jonah," she whispered, under her breath. "I'm here, baby boy."

Sarah rushed alongside the first car, looking through the gauzy windows. Images floated within, faces that loomed up from a grey nothing beyond the glass. Some of them seemed to be in pain, while others only looked lost, their eyes vacant. The transparent figure of a little girl gazed out at Sarah with hope in her eyes. Sarah shook her head and ran on. She did not want to linger on any of those faces.

The second car gave her no answers and so she moved on to the third, wondering if she should have tried the other side of the train—wondering how long she had before the train began to move again and whether she should just try to get on board. Had enough of her blood been left behind on the tracks for that?

After the third car, she began to panic. Sarah ran.

"Jonah!" she called. "Where are you, sweetie?"

Halfway along the fourth car, she staggered to a halt. One hand fluttered to her mouth, smearing blood on her face. She laughed into her hand.

Jonah waved to her from the window. Then he retreated, as though getting up from his seat.

Sarah ran to the door at the end of the car. She could see through it to the trees on the other side and the river beyond, but the train itself had substance. It pulsed and gave off a strange luminescence, which might only have been the influence of the moon. The 3:18 was a ghost in and of itself, ridden by phantoms. But Sarah had not forgotten the story that had first brought her here. Near death herself, she could see it well enough.

Now she reached toward the handle beside the door, expecting her fingers to pass through the misty nothing of that spectre. Instead, her bloody hand gripped cold metal.

"Oh, my God," she whispered. "Thank you."

She put a foot on the metal step below the door, and hoisted herself up into the open door at the rear of the car. Immediately, the train hissed and lurched, slowly starting forward once more. She could hear the clack of the rails and the breeze as it began to depart.

Sarah looked up and saw Jonah standing in front of her, on the platform at the back of the car. His precious face was just as she remembered, open and smiling, eyes full of love. Jonah reached for her. A shadowed figure loomed behind him, but she paid the other ghost no mind as she put out her arms to her son.

Strong hands snatched him backward, lifted him up and away from her.

"No!" Sarah cried.

The ghostly figure coalesced from the shadows, and she saw the face of the man who held Jonah.

"Daddy?"

He held Jonah against his chest. The boy wrapped his arms around his grandfather's neck, clinging to him, resting in that embrace.

Sarah's father stared at her, his eyes somehow more real than the rest of him, peering out at her from the grey realm of spirits.

"Stop holding on to us, honey. We're fine. The only thing that hurts us now is you not living the life we can never have. We'll see you again, when it's time."

Turning Jonah away from her, he reached out with his free

hand—a gossamer thing, translucent and floating, a bit of nothing and shadow—and touched her face. He gave her a wistful smile, and then he shoved her.

Sarah tried to reach out and grab hold of the door frame, but her fingers passed through it like smoke.

She fell backward from the slowly moving train, hit the ground and rolled. By the time she looked up, she could hear it picking up speed, could feel the breeze of its passing, but she couldn't see it any more.

The 3:18 had come and gone.

Sarah stared at the place where it had been until even the most distant whistle had disappeared, and all she had left was the memory of it. Somehow she knew that she would never hear the whistle of the 3:18 again.

For what seemed an eternity, she sat and waited to die. And when she did not die, she held her hands up in front of her face and looked at her wrists. The right still bled, though not much, and the other had begun to close already. Blood clotted and dried and crusted over. She had not cut deeply enough.

Sarah screamed, enraged that she still lived.

And then she cried.

So lonely, but alive.

In time she rose, weak and disoriented from blood loss, and followed the train tracks until she found her car. She managed to open the door and slid behind the wheel. Sarah wrapped her jacket tightly around her wrists, tangling herself up to stop any further bleeding, but could do no more. Unconsciousness claimed her.

Some time later, with the sky beginning to lighten in the east, her eyes fluttered open. Her cell phone had been in her jacket pocket, and it was ringing. Freeing one hand, she managed to retrieve it.

Paul.

Sarah opened the phone and fumbled it to her ear.

"Hello?"

"Oh, God," he said, "you had me so scared."

"I miss Jonah," she mumbled.

He cried then, for the first time in a very long time, and Sarah knew that they had both bid farewell to ghosts that night.

UNDER COVER OF NIGHT

Long past midnight, Carl Weston sat in a ditch in the Sonoran Desert with his finger on the trigger of his M16, waiting for something to happen. Growing up, he'd always played army, dreamed about travelling around the world and taking on the bad guys—the black hats who ran dictatorships, invaded neighbouring countries, or tried exterminating whole subsets of the human race. That was what soldiering was all about. Taking care of business. Carrying the big stick and dishing out justice.

The National Guard might not be the army, but he had a feeling the end result wasn't much different. Turned out the world wasn't made up of black hats and white hats, and the only way to tell who was on your side was looking at which way their guns were facing. Weston spent thirteen months in the desert in Iraq, and for the last three he'd been part of a unit deployed to the Mexican border to back up the Border Patrol.

One fucking desert to another. Some of the guys he knew had been stationed in places like El Paso and San Diego. Weston would've killed for a little civilization. Instead, he got dirt and scrub, scorpions and snakes, land so ugly even the Texas Rangers had never spent that much time worrying about it.

Army or Guard, didn't matter that much in the scheme of things. None of it was anything like he'd imagined as a kid. All just waiting around. If he'd earned a trip to Hell, he was living it. Never mind the heat, or the grit and desert dust in his hair and every fucking orifice . . . the boredom was Hell enough. It was all just so much waiting around.

Once upon a time, he'd have been excited about a detail like tonight. Border Patrol and DEA were working together to take out a cocaine caravan, bouncing up from South America on the Mexican Trampoline. The traffickers were doing double duty—taking money from illegals to smuggle them across the border, and using them as mules, loading them up with coke to carry with them. Where the DEA got their Intel was none of Weston's business. He was just a grunt with a gun. But from the way the hours were ticking by, it didn't look good. They hadn't seen shit all night, and it had to be after two A.M.

South of the ditch, Weston couldn't see anything but desert. Out there in the dark, less than half a mile off, locals had strung a barbed wire fence that ran for miles in either direction. The idea that this might deter illegals from crossing the border made him want to laugh and puke all at the same time. Yeah, Border Patrol units traversed this part of the invisible line between Mexico and the U.S. on a regular basis, but if you were committed enough to try crossing the border through the desert, you had a decent shot at making it. Border Patrol captured or turned back hordes of illegals every day, but plenty still slipped through.

And that was just the poor bastards who didn't have transport, a bottle of water, or a spare sandwich. You had a little money and wanted to get some drugs across, all you needed was a ride to the border and a pair of wire-cutters. Came to it, you didn't need the cutters, either. If you drove a little way, you'd find an opening.

The whole thing was a game. That was what bothered Weston the most. Over in Iraq, the other guys were full of hate and trying to take as many Americans out of action as possible. That was war. This whole business, sitting around in the ditch, was hide-and-fucking-seek.

"Weston."

He blinked, turned and glanced at Brooksy. The guy hadn't been in Iraq with Weston's unit. He was brand new to the squad; eighteen years old and thinking this shit was war. Grim motherfucker, skinny as a crack whore, hair shaved down to bristle, and twitchy as hell. The squad leader—Ortiz—had made Weston the kid's babysitter, which meant they were sharing the ditch tonight. Six other guys in the squad, but Brooksy had to be Weston's responsibility. He wasn't sure if Ortiz was punishing him or complimenting him, making him look after the kid.

"Shut up," Weston said, voice low.

He held his M16 at the ready and glanced around to see if anyone was picking up on their chatter. No sign of movement from the rest of the squad, never mind the Border Patrol grunts or the DEA crusaders.

"I gotta piss, man," Brooksy said.

Weston's nostrils flared. "Not in this ditch."

"What do I do?"

"Hold it, dumbass."

"And when I can't?"

"You piss in this ditch, I swear to God I'll shoot you."

Brooksy's eyes narrowed. He gripped his M16 and scanned the desert in the direction of the border.

Weston rolled his eyes. He turned and looked north. In the moonlight, the black silhouettes of a dozen or so small buildings were visible. They were all single-story, slant-roof shacks, most of which had once been houses. One had been offices, one a gas station, and one a saloon. The tiny desert town had never had a name—though one clever prick had painted a sign and planted it at the south end of the cluster of shacks. It read WELCOME TO PARADISE.

From what Ortiz had told the squad, passed down from the DEA briefing, the place had been hopping back in the days when heroin production had been huge in Mexico—before they'd realized that their greatest asset wasn't crops, but the border itself, and started putting all of their efforts into trafficking instead. There'd been a big operation going in this little shithole, but the DEA had compromised it then and it had been abandoned ever since. The few people who'd actually tried to live there had long since wandered off.

Paradise Lost.

"Seriously, man," Brooksy began.

Weston laughed softly, reached out with his foot, and kicked the kid's pack. "Drain your canteen and piss in it."

"I'll never get it clean, man. I'll never be able to use it."

That might be true. Weston gave him a hard look. "Go in the corner over there. Dig yourself a little hole, piss in it, then cover it up again. And you better hope the wind doesn't shift."

Brooksy nodded, propped his weapon against the side of the ditch, and went over to the corner. He used the heel of his boot to dig into the ground, then got down and deepened the hole with his hands. When he stood and unzipped, Weston laughed.

"Keep your head down, Brooks."

The kid bent his head and his knees, half-crouched, and it was just about the most foolish-looking thing Weston had ever seen. For a few seconds, it seemed inevitable that Brooksy would stumble into his hand-dug latrine.

From out across the desert came the distant growl of an engine. Weston swung round, propped the barrel of his M16 on the top of the ditch, and sighted into the darkness. The sound of the engine cut off abruptly. Maybe there had been more than one. Regardless, it had come from the other side of the border, and no way anyone was joyriding the Sonoran in the wee hours of the morning.

"It's on," he whispered.

Brooksy might have been a kid, but instead of losing his cool and flopping all over the place, he turned pro. Quietly, he sat backward on the floor of the ditch, used his boots to cover the hole he'd made with dirt, then lay back and zipped up. He was back at his post with his weapon up in a handful of seconds, eyes gleaming in the dark. All the nervous energy that made him so twitchy had gone away. Weston nodded to him, then settled in to wait. Maybe the kid wouldn't be a liability after all.

He imagined he could hear the twang of the barbed wire being cut, but at this distance, that might have been in his head. For long minutes they sat in the ditch, barely breathing. The other six members of the squad were broken into three two-man teams in different locations, but all on the obvious approach to the empty husks of Paradise.

At first, the rhythmic sound was so muffled that it could've been his own pulse in his ears. But when it grew louder, Weston knew the mules were on the move. Ortiz had told them the DEA expected a couple of dozen, but as the noise of running feet multiplied, it sounded like a hundred or more. The illegals would all have backpacks full of coke. They'd been warned some of them would be guards sent along to protect the coke—coyotes herding the mules—and those guys would be armed. Weston tried to do the math. If he figured twenty-five pounds of coke per mule—over ten kilos—at a hundred mules, they were talking about over a thousand kilos of cocaine.

How the DEA knew about the whole setup, he had no idea. That was their job. But obviously the traffickers had to be pretty confident to risk that kind of product on a bunch of desperate Mexicans looking for a better life in the goddamn desert.

Shadows out on the desert began to resolve into running figures. They were coming, but after crossing through the hole they'd cut in the fence, they'd spread out. DEA and Border Patrol were set up in the ramshackle buildings of Paradise, hiding behind and inside them, just waiting. There were big black Humvees and somewhere—not far off—a DEA chopper was waiting to be deployed.

Weston sighted down the barrel of his M16. He almost felt bad for the mules. They didn't stand a chance. They expected to show up in Paradise, get a meal and a blanket, and transport deeper into the U.S. But their ride wasn't ever going to show up. DEA had already taken care of that.

A night wind blew over the desert and Weston shivered. During the day, the Sonoran was a frying pan. But at night, it could get cold as Hell.

He watched the tiny figures running closer, moving in and out of patches of moonlight. The night played tricks on the eyes. It was hard to track them closely from this distance. But the sounds of their running grew louder and pretty soon he motioned to Brooksy to duck down inside the ditch.

They slid down, their backs to the dirt wall. The mules started running by, some of them so close he could hear their laboured breathing and their grunts of exertion. A voice snarled, let off a stream of abuse at one of the mules. Had to be one of the shipment's guards. Weston forced himself to take his finger off the trigger to fight the urge to rise up from the ditch and blow a hole in the bastard's skull.

He kept his own breathing steady. Their assignment was simple. Let the mules and the coyotes pass on by, then close ranks behind them so that when the shit hit the fan in Paradise, none of the coke fled back across the border.

Simple.

Until the screaming started.

In the dark, he saw Brooksy glance at him, wondering who the fuck was screaming. There'd been no gunshots yet. Nobody was supposed to make a move until they got the go signal from DEA, and that wasn't intended to happen until all of the coke-carrying illegals and their guards had marched into Paradise, putting them between the DEA and Border Patrol on one side, and the National Guard on the other to keep them from retreating. But to the south, toward the border, a grown man had started shrieking like someone had just cut his dick off. It sent a chill up Weston's spine, and he wondered how the other guys would be taking it.

The sound of running footsteps slowed, became hesitant.

Voices barked, urging the illegals on. The guards couldn't let the mules change their minds now. Whoever was hurt or dying out there, it didn't concern the drug runners.

Then the screaming died abruptly, a second of silence followed, and several other voices started a chorus of screams. At least one of them had to be that of a child, badly injured or at least in terror.

"Damn," Weston whispered.

Brooksy flinched and stared at him, almost like the kid was judging him for breaking silence. Punk could fuck off as far as Weston was concerned. You got to the point where the terrified, maybe dying screams of a child didn't rip your heart out, you might as well eat a bullet right there.

The comm. unit in his ear crackled. "Go. Word is go."

Engines roared—the Humvees coming to life. Shouts began to arise, in English. "Go, go, go, go!" over and over. Weston took one glance at Brooksy and saw that, indeed, the twitchy motherfucker had vanished, leaving one stone cold bastard behind. No more babysitting for Weston.

"Go, go!" Brooksy chimed in.

They ran up out of the ditch, weapons up and ready. Instantly, Weston saw what had happened. The screams back there in the darkness of the border had made the flood of illegals hesitate. They'd slowed down. Some had maybe even started to turn back, going to check on friends or family members who were stragglers, worried that they were the source of the screams. Whatever it was, the DEA cowboys had gotten worried that they might lose part of their score—or they'd just gotten impatient, which was typical. Grunts like Weston were used to waiting around for the world to explode. From what Ortiz had said, DEA cowboys spent too much time in offices, doing paperwork, and got stir crazy enough that once they hit the field, they couldn't wait for shit to go down.

The mules started shouting in Spanish. Weston didn't have to be fluent to know what they were yelling. "Fuck. We're fucked. Get the fuck out of here." Pretty much a universal language.

The Mexicans started dropping the backpacks full of cocaine—mules couldn't run very fast with kilos of blow strapped to their shoulders—and turning toward the border full speed. One of the guards—they were better dressed, healthier looking, and didn't carry any coke—started screaming at them, raised a 9mm, and put a bullet in the head of the nearest mule who'd dared to dump his drugs.

Weston stitched him with a few rounds from his M16 and the guy danced a little, spraying blood, and then sprawled onto the desert.

That didn't accomplish anything except to start more shouting and make them run all the faster, like a starter pistol. Only about two thirds of the hundred and fifty or so Mexicans had made their way past the ditches the National Guard squad had been waiting in, not even all the way into Paradise. Now they were fleeing.

"Stop right there!" Brooksy roared.

Like they were going to listen.

"Hustle!" Weston told him.

Brooksy fired a few rounds into the air and they started running alongside the illegals, watching for more coyotes—more guns. Not one of them slowed down. They all figured to take their chances that it would be some other guy who got dropped. Ortiz and the other guys in the squad were on the other side of the stampede. If it was only the eight of them, they'd have had to let most of them go.

"Get the guards," Weston said.

Brooksy nodded and they started scanning the throng.

Then the Humvees tore past them, half a dozen of the roaring machines kicking up clouds of sun-blanched desert dust as they began to herd the stampede. Two vehicles reached the far end and cut in, blocking the way. Doors popped open and DEA agents leaped out, jackets emblazoned with the bold yellow letters of their agency. Jeeps followed, loaded with Border Patrol.

The stampede slowed. The mules didn't know what to do with themselves. The guards were fucked. Now it was just a matter of containing the herd and getting them all into custody. For a minute, it had looked like the operation might fall apart. But the DEA and the Border Patrol guys had moved fast.

"Look at you," Brooksy said, eyes bright. "Taking that guy out. You had him fuckin' dancing, man."

Weston's nostrils flared. "I did what had to be done. That shit isn't fun for me."

"Would be for me," Brooksy replied, that skittery grin returning.

The comm. in Weston's ear clicked and Ortiz came on, sounding like he'd climbed right inside his skull.

"Weston, come in."

He adjusted the comm. so the mouthpiece was in place. "This is Weston."

"We've got plenty of runners, including at least a couple of coyotes. Take Brooks. Stop as many of the illegals still carrying as you can, but first priority are the guards. Do not let them back across the border. Improvise. You read me?"

"Affirmative, Sergeant."

"Go."

But Weston was already moving. He grabbed Brooksy by the arm and started dragging him away from the cluster of DEA and Border Patrol officers who were closing ranks around the corralled mules.

"What the fuck?"

"Come on. We're moving," Weston said.

"Where to?"

"Give me a minute."

Brooks fell into step and the two of them ran outside the circle of vehicles. A Border Patrol Jeep had slewed sideways in the dirt and sat there, engine still purring. An officer stood beside the open door, talking into a two-way radio. From somewhere far off, Weston could hear the distant staccato of helicopter blades.

"Drive!" Weston snapped.

He ran around the Jeep and pulled the door open at the same time Brooksy was climbing into the back. The Border Patrol officer stared into his vehicle at them.

"Get the fuck out of there. What do you think you're doing?"

Weston leaned over and shot him a hard look. "We've got coyotes on the run and orders to stop them. You want to explain fucking that up, or you want to drive?"

The officer hesitated, but only for a second.

"Fine," he said as he slid into the driver's seat. "But I want your names."

He dropped the Jeep into gear and hit the gas, the tires spinning and spitting dirt behind them as they tore off across the desert. Brooksy clutched his M16 like he was bringing flowers to his mother.

"I'm Weston. This is Brooks."

"Austin," said the Border Patrol man. He drove past the last Humvee and then they were in open desert, headlights illuminating the ground straight ahead but somehow making the rest of the landscape around them even darker.

"That your first or last name?" Brooksy asked.

"We on a date?" Austin snapped.

He picked up the radio he'd tossed aside and got his boss on the line, told the guy he had two Guardsmen on board and they were running down the last of the coyotes the cartel had sent to protect the coke. He had the accelerator pinned. The Jeep jittered in the ruts and bounced across the ground, closing the gap between Paradise and the Mexican border. They passed a bunch of backpacks full of cocaine that had been tossed aside in favour of getting the hell out of the U.S.

Austin's boss told him to carry on, inter-agency cooperation, and some other bullshit that meant any pissing matches that were going to happen would take place above their pay grade. Let the DEA, Border Patrol, and the Guard work it out after the op was over and they jostled for credit or blame.

The first of the strays came in view up ahead. They should've rabbited in either direction but they kept going in a straight line, which confused Weston until he remembered the fence. They went right or left, they'd never get back across the border before they were caught. The opening in the fence was dead ahead.

An old man stumbled. A younger guy collided with him from behind, managed to stay on his feet, grabbed the old man by a fistful of white hair and shoved him out of the way. The old guy fell in a tangle of arms and legs, probably breaking something—bones were brittle at that age. The one who'd tossed him aside had a 9mm in one hand and was shouting to some of the other mules. Two young women and a small boy were just ahead of him. He raised his gun and fired once like he was trying to get them moving faster.

Instead, they stopped short.

"What the fuck?" Austin barked.

But Weston understood. The young guy—one of the guards—ran between them and kept on running. He'd commanded them to stop or he'd shoot them, made them stand still, block the Jeep to buy him a few seconds.

It worked. Austin hit the brakes, swerved around them, then gunned it again.

"We want that guy," Weston said. "Probably at least one more. But let's do this the easy way. Go right past him."

"What?" Brooksy snapped.

"Shut up." Weston glared back at him, then turned to Austin. "Just do it."

Austin held the wheel tightly, went around the guard. They caught a glimpse of his confused expression and he seemed to slow down, wondering what the hell was going on. They passed maybe a dozen others, all mules, some of them still wearing their backpacks.

"There's the fence," Austin said.

The headlights instantly picked up the hole that had been cut in the border fence. They caught just a glimpse of a few Mexicans returning to their homeland through the opening.

"Block it with the Jeep," Weston said.

"My thought exactly." Austin actually smiled. He'd been uptight about working with them, but now he was on the hunt, doing the job he'd signed up for. Weston thought maybe he wasn't an asshole after all.

The Jeep hurtled across the hard-packed earth. Brooksy let out a rebel yell.

Austin hit the brake and cut the wheel. The Jeep slewed badly to the left and skidded on the baked desert earth, bumped right up against the fence, and then was still. Austin killed the engine and had the door open instantly. Weston knew he shouldn't even step across the border, which didn't leave him many options. The window of the Jeep was open but the door was almost up against the fence. He pushed himself out the window and climbed onto the rack on the Jeep's roof.

Brooksy and Austin brandished their weapons at the exhausted, pitiful, starving people who had already had their worst night ever. Weston had nothing against the Mexicans. They were breaking a shitload of laws, bringing coke into the U.S., never mind crossing the border illegally. If he lived their lives, he'd do the same goddamn thing. But the coyotes worked for the scum who couriered the drugs into the States and were taking advantage of desperate people at the same time. He would've loved to get his hands on the bosses, the guys who actually hired the guards. But since that wasn't going to happen—those guys weren't running coke mules across the border themselves—he'd make do with the guards.

The one they'd passed—the one who'd shoved the old man— had slowed to a walk and now held up his 9mm, hands raised in surrender. The mules dropped to their knees in exhaustion, knowing it was all over, that they'd likely be shipped back home, where they'd try to cross the border again as soon as possible.

In the moonlight, Weston studied one of the mules. He had no backpack, but a lot of them had dropped the drugs while running. But this guy wore a decent shirt and, though he had stubble on his cheeks, he'd had a haircut recently.

"Better watch—" he started to say.

The guy—a guard pretending to be a mule—pulled a pistol from the waistband of his pants and shot Austin in the face. The mules screamed and the echo carried across the Sonoran desert. For an instant, Weston could do nothing but listen to those screams and the echo of the gunshot, and he remembered the other screams they'd heard, right before the whole op went off the rails. Out there in the darkness of the border . . . not far from here.

"Fuck!" Brooksy shouted.

He put three rounds in the cartel guard's face and chest at close range. The back of the guy's head exploded, spattering a teenaged girl beside him with blood and flecks of bone and brain matter. She screamed, closed her eyes tightly, and crumbled to the ground as though wondering when she'd wake up from this nightmare.

Weston trained his M16 on the other guard. "Drop it."

The coyote let the gun fall to the dirt. Brooksy rushed over and picked it up, stuck it inside his jacket, then smashed the guard in the face with the butt of his M16. The guy went down hard and didn't get up again. He was still breathing.

"Beautiful," Brooksy whispered.

"You're psycho, Brooks. We got a guy down, and this is beautiful?" Weston slid off the roof of the Jeep.

Brooksy sniffed. "Border Patrol, man. Sorry to see him go, but he ain't one of ours."

A chill ran through Weston.

Then the screams began again, from behind them this time— from beyond the border fence. Weston stepped to one side, trying to keep his weapon trained on the illegals even as he moved around the Jeep to get a look across the border.

Something thumped against the Jeep. He heard the chain link fence shake and a scrambling against the vehicle, and then a face came over the top.

"What the fuck?" Brooksy shouted.

A young guy, no more than twenty, crawled onto the roof of the Jeep. His face had been slashed, long wounds that pouted open, weeping blood. His eyes were wide with madness and fear—had to be crazy to try to cross the border by scaling a Border Patrol vehicle. But this guy wasn't even seeing the Jeep, barely even seeing them.

"Stop right there!" Weston shouted. "Alto! Alto!"

The wounded man noticed the guns, then. He stared at Weston, lower lip quavering in shock or terror, then glanced over his shoulder. With a low, Spanish curse, he turned toward them again, brought his legs up beneath him, and tensed to lunge at them.

Weston pulled the trigger.

The dead man staggered backward and fell off the Jeep. Weston heard the body hit the ground on the other side, then he turned to Brooksy.

"Cover them."

Brooksy nodded, training his weapon on the twelve or thirteen illegals they'd rounded up. He stood right beside Austin's body, one boot sunken into parched soil made wet by the Border Patrol officer's blood, but didn't seem to notice.

The whole thing was fucked. Weston hesitated only a second and then went around the Jeep. The last thing he needed was an incursion into Mexican territory. But there was a space of about two feet between the Jeep and the fence. He hesitated a second and then slipped through that space to the opening in the fence. The corpse lay in the moonlight, and Weston saw that he'd suffered more wounds than the gashes in his face. The dead man had landed on his belly with his arms and legs splayed out. The back of his shirt had been torn to bloody ribbons, and it looked like the skin beneath it was just as badly damaged.

What the hell happened to this guy?

He remembered the other screams, the ones that had come from down here right before the op started going bad. Standing on the border, he looked out across the moonlit Sonoran. The Mexican side looked no different from the American side. It was all hellscape, no matter what country you were in. But the moonlight picked out dark forms crumpled on the ground. He counted at least six bodies out there, and there might have been more. One of them looked like only part of a person. If he'd had any thoughts that some of them might still be alive, that banished them.

Something moved out there in the desert, a black silhouette that crouched like an animal, running from one body to the next. Weston stared at that strange, slender figure as it bent over a corpse. It moved its head in curious dips and sways like an animal, but walked on two feet. In that crouched position, it lifted a dead man from the ground with ease, as though the body weighed nothing. In the moonlight, Weston saw its head rear back and a long, thin tongue dart out. The sound that carried to him across that killing ground was the dry crack of bone, followed by a terrible, wet slap.

The thing had driven its tongue right through the dead man's skull, and now it began to suck. The noise made him retch, but he forced himself not to vomit, not to look away from the horror unfolding out there on the desert. These people had to have been the source of the earlier screams. This thing had murdered them and now it was moving from body to body, feasting on the dead.

"Weston, what's up?" Brooksy called from the other side of the Jeep.

The creature froze, cocked its head, listening. It thrust out its tongue, tasting the night air. Slowly, it turned to look right at Weston.

He couldn't breathe. Long seconds passed while the thing stared at him. At last it turned away, dropped the body, and scurried across the desert to the next corpse to start the whole process again.

Weston raised his M16 and sighted on the creature, but his finger paused on the trigger. If he missed it, somehow, or if there were more of them, he would be endangering the civilians now in his care. They might be illegals, but they were still people and were his responsibility.

Silently, he slid once more between Jeep and fence and moved around the front of the vehicle. It felt like stepping between worlds. Brooksy looked up sharply.

"Where you—?" he started.

Weston silenced him with a look and a raised hand. "Get them in the Jeep," he whispered, gesturing to the Mexicans and then to the vehicle. He glanced again toward the other side of the border and when he looked back, Brooksy had a dubious expression on his face, like he might challenge that order or take it upon himself to go see what they were running from.

"Go," Weston whispered.

Brooksy must have heard the edge in his voice, then, for he started moving as quickly and quietly as he could. A fortyish guy tried talking to them in thickly accented English, but Weston hushed him and gestured for him to get into the vehicle. The man did, and others followed. Quickly enough, the Jeep was full, leaving six illegals still on foot. The girl who'd nearly been killed by one of the cartel guards looked at him in confusion and fear, her face still dappled with drying blood.

"You drive," Weston whispered to Brooks. "I'll escort the others. Don't rev it. No lights. Roll out quiet and dark."

"What's going on?" Brooksy asked, a little twitchy but not smiling.

Weston shook his head. "Later. Just go."

"What about Austin?" He pointed to the dead Border Patrol officer.

"We'll come back," Weston whispered.

Brooksy shrugged. He got behind the wheel of the Jeep, closed the door as quietly as possible, then fired up the engine. To Weston, it seemed the loudest thing he'd ever heard. But then it dropped to a purr and he heard Brooksy put it into gear.

"Vamanos. Let's go," he said, using the barrel of his M16 to gesture toward Paradise. He put a finger to his lips and shushed them. "Quietly."

The Jeep pulled away from the opening in the fence and for a second, Weston was sure one or more of the Mexican men with him would bolt for the border. The girl wasn't going anywhere, and he didn't think the older woman would try to run it out. But the men . . .

He glanced back toward the bodies scattered on the desert and saw that slender silhouette again. It crouched by a corpse with its head cocked and in the moonlight he saw the glint of its eyes, watching the Jeep pull away.

His pulse raced and his finger twitched on the trigger. Weston forced himself not to run, instead urging the others on. They were focused on him, and he had to keep them from panicking. They all fell in step alongside the Jeep, which rolled slowly back toward the ghost town. The sound of helicopter rotors came from that direction. The headlights of Jeeps and Humvees had made a circle, like a wagon train preparing for attack. If they could just get back there, they would be safe.

Finally on the move, he snapped the mouth piece of his comm. unit into place. "Weston for Squad Leader. Weston for Squad Leader."

Seconds ticked by and he was about to radio again when he heard a pop on the line. "What the hell are you whispering for, Weston? It's all over but the paperwork."

"Maybe not, sir,"

"What happened? You didn't catch the coyotes?"

"Got 'em, sergeant, but it's a mess." He glanced back, saw the thing—the scavenger—framed in the opening in the fence, standing in the very same spot he'd been in just a minute ago, watching them. Fear ran up the back of his neck and prickled his skin. "And there's . . . there's something else over here, sarge. We're not alone."

"What the hell are you talking about?"

Weston thought about that a second. He looked back again.

Only that gaping hole across the border remained, and beyond it the scattered dead. The creature had vanished.

It darted out of the night so swiftly that he barely had time to aim the M16. The creature came from the left, a paint stroke of fluid black across the moonlit landscape, grabbed hold of the Mexican at the front of their little march and tore open his throat and abdomen in a single pass.

The screaming started.

Weston ran past the others, up to the front of the Jeep, and squeezed off a couple of rounds without a chance in Hell of hitting the thing. It blended too well with the desert and the dark.

"What the hell?" Brooksy roared from behind the wheel of the Jeep.

"Weston. Do you read? Are you under fire?" Ortiz barked in the comm. in his ear.

"Under attack!" Weston snapped back. "Not under fire. That was me shooting."

Ortiz asked half a dozen questions in as many seconds, but Weston wasn't listening anymore. He pulled the comm. from his ear and tossed it into the dirt. They were three or four hundred yards from the lights and vehicles and weapons of the DEA and Border Patrol. Not far at all.

Not far, he told himself.

But those Mexicans hadn't made it very far, back at the border. They'd been picked off one by one, the stragglers, killed quickly. The thing only slowed down to start its banquet when they were all dead and the screaming was over.

Weston swung the barrel of his M16, searching the darkness all around, knowing the thing could come from anywhere. The Mexicans not inside the Jeep huddled nearby him. Afraid as they were, no way were they making a break for the border now.

"Damn it, Weston, what was that?" Brooksy asked.

"I don't know," he said, without sparing the other grunt a glance.

"Fuck this."

Brooksy gunned it. The Jeep's engine roared and the tires spit hard-baked earth and stones as the vehicle leaped forward.

"Goddamn it, no!" Weston yelled.

Two of the Mexican men started running after the Jeep, shouting. The others hesitated only a second before following. Weston yelled for them to stop, but they were beyond listening. Exhaustion, starvation, and despair had plagued them earlier— people who'd been taken advantage of by nearly everyone they'd encountered—but now fear drove them to madness.

Weston pursued them. The night loomed up on either side of him. He could feel the vulnerability of his unprotected back, but knew that they were all vulnerable. The darkness shifted. Every shadow, every depression in the desert floor, seemed about to coalesce and take shape and rush at him with its claws out.

The illegals were stretched out in a line, scattered in their pursuit of the Jeep. The thing came out of the night and killed the woman, punching a hole in her chest. Weston brought up his weapon and fired at it. Two bullets hit the woman as her corpse fell. The thing flinched and he thought he'd winged it, but it rushed off into the dark again, merging with the night.

The taillights of the Jeep grew smaller.

Weston swore, catching up with the four survivors. The teenaged girl fell to her knees beside the dead woman, and Weston heard her saying "Tia" over and over, and knew she had been the girl's aunt.

They all clustered around the sobbing girl. Weston heard the Humvees revving. One of them pulled away from Paradise, headlights turning their way.

"We'll be all right," he said. "They're coming."

But his fingers felt frozen on his weapon. Ortiz would be coming to get them, maybe with inter-agency backup, but seconds counted. He swung the M16 around, jerking at every sound—real or imagined—from the desert. The survivors stayed low, out of his way. Maybe they hoped the thing would come for him next.

One of the men had begun to cry with the girl.

When Weston saw it, at first he didn't even know what he was looking at. The thing stood forty feet away, entirely motionless. On instinct he raised the M16 and squeezed the trigger. The thing darted aside, slipping through the darkness, too fast to hit. It stopped, studied him again, cocked its head and gazed with a terrible intelligence. It thrust out that long, thin, snaking tongue and tasted the air with it.

"El Chupacabra," one of the men whispered.

Engines roared and headlights splashed across them. A pair of Humvees arrived, one on either side of the group, bathing the

Chupacabra in yellow light. It bolted instantly, heading for that gap in the border fence.

"Oh no you don't," Weston whispered.

Fast as it was, the thing was making a run for the fence in a straight line. He sighted on its back as Humvee doors popped open and DEA agents jumped out. Ortiz's voice called out, so Weston knew his squad leader was with them.

Once again the creature paused, framed in that opening in the fence.

Weston squeezed the trigger.

An arm came up under the barrel, knocking the gun's nose up, and the bullets fired into the desert sky.

Enraged, Weston spun on a man wearing a DEA jacket.

"Back off!" he snapped, shoving the man away. When he glanced back toward the fence, the creature had vanished once more, and he knew that the opportunity had passed. "What's wrong with you? Did you see that thing? Do you have any idea what it just did? What you let get away?"

Ortiz had come up by then. The DEA agent grinned and Weston wanted to break his face with the butt of his M16. But the Squad Leader glared at him.

"Stand down, Weston."

Weston glared at the DEA prick. "Tell me you saw that thing."

"I didn't see anything." The grin remained. "And neither did you. We've got thousands of miles of border to worry about. If there's something else that keeps them from trying to get across, then it's doing us a favour."

Behind Weston, the teenaged girl still sobbed over the corpse of her dead aunt. She'd wanted a new beginning, but instead she'd found an ending to so much of her life. All he could think about was that if the girl had been torn open by that thing out in the desert, this son of a bitch would have kept grinning.

Doing us a favour.

Weston looked at the grim, cautious expression on Ortiz's face. The staff sergeant was silently warning him to keep his mouth shut. More than anything, that made him wonder. Was the grinning DEA man just happy the scavenger was out there in the desert, helping him do his job, or had he and his people put the thing there in the first place? And if they had, were there others?

But he did not ask those questions.

"A Border Patrol officer—Austin—one of the coyotes shot him. He's down by the fence, DOA," he said.

"A tragedy," said the grinning man. "Died in the firefight that cost the lives of a number of illegals as they attempted to enter the country carrying cartel cocaine. A hero of the border wars, this Austin. You were lucky to survive yourself."

Weston slung his M16 across his back. One last time he glanced at Ortiz. They already had their version of tonight's op ready to go. If he tried telling it differently, who would listen?

Slowly, Weston nodded.

"Sir, yes sir."

PUT ON A HAPPY FACE

The blood seeping out of the midget car was Benny's first clue that something had gone awry. The audience kept laughing—either they hadn't seen it yet or they thought it was part of the show—so Benny didn't slow down. He waddled on his big shoes, storming with exaggerated frustration toward Clancy the Cop, and slapped the other clown in the face with a rubber chicken.

It looked like it hurt.

The audience roared.

Back up.

The night before—a Friday—the circus had ended at quarter past nine on the dot. Appleby, the manager, was a stickler for punctuality. The last bow took place between ten and fifteen minutes past the hour every performance, and when the thunderous applause—which, honestly, wasn't always thunderous and was sometimes barely more than a ripple—had died down, the ticket sellers became ushers . . . ushering folks out of the tent as quickly as possible. The ushers didn't hurry people because anyone was in a rush to get their makeup off, but because once the little kids started moving, all the popcorn and cotton candy and soda and hot dogs started to churn in their bellies. Much better to hose the vomit off the ground outside than in the tent.

The clowns ran out of the tent the way NFL teams came onto the field, arms above their heads, whooping and hollering, before the last of the crowd had departed. Benny had always thought it looked stupid, but Zerbo—the boss clown and the troupe's whiteface—wanted to leave the straggling audience members with an image of the clowns as a kind of family.

Out behind the tent, the family fell apart. The tents and trailers that made up the circus camp were a tense United Nations of performers and labourers without any real unity. Like a high school full of jocks and geeks and emo kids, the clowns and workers and animal trainers and acrobats each formed their own caste, every group thinking themselves above the others. Friendships existed outside the boundaries of those castes, but when it came to conflict, they stuck together like unions. The acrobats were effete, the animal trainers grave and sensitive, and the workers gruff and strong.

But nobody fucked with the clowns.

"You mess with the clown, you get the horns," Zerbo was fond of misquoting, right before blasting you in the face with an air horn. His idea of a joke. Most people laughed, but Benny had never found the boss clown all that funny.

The Macintosh Traveling Circus Troupe had been playing sold-out audiences in a field in Brimfield, Massachusetts for a week. Normally, the grounds were used for the huge antique flea market the town held a couple of times a year, but the circus had been a welcome novelty, as far as Benny could tell. Not that Appleby talked to him about it. Clowns were beneath the manager's notice, except when it came time for him to talk to Zerbo about renewing contracts. Even then, nobody bothered to ask Benny what he thought.

In the hierarchy of clowns in the Macintosh Traveling Circus Troupe, Benny Martini was on the bottom rung. The runt of the litter. The red-headed stepchild. Shit, that last one was probably offensive in these sensitive modern times. No matter. The point was that Benny was an afterthought to everyone, even the audience.

He'd often thought about how much happier he would have been if, like Tiny and Oscar—two of the other character clowns in the troupe—he'd been too stupid to know it. But even Tiny and Oscar were above him. If the troupe had been a wolf pack, Benny would have been on his back, baring his throat for everyone who came along. And why?

It was all about the laughs.

Laughter and his status in the circus, nearly always the only two things he thought about, were foremost on his mind as he followed Zerbo, Oscar, Tiny, Clancy the Cop, and the rest of them into clown alley. Tiny bumped Oscar, then clapped him on the back—they'd successfully completed the Hotshots gag after having totally bungled it the night before. On a façade so rickety even old-time Hollywood stuntmen would've shied away from it, three-hundred-pound Tiny dressed in drag and pretended to be a mother trapped with her infant on the third story of a burning building. The fire effects were minimal—gas jets, a low flame, a lot of orange lighting, the whole thing designed by a guy who'd helped put together the Indiana Jones Stunt Spectacular at Disney World, before he'd been fired for drinking on the job—but it looked great, as long as Tiny didn't set his wig on fire.

Oscar, in character as a clown firefighter, pushed a barrel of water back and forth across the ring, exhorting Tiny to throw him the infant and then jump into the water. The culmination of the whole thing was that Tiny's aim would be off, forcing Oscar to step into the water barrel in order to catch the baby—only a doll, of course. At the moment he caught it, the trap door would give way beneath the ring, dropping Oscar and the baby and the water through and giving the audience the impression that the baby had been heavy enough to drive him into the ground. It was a pain in the ass to set up the gag, but when it went off, the surprise always led to real laughs, especially when Tiny theatrically threw up his hands, mopped his sweating face with his wig, took a deep breath, and blew out the fire around the windows like candles on a birthday cake. The lights would go dark. Cue the applause.

Thursday night, Tiny had stumbled, throwing off his timing. The doll—to the eyes of the crowd, an infant—had tumbled down to splat in the middle of the ring while Oscar stood watching like a fool, until the trapdoor gave way and shot him down into the space beneath. The audience had to know the baby wasn't real, but they'd screamed all the same.

Timing was everything, Benny always said.

How Tiny and Oscar could screw up the gag so badly and still be above him in the pecking order, he would never understand.

In clown alley that Friday night, he washed off his makeup without a word to any of the others. Most of the time he shot the breeze with them and tried to ignore the fact that, four years since he'd joined up, they still treated him like a mascot, but not tonight. The cold cream took off most of the makeup and then he splashed a little water on his face and dragged on a pair of stained blue jeans and a Red Sox sweatshirt—it had been strangely cool the past few nights, uncommon for July in western Massachusetts.

As he left the others behind and went out to wander the grounds and clear his head, he ran into the lovely blonde contortionist, Lorna Seger. There were tears in her eyes and she gave him a helpless, hopeless glance that made him think maybe she wanted to talk about her breakup with the stunt rider, Domingo.

"Hey," he said, shaken from the reverie of his self-pity by her sadness. "You okay?"

Lorna smiled and wiped at her eyes. "Could be worse, I guess," she said. "I could be a clown."

Benny flinched. Lorna chuckled softly to let him know it had been a joke. He hoped Domingo ran her down on his motorcycle.

"You're such a bitch," he said.

Lorna rolled her eyes. "Why is it clowns never have a sense of humour?"

He walked on, fuming, wanting to scream, wanting to get the hell away from the circus but crippled by the knowledge that—like everyone else who performed under the tent—he had nowhere else to go.

Put on a happy face, his mother would have said. Remembering did make him smile, but it faded quickly.

The wind picked up as he walked the grounds, which were rutted and pitted with tire tracks from decades of vehicles moving through the fields in all weather, turning up muddy ridges, which had then dried and hardened. Loud voices came from the trailers where the workers had made their own small camp, and he could smell sausages cooking on a grill. When he passed a tent, he saw them, standing in a semi-circle, drinking beer, a small radio picking up a static-laced broadcast of tonight's Red Sox-Yankees game. Summer in New England. These guys looked like their entire life was a tailgate party. They worked hard and were content with the cycle of labour and paycheque, beer and cookouts and Red Sox games. In a way, Benny envied them.

The stencil on the side of the converted school bus read ROSE'S MOBILE BOOK FAIR. In a side window there hung a cardboard sign, "New, Used, and Antiquarian—Something For Everyone," written in thick black magic marker. Benny had seen the bus several times this season, in Vermont and New Hampshire and upstate New York. It might've been there when they'd played Bangor back in May, but he couldn't be sure. He'd never been inside—he'd never been much for books, unless they were about clowns or vaudeville or something useful.

Tonight, he just wanted a distraction.

The accordion bus door was open and a sign indicated that the mobile book fair was as well, so he went up the couple of steps, ducking his head though he'd never be tall enough to bang it. Oddly enough, he didn't notice the woman right away. At first, all he could see were the books, and he wondered how she managed to keep them all from falling off the shelves while she drove the old beast of a school bus around the northeastern United States. The metal shelving units had been secured to the walls and lined both sides of the bus. Each shelf had an ingenious device, a bar that went across the spines of the books to hold them in place and could be locked into different notches to accommodate racks of books of different sizes.

"Looking for something to read?" the woman asked, and he blinked and stared at her.

She'd been there all along, of course, but it felt almost as if he'd dreamed her into being. Slender and fit, perhaps forty, she wore black pants and shoes and a tight pink tank with a bright red rose silhouette stretched across her breasts. Rose—for how could she have been anyone else?—had an olive complexion and a proud Roman nose, and she wore a kindly expression, her gaze alert and attentive. Though the interior of the mobile book fair was lit mainly with strings of old white Christmas lights, he could see that her eyes were icy blue. It both pleased and unnerved him to have someone study him with such intensity—such intimacy. People looked at him all the time when he had his clown makeup on, but he couldn't remember how long it had been since anyone had really *seen* him when he didn't have it on.

"I doubt you'd have anything for me," he said. "I'm not a big reader."

"Didn't you see the sign," she said, amused. "Something for everyone. What do you do here?"

He almost lied, but she would've taken one look at his little pot belly and stiff shoulders and known he wasn't an acrobat.

"I'm a clown."

Her eyes lit up. "I've got a small section back here. Not a whole shelf, but a handful of interesting antiquarian books I picked up from an old guy in Cheektowaga, when his carnival went belly up."

Most of the books were things he'd seen before. Way back in high school, he'd researched Grimaldi and Tovolo and Ricketts, studied the Fratellinis, and watched the films of the great movie directors who had started their careers as circus clowns, like Fellini and Jodorowsky. Charlie Chaplin had become his god, and he mastered the rolling walk of the Little Tramp. There were many schools of comedy, but Benny had never been much interested in telling jokes or doing stand-up. In his heart, he had always been a clown. Though some of them were probably quite valuable, none of the books Rose's Mobile Book Fair had on her shelves were unfamiliar to him.

He'd just begun to turn away when he noticed the frayed spine of a book lying on its side atop the dozen or so she had shelved at the end of her boys' adventure section. The worn, faded lettering was almost unreadable in the shadows, but when he slipped his slender fingers in and slid the volume out, the cloth cover made him stiffen in surprise. The comedy and tragedy masks were there, along with the initials G.T.

Quickly he leafed to the title page and a warm feeling spread through him. *Charade: The Secret to Being a Clown*, by Giovanni Tovolo. He had never even heard of the book, had not run across it in any of his reading and research, even in the biography of Tovolo he'd read. The famous Italian character clown had retired after a horrifying accident had taken sixteen lives in a big top fire outside Chicago in 1917. All but forgotten, Tovolo had been a particular fascination of Benny's because the man had earned his reputation doing characters. Most of the famous clowns were whitefaces or augustes. Tovolo could do anything, at least according to what Benny had read . . . but now, to read it in Tovolo's own words.

Maybe Tovolo could help him figure out how he ended up spending four years at the wrong end of clown alley. He glanced up at Rose, unable to stifle his excitement and hoping she didn't take advantage of him.

"How much do you want for this one?" he asked.

She took it from his hand, opened it to see the price she'd penciled on the first page. "Twenty-two dollars."

Benny swallowed hard, knowing his smile was too thin. Did she not realize that, to certain collectors, this book would be worth a hundred times that? Or did she simply not care, having paid next to nothing for it herself.

He smiled. "I'll take it."

Benny's mother always thought he was funny. All through his

childhood he had been encouraged by her laughter, egged on by the way her face would redden and she would wipe at her eyes when he made silly faces or did the big, galumphing walk that would one day become his trademark. At the age of nine he had begun rearranging living room furniture so that he could stumble over it, practicing pratfalls and somersaults and rubber-leg gags—anything that might elicit laughter from his mother. Once she had laughed so hard that she had to wave at him to stop so she could catch her breath. Her chest ached for days afterward, and she had joked often that if he wasn't careful he would give her a heart attack.

That's how funny Benny Martini was as a kid.

He loved to make her laugh. He watched the Three Stooges and the Marx Brothers and forced his friends into helping him reenact their gags. Mrs. Martini took young Benny to the circus every year, and when the clowns made the audience roar with their hilarious antics, he watched with fascination and a dawning envy. For weeks after a circus trip, he would mimic the clowns, practising the faces they pulled, their walks, their timing.

In school, he put whoopee cushions on the seats of teachers and thumb tacks on the chairs of the girls he liked. In the eighth grade, he had taped a sign to Tim Rivard's back that read HONK IF YOU THINK I'M A MORON. Only other jocks had been brave enough to make honking noises when Rivard walked down the hall, but it took the football player until fourth period to really start to wonder what all the honking was about. He'd slammed Benny's head into a locker, but the sign alone hadn't been enough to prompt the violence. That had come when Benny had pointed out that Rivard going most of the day without noticing the sign pretty much proved his point.

When Benny told his mother what he'd done, she'd put a hand over her mouth to hide her laughter. And when he confessed that he'd been suspended for three days—even though he was the one with the black eye—she'd laughed so hard she had cried, tears streaming down her pretty face, ruining her makeup.

Benny had become the class clown by design. He knew every class had to have one, and he'd be damned if he let some other guy take on that role. His classmates—hell, the whole school—would remember him forever as *that guy*, the one with the jokes, the one with the faces, the one who couldn't be serious for two seconds.

There were dark moods, of course. Who didn't have them? Who hadn't spent a little time studying his own face in the mirror, trying to recognize something . . . anything of value? Who hadn't tested the edges of the sharpest knives on the hidden parts of their skin just to see how sharp they really were, or sat in the dark for a while and wondered if people were laughing with him or at him?

By the time senior year of high school rolled around, Benny didn't know how to be anything but funny, and he didn't want to learn. His mother had told him he ought to try to do birthday parties, paint himself up as a clown and make children laugh. Benny would rather have cut his own throat. He didn't want to do gags at birthday parties for a bunch of nose-picking brats; he wanted to perform in a circus.

The Macintosh Traveling Circus Troupe came to town in the spring of his senior year. The Macintosh was small enough that it still relied on posters hung at ice cream stands and grocery stores and barber shops to pull in an audience. In a little town like Corriveau, Vermont, that sort of thing still worked.

He'd gone to the circus every day, hung around before and after shows, talked to the workers, the animal trainers, the ticket takers, and eventually worked up the courage to talk to the clowns. By the third day, after hours, they invited him into clown alley to talk with them while they removed their makeup and hung up costumes and props. Benny could barely breathe. It had felt to him as though he had stepped into a film, or into history. He could smell the greasepaint, could practically feel the texture of the costumes, could hear the roar of the crowd, even though the tent had stood empty by then.

The second-to-last night, his hopes of an invitation fast

fading, he confessed his hopes and dreams and begged for an apprenticeship. The clowns had indulged him, patted him on the back, told stories of their own glory days, but none of them had encouraged him. It was a hell of a life, they'd said, something they would never wish on anybody. It was brutal on family and worse on love. Circus life set them apart from the rest of the world, created a distance that could never be bridged. Once you were in, you were in. They were trying to scare him off, but Benny had persisted.

Two hours after their final performance, as they were packing to move on, Zerbo—the boss clown—had given him the word. They'd take him on for the rest of the season, no pay, just food and a place to lay his head. If he was good enough to take part in the act by the season's end, and could get some laughs of his own, the circus manager—Mr. Appleby—would hire him on. If not, he'd be sent home.

Benny had given it his all, pulled out every gag, every funny face, every silly walk he had ever learned. He had studied the troupe, could stand-in for almost any of them if someone fell ill. At the end of the season, on the fairgrounds in Briarwood, Connecticut, they were as good as their word—a spotlight of his own, a chance to prove himself.

The laughs had been thin and the applause half-hearted, but Zerbo had given him the thumbs up. Tiny had told him later that it had been a near thing, but he'd worked so hard they had wanted to give him a second chance.

Now, four years of second chances later, he still felt like an apprentice.

That Friday night, Rose moved on. She'd mentioned a carnival somewhere, and a little league baseball tournament later in the week, but Benny hadn't really been listening. Kind as she'd been to him, a woman as attractive as Rose wasn't interested in doing more than selling him a book, and she'd done that already.

He stayed up all through that cool night, reading Tovolo's words over and over until the battery of his flashlight began to give out, the light to dim. By then, the horizon had begun to glow with the promise of dawn, but Benny read the final chapter of the book over a few more times. At first, he'd thought the whole thing was some kind of joke, Tovolo trying to pull one over on the reader, or attempting some tongue-in-cheek social commentary about circus life that didn't quite translate in his imperfect English. The book had been broken down into thirds—part one a memoir of his life, part two a kind of compendium of what he considered the funniest gags, and part three a reminiscence about his lifelong interest in the darker aspects of the history of clowns, everything from suicides and murders to haunted circuses and black magic.

The final chapter concerned Tovolo's lifelong struggle with his own talent, and his belief that he had never been funny enough. Two small circuses had merged, forcing him to perform alongside his longtime rival, Vincenzo Mellace, and every time the audience laughed for Mellace, Tovolo had wanted to set himself on fire. The reference to self-immolation made Benny shiver every time he read it, and he wondered if it had been written before or after the tragic blaze that had led to the Italian's retirement.

Tovolo had befriended a Belgian fire-eater who had come over from the other circus and who shared his hatred of Vincenzo Mellace. The fire-eater's mother travelled with her son, and sometimes told fortunes on the show grounds after the audience had gone home and the circus folk had drunk too much wine.

She had been the one to instruct him as to the ingredients for the elixir, and to explain to him precisely how to summon the spirit of *Polichinelle*, the patron of clowns, the demon known to children as the jester puppet Punch.

As the circus folk began to rise that Saturday morning, the day arriving overcast and bleak, Benny read Tovolo's final chapter over and over. Each time, he held his breath as he read the last few lines.

Mellace's routine was a disaster, he had written. *He has performed Busy Bee thousands of times, and yet it seemed like his first. Laughter was sporadic at best, and mostly sympathetic at that. There were boos. For myself . . . I could do no wrong. They laughed at a simple chase on the Hippodrome Track. They howled when Rostoni and I performed the Shoot-Out. And when I went out to do the Cooking Class gag on my own, it felt like a dream of how smoothly I have always wished for a performance to unfold.*

God, how they laughed.

I cannot say for certain that Polichinelle was in my corner tonight, but he was certainly no friend to Mellace. If offering the demon a little of my blood and a handful of days at the end of my life is all that is required for me to become the greatest clown in the world, it is a small price to pay.

When Benny heard Oscar and Tiny calling for him, he closed the book, yet as he went about his morning, he could think of nothing but the elixir and the summoning spell that the fire-eater's mother had given to Tovolo. One line kept repeating itself in his head.

God, how they laughed.

The blood seeping out of the midget car was Benny's first clue that something had gone awry. The audience kept laughing—either they hadn't seen it yet or they thought it was part of the show—so Benny didn't slow down. He waddled on his big shoes, storming with exaggerated frustration toward Clancy the Cop, and slapped the other clown in the face with a rubber chicken.

It looked like it hurt.

The audience roared.

He'd asked the demon Polichinelle for his heart's desire—to be the funniest clown in the circus. As blood flew from Clancy the Cop's split lip, Benny began to have second thoughts. He staggered backward, tripped over his own big clown feet, and let himself roll with the fall. His whole life had been spent performing such antics, so if there was anything he knew how to do, it was fall. He rolled on his curving spine, then flipped back up onto his feet and executed a fluid bow.

Clancy, snorting like a bull, eyes bulging with his fury, barrelled toward him running on an engine of vengeance. Benny saw him coming just in time, spun in a circle to avoid his outstretched hands, and whacked Clancy in the back of the head with the plucked, frozen chicken—it wasn't made of rubber anymore. The impact dropped Clancy to the ground, where he began to spasm and seize.

Benny lifted the chicken by its legs, examining it in full view of the audience. From their seats, they couldn't have seen the blood on the chicken, would presume his horror just a part of the act. He turned and looked at them, a wide-eyed clown mugging for the paying customers, and they ate it up. The stands were shaking with laughter.

Stunned, a dead, frozen chicken dangling from one clenched fist, Benny remembered the midget car. He turned, saw the blood dripping from the door seam, and started to run toward it. A scream filled the air and Benny spun to see Tiny standing in the window of the Hotshots building façade, his striped dress and blond wig both in flames that spread quickly to his arms and the baby doll bundled in his arms.

But from the way Tiny stared at the swaddled infant—and from the high, shrieking noise that could really be nothing else—Benny had the terrible idea that maybe it wasn't a doll in Tiny's arms. Not anymore. Not thanks to Polichinelle.

Burning alive, screaming baby in his arms, Tiny jumped from the façade, which was now engulfed in flames, and plummeted toward Oscar, who stood knee-deep in the water barrel below. Too late, Oscar realized his situation. He tried to climb out of the barrel, but tripped on the rim and fell half-in, half-out of the water, where he lay when Tiny and his baby struck Earth in a comet-like blaze. The trap-door opened and all three of them crashed through, water barrel and all. Steam and smoke rose with a hiss and the stink of burning hair and flesh began to fill the big top.

The applause was deafening. The laughter rolled through the tent like a hurricane.

Bobo shot Zerbo through the head during the Shoot-Out. The guns were supposed to be made of rubber. When Zerbo's only bullet went astray and killed a young father, passing through his popcorn tub on the way and spraying butter and popcorn onto a dozen people, the laughter turned to breathless, teary-eyed hysteria that reminded Benny of his mother.

Numb with shock, Benny staggered over to the midget car—what the public called a clown car—and vomited across the hood. Crimson leaked from every crevice in the miniature vehicle, pooling on the floor and running across the ground. The stink of blood and offal wafted off the midget car, and he felt as if he stood in an abattoir.

The driver's door popped open. A colourfully clad leg slipped out, and then Polichinelle climbed from the car. He wore a red and black jester costume, complete with ruffles at the shirt cuffs and bells atop his pronged hat and at the toes of his shoes. His alabaster skin did not appear to be makeup, nor did the bright red circles like burn scars on his cheeks.

Benny caught a glimpse of the carnage inside the midget car. The trap-door meant to be beneath it no longer existed. Eight clowns had been broken and twisted and jammed together to make sure they could all fit in a space that would've been cramped for two, and somehow Polichinelle had fit into the driver's seat.

Bobo stood in shock above the corpse of Zerbo, shaking and weeping. As Polichinelle pirouetted toward him, Bobo could only stare, but as he looked into the demon's eyes, he screamed.

Polichinelle plucked a trick flower from Zerbo's corpse and held it as if offering it to Bobo for a sniff. When he squeezed the rubber bulb dangling from the flower, an acrid-smelling liquid jetted out of it, coating Bobo's head. His scream rose to a shriek as his face began to melt and his eyes sank into his skull. When he crumpled to his knees and then toppled sideways to land beside Zerbo, his scream died.

Benny had never heard laughter so uproarious. The audience

cheered. Some stood and others doubled-over, clutching their bellies. Some slapped hands across their chests as their hearts burst and they slid into the aisles, gasping into cardiac arrest. Throats went hoarse, faces turned red, hands blistered from applause, but they couldn't stop. Their faces were stretched into grins that split the corners of their mouths and they wept tears of terror and pain and amusement, but they simply could not stop. It was, after all, the funniest thing they had ever seen.

God, how they laughed, Benny thought, and then, at last, he began to laugh as well.

Polichinelle performed a mad, capering little dance, part ballet and part mincing, mocking swagger, and then mimed a curtsy to the audience.

Through his laughter and his tears, Benny managed to choke out a single word.

"Why?"

Polichinelle gave him an apologetic shrug, an angelic look on the demon's face.

"You wanted to be the funniest clown in the circus."

Trying to catch his breath, Benny forced out the words. "All . . . all the others . . . are dead."

Polichinelle giggled. "Don't blame me, Benny. Blame your mother for all those years of lies."

Benny stared, eyes widening in horror. "My . . . my . . ." he gasped, but he couldn't get the word out.

"Sorry, pal," Polichinelle said. "But you're just not that funny."

The giant mallet seemed to appear from nowhere. Polichinelle gripped it in both hands as he swung, and Benny knew it wouldn't be made of hollow plastic or rubber. The crowd roared, laughing themselves to death.

God, how they laughed.

BREATHE MY NAME

There came a time when Tommy Betts thought they'd all have been better off if the mine had collapsed on top of them, crushing them under tons of stone and earth and coal. Better that, by far, than dying a little bit with every breath of poison air. Better that than seeing the fear in the faces of men he'd looked up to all his life, and desperation in his own father's eyes.

As a boy, Tommy had told his dad to be careful, worried that if they dug too deep, the miners might break through into Hell. His mother had still been making him go to church in Wheeling every Sunday back then, and Hell presented a special terror for him. His father and the other miners would come back with their clothes caked with black dust, faces painted with the same crap that filled their saliva when they'd spit, and Tommy worried they might one day encounter demons down there.

At eighteen, Tommy had gone into the mine for the first time and discovered that the church had a pretty simple vision of Hell, and what waited in Shaft 39 was a different sort of damnation altogether. In the seven years since, he'd learned that even the bravest man discovered claustrophobia in the deep underground, with the walls pressing in and the weight of a mountain hanging above him. The slightest tremor might be the end of days. Two miles into the heart of a mountain, they might as well have been floating in space. That first trip down, Tommy had understood that no matter how many precautions might be taken, the miners were on their own.

Rick Nilsson, one of his father's drinking buddies, had said the life of a miner was like playing Russian roulette every day for the rest of your life. You could find the chamber with the bullet any time, without warning. For Tommy and his dad, Al, and for Nilsson and Jerry Tolland and Rob McIlveen and Randy Wisialowski and a dozen other guys, it happened on the tenth of April.

It was raining, but no one complained about the black storm clouds or the soaking they got on the walk up from the parking lot. Underground it didn't matter what the weather was like outside. In fact, as far as Tommy was concerned, the shittier the day the better. It was the beautiful days when he wished he could be at home with Melissa, tossing a ball in the backyard with their boy, Jake, doing a little barbecue. Jakey was only five, but sometimes Tommy let him flip the burgers.

Stormy days, though, he didn't mind the mine so much. At least it was dry down there.

At the entrance to the mine, they waited for Wisialowski to show up. The guy was always fucking late and almost always hung over when he did show up. But Hanson, the shift supervisor, wouldn't let them go down until the whole shift had arrived. They were supposed to be there by 7:30. At a quarter to eight, just when Hanson was about to let them go down and dock Wisialowski for the whole day whether he showed up or not, the guy pulled into the lot.

"Standing out here in the rain waiting on this asshole," Tommy's dad muttered, standing next to him.

"I'm in no hurry to get down there," Tommy replied.

His father grunted. "Ain't the point."

Tommy didn't say anything to that. There was never any arguing with the old man. Even his eyes seemed chiselled out of stone, made of the same stuff they were digging into. He had a scar on his left temple from a fight years back when one of his crew had gone stir crazy down in the mine. Al Betts had been the one to finally subdue the head case, but not before the guy tried bashing his skull in. The rest of the crew looked up to Al. He wasn't the kind of man who started shit, but he'd be the one to put an end to it.

Hanson walked into their midst, hands up to get their attention. "All right, listen up! Wisialowksi, you paying attention?"

With the rain streaming down his slicker and spotting his glasses, the supervisor looked like an alien species standing amongst the miners. Wisialowski nodded, red-rimmed eyes anxious.

"This is the last time you're late, Randy," Hanson told him. "I'm saying this in front of everyone, so nobody can complain you weren't warned. Every time you're late, you cost us money. You're all going down twenty-five minutes later than scheduled. Multiply that by eighteen, and you're looking at seven and a half hours of accumulated time. So the next time you're late, I'm docking you— and only you—for the total accumulated time you've delayed the entire crew. And if there's a time after that, you'll be fired."

Nobody said a word. They stood in the rain and waited until Hanson sent them on their way. The whole crew climbed aboard the mantrip—the cable car that lowered the men into the mine and drew them back up again later. Only when they were on their way down into the ground with the lights flickering around them and the mantrip's wheels squeaking on the metal rails did the miners start to grumble. They cussed out Hanson, now that the supervisor wasn't there to hear them. Tommy said nothing. Every member of the crew had said much worse about Wisialowski themselves, but now that management had singled him out, the wagons would be circled. The guy was a drunk and a slacker even when he made it to the job on time, but he'd been down there in the tunnels with them and Hanson had probably never had coal dust under his manicured fingernails. At least, that was the way they looked at it.

Tommy thought the warning to Wisialowski had been more than fair, but he wouldn't dare say so.

Jerry Tolland sat next to him in the mantrip. He scowled and looked at Tommy. "Fucking Hanson."

Tommy just nodded, rolling his eyes.

"What'd you guys do this weekend?" Jerry asked.

That brought a smile to his face. "I'm building a tree fort for Jake. Ain't much of a carpenter, but it's coming out all right. Took

Melissa out to dinner Saturday night to that new place, Evergreen. No place to go for beers, but you want to make the wife happy, bring her there."

"Expensive?"

"Not like you'd think. Shit, they know nobody around here can afford expensive."

They fell silent after that. Something about the mine had that effect. The deeper they went, the quieter the miners became. It often lasted well into the first hour after work began, until they became acclimated again. Some people might have thought it was fear that made them quiet, but Tommy thought of it as respect. You worked down there in the ground, you had to give the mountain its due.

The mantrip squealed as it slowed, then rocked them a little as it came to a stop.

The crew stepped out of the contraption, cables swaying. There were burned out lights along the length of the shaft, but down here, they were all working perfectly. Not so much as a flicker. When it came to the workspace, they didn't fuck around. The dim yellow light washed over the stone.

"You smell something?" Jerry asked.

Tommy didn't. Jerry was always smelling something. Of the entire crew, he was the most paranoid, but nobody thought of it like that. More than once, Al Betts had told his son that paranoia could save his life. So Tommy took another whiff.

"I got nothing."

Jerry nodded. "Probably just me. McIlveen and I found that methane leak on Friday while we were drilling a bolt hole in the roof. Patched it up ourselves, so I'm not worried about that. But it's got me on edge."

"I'm never *not* on edge," Tommy said.

They fell into line with the rest of the crew, shuffling down the tunnel and into Shaft 39. Tommy's dad shouted something to

Nilsson and the two older guys—closing in on fifty and the senior members of the crew—laughed in such a way that Tommy knew whatever it was had been filthy. The second shift had a few women on the crew, but they'd never had any. Tommy thought maybe the big bosses knew what they were doing, keeping his father and Nilsson away from women miners. What a combination that would be.

They were deep in Shaft 39 when a frown creased Tommy's forehead. He caught a scent that made his nostrils flare and his upper lip curl. It reminded him of the odour that filled the house every time Melissa ran the self-cleaning program on the oven.

Jerry Tolland moved up beside him. "You sure you don't smell something."

"I smell it now," Tommy replied.

"What the fuck is that *stink*?" someone called from the back of the line, which made Tommy realize that the smell was coming from behind them.

A dull whump echoed along the shaft and the ground shook, just once. A kind of grinding noise reached them, and then only silence. Tommy searched the faces of the miners around him and saw them blanch. He glanced at his father and saw a momentary flicker of fear before Al Betts recovered from the moment.

"Holy shit," Rob McIlveen said.

Wisialowski put his head into his hands. "We're screwed." Jerry started to cough and then to choke. He covered his mouth and nose, panic in his eyes. Tommy tasted the gas on his tongue and then black smoke started billowing down along the tunnel after them.

"Fuck," Al said. "All right, this way. Everybody with me, and follow procedure. We're gonna be fine. We've just gotta buy ourselves some time until Hanson gets a team down here to get us out."

Nobody but Tommy had seen the flicker of fear in his father's eyes. They all nodded and fell into step behind him. But Tommy couldn't ignore the fact that they were going deeper into the mountain, farther away from the surface and clean air with every step.

Tommy watched as McIlveen and Jerry Tolland hung a plastic curtain across the shaft. All three of them wore emergency oxygen packs—rescuers, the miners called them—and over the top of Jerry's rescuer, his eyes were wild. His hands shook as he tucked the curtain up as best he could.

A steady, clanging noise came from behind Tommy. He turned and watched as his dad swung a sledgehammer against the plates and bolts that supported the walls and ceiling of the mine around them. Normally that kind of thing was ill-advised, but right now all they wanted was for someone up above to hear them. By now there would be a rescue attempt going on; folks would be looking for some sign of their location. The hammer on metal might be the only way to signal them.

Nilsson had found the sledgehammer, but now he sat on the floor against the back of the coal rib, his face covered with a bandanna— no rescuer for him. Of the eighteen men, only ten had working oxygen packs. The other rescuers were faulty. The guys who had working oxygen packs were taking turns, just like they were taking turns with the sledgehammer. Tommy felt like puking when he thought about it. These things were supposed to save their lives, give them enough air to last until someone could get to them, but nobody bothered to test them now and again to make sure they were working?

Someone tapped his arm and he turned to see that Jerry and McIlveen had gotten the curtain up.

"What do you think?" Jerry asked. "Cozy, huh?"

"Just like home," Tommy said.

Home. He'd been trying not to think of home, of Melissa and

Jake. Had they heard the news by now? Would Melissa tell Jake that Daddy was trapped down in the mine? No way. She wouldn't do that to the kid; he was only five years old. But Melissa would be trying to find someone to stay with him so that she could come and stand out there at the mouth of the mine, waiting.

She wouldn't be there yet. But soon, she'd be out there waiting on him.

Tommy didn't want to let her down. When he thought about leaving her alone, leaving Jake to grow up without his dad, his heart hurt so much he thought he might scream. No, better not to think of home.

The curtain had created an enclosure about fifty feet square. Not a lot of room for eighteen guys. Not a lot of air, even with the curtain up. The guys without working rescuers would suck up the remaining oxygen in no time.

Tommy watched his father swinging the sledgehammer. Al Betts had come home from the mine every night, black with coal dust and too exhausted to play very much with his son. Tommy had done his damnedest to be different, to make time for Jake whenever he could. But even with the best of intentions, sometimes he just couldn't.

The tree fort wasn't finished yet.

Jake had never even asked what would happen if the mine collapsed. At five, the possibility hadn't even occurred to him. Somehow he'd managed to avoid the fear that lay always beneath the friendly conversation of the entire community. Tommy hadn't been that lucky. He didn't remember how old he was when he first asked his father about what would happen in a cave-in. He had seen something about it in an old movie on television.

Watching his father now—still so strong and grim while closing in on fifty—he remembered the way the man had softened. He'd crouched down to get even with Tommy and ruffled his son's hair.

"You've got nothing to worry about, Tom-Tom. Anything goes wrong down there, the Lost Miner will get us out."

Tommy's eyes had gone wide. "The Lost Miner?"

That had only been the first time his father told him the story. For years, Tommy had asked for stories of the mysterious, ghostly miner. His father had spun tales, mostly of his own invention, but some of them surely local legend, of a man who had died underground, and who would always appear to save trapped miners who called to him. By the age of eleven, Tommy had realized that they were only stories, but some part of him had still believed. When his father decided he was too old for such stories, he had felt a terrible loss.

Al swung the sledgehammer. He turned to glance at Nilsson and the others who were without oxygen packs, then wiped the sweat from his brow. Al Betts was no ghost, and he wasn't lost, but Tommy thought his old man might be their best hope.

He went over to his father and reached out to take the sledgehammer. "Have a rest, Dad. Let me take a few whacks."

His father nodded slowly and bent over, winded.

Tommy stared at him. "You all right?"

"I will be. Give it a go, Tom."

As he turned to go and sit with the others against the coal rib, Tommy called to him. Al came back and put a hand on his arm, gave it a brief squeeze.

"We're gonna be all right. Just gotta hunker down, now, try not to suck up any more air than we need. Sip at it, make it last. They'll be here."

Tommy studied his face, searching for a crack in his father's mask of confidence but finding none. Maybe it was for his benefit—his and the rest of the crew's—but right then he thought his father actually felt confident that, even with so little air for so many of them and with the toxins seeping in around the edges of the curtain, they would be rescued in time. Two miles into the mine, out of contact with the surface, Al Betts believed in salvation. Blind faith.

"Hey, Dad?"

Al looked at him over the top of the rescuer's mask.

"You remember the Lost Miner?"

Tommy thought that, behind the mask, his father smiled. "I've been thinking about him, too."

"Did he have a name? The original guy, I mean. The one who died."

The older man narrowed his eyes in contemplation a moment. "Ostergaard, I think. Something like that."

Ostergaard. For some reason, having the name made Tommy feel better. He gripped the handle of the sledgehammer the same way his mind wrapped around the name of the Lost Miner. Something to hold on to.

He swung the hammer against a metal support plate and the clang reverberated up his arms. Tommy barely noticed his father walking away. Barely noticed anything at all after that first swing. He counted the hammer blows just to keep his mind busy. At thirty-two, he took a break. Rob McIlveen was sprawled on the floor, a t-shirt over his face. He looked asleep or dead, but the rise and fall of his chest made it clear he was still breathing. In the flickering light, Nilsson had gone awfully pale. He had a rescuer covering his nose and mouth now, getting oxygen, but the way he clutched at his chest, Tommy thought maybe he was having a heart attack.

At fifty-seven strikes of the hammer, Jerry Tolland took over. Tommy hesitated, hating the thought of just sitting there waiting to run out of air. But he could barely lift the hammer anymore.

He staggered to the far wall and sat down. After a few minutes he tried to offer his oxygen pack to Randy Wisialowski, but the guy waved it away.

"I just gave mine up a few minutes ago," he said through the front of his sweatshirt, which covered his nose and mouth. "Besides, you've been trying to signal, working your lungs. Wouldn't be fair to cut off your air now."

Tommy stared at him a moment, then nodded and slumped

back against the wall. He studied the curtain, wondered how toxic the air had become. Above their heads, the tunnel had a thin layer of smoke. Keeping low to the ground was safer, but it wouldn't save their lives.

"Randy?"

Wisialowski looked up, his reaction time slow, like he'd had too much to drink and might pass out any second.

"Hmm?"

"You ever hear about the Lost Miner?"

"Sure. Everyone knows that story. You don't grow up with family in the mine and not hear that old tale."

"So you think it's just a story."

Tommy saw the doubt in the man's eyes. "Of course it is. Jesus, kid, you better just sit there a bit, soak up some oxygen."

"But if the story's based on a real guy who died in the mines, how do we know, right? I mean, every legend starts somewhere, right?" Wisialowski knotted his brows. "Did you miss the part where the guy died?"

Nine or ten guys had taken turns with the hammer before, at last, none of them were strong enough to lift it. McIlveen and Bob Landry had fallen unconscious. Bob had been in and out for a while, but nobody could wake McIlveen.

They didn't talk much, trying to conserve air. What little conversation took place down there in the heart of the mountain was in whispers, men sharing regrets and fears. Wisialowski talked about the way his drinking had driven his wife, Lorraine, away, and how he would have done it all so differently if he had it to do over. Some of the men were writing notes on scraps of paper from their wallets or on torn pieces of clothing, just wanting to leave something behind, some reassurance or a farewell or a last expression of love. They told each other it was just in case.

Just in case.

Tommy stared across the small enclosure at his father, and Al stared back, never looking down at Nilsson, who lay with his head on Tommy's dad's lap, unmoving.

"Christ," Wisialowski said at one point. "Is he . . . ?"

Al froze him with a look and Wisialowski never completed the question. That grim expression was answer enough. None of the others had been foolish enough to ask. Or, Tommy thought, perhaps they just hadn't wanted to acknowledge the death that had taken place in their midst.

"Ostergaard," Tommy said.

The name echoed against the stone and the coal rib and the curtain. The men who were still alive and conscious all turned to stare at him.

"What's that?" Jerry said.

"The Lost Miner," Tommy said, pulling the mask of his rescuer down. "We've gotta call on him. Nobody else is coming, Jer. We're gonna die down here, we don't get some help."

"Are you fuckin' thick?" Dan Raymo snapped. "We tellin' ghost stories, now, or you got brain damage from the fuckin' methane?"

Tommy blinked. His eyes felt heavy. "Gotta call him." He sat up straighter, looked around at the walls, settled his gaze on the coal. "Ostergaard! You gotta come, man. We need you, now. Ostergaard. We need your help or we're gonna die down here."

"Tom," his father snapped.

Tommy looked at him.

"Shut it, boy," his old man rasped.

It felt like a slap. He flinched, then hunched down a bit. Tommy pulled his rescuer back over his face. He closed his eyes and whispered the name into his mask, over and over. *Ostergaard*.

He woke, suffocating. His chest clenched and the muscles in his throat began to seize up. Eyes wide, Tommy reached up and scrabbled at his face, tearing away his mask. The oxygen in his rescuer had run out. He clawed it off and dropped it to the ground.

In his mind, he began to roll over and sit up, but his body was sluggish in its reply. He managed to loll his head to one side and then prop himself up enough to look around.

Sometimes he drank a little, but this wasn't like being drunk. It was more what he imagined it must feel like for people who took too many sleeping pills or Hollywood types into heavy narcotics. The small space between the curtain and the coal rib seemed to shift and blur. His eyelids felt heavy. Nearby, Wisialowski had curled up into a fetal ball, softly crying. Raymo had sprawled onto the stone floor of the tunnel on his face, breath coming in long, shallow hisses, body twitching. Jerry Tolland sat against the wall with his knees up under his chin, arms draped over his legs. Staring at him, Tommy frowned. It took him a moment to understand that Jerry was dead.

"Dad?" he whispered. He gazed toward the far wall, where his father had been sitting with Nilsson. Someone shifted there. In the fading glow of their remaining lights, a hand rose up—his father, signalling that he had not yet breathed his last.

But it wouldn't be long for Al Betts. Whatever rescue might be in the offing, it needed to happen now. The sledgehammer lay on the floor, forgotten.

Tommy ran out his tongue to wet his lips, opened his mouth in a last prayer. But instead of Jesus, the name that came out of his mouth was *Ostergaard*.

His eyes felt even heavier. He slumped back to the ground, unable to keep himself propped up any longer. As he lay there listening to the silence, to the weight of the mountain closing around them, he knew that there would be no rescue. They were alone.

Pain began to spread in a band across his chest. Every breath felt more difficult than the last. For several long moments, he succumbed to unconsciousness again. Then a sound made his eyes flutter open—a low moan, accompanied by a hideous choking noise.

Again he rolled his head to the side, searching for the source of that sound. His upper lip curled and for a moment he ceased breathing at all. A man stood in the midst of the enclosure. He was dressed in full mining gear, but wore an old-fashioned sort of miner's helmet with a light on the front and a black gas mask beneath it.

A flutter of hope went through Tommy. *Him.*

Barely conscious, he managed a smile.

Until that figure leaned down and touched Wisialowski on the shoulder, and the crying man went silent and still. No weeping. Not so much as a shudder of breath. And then the strange figure, a coal-smeared silhouette, began to move through the enclosure, pausing to reach down a comforting hand to the other men. As he passed amongst them, he almost seemed to float, and the edges of the figure blurred like heat haze over summer blacktop. And when he touched them, one by one, they became still.

As the Lost Miner moved toward the coal rib—toward the place where he had seen his father raise one weakened hand—Tommy closed his eyes. He heard a rattling hiss of breath and then nothing.

He felt so cold.

Something jostled him awake. Tommy winced at the smell of exhaust. Only vaguely aware of his surroundings, of a sense of motion, he felt the rubber strap against the back of his head and plastic over his nose and mouth.

"Fuckin' sick irony," a voice said.

Tommy tried to open his eyes. He caught a glimpse of the two paramedics working to keep him alive, and he heard them talking about him . . . about the sole survivor of the collapse, and how if those other poor bastards had lived any longer, he wouldn't have made it either.

"The only reason he had enough oxygen is 'cause the other guys died first."

The ambulance went over another bump and he felt himself slipping into darkness once more. Fading to black.

"Babe? You all right?"

Tommy stood just inside the screen door off the kitchen, looking out onto the backyard. June had come so fast. He held a cold beer in his hands the way a child might hold a doll, close against him, fingers wrapped around the neck. Out in the yard, Jake ran through the spray of water thrown by the sprinkler, whipping his arms around and cackling like a lunatic. Katie Hoyt from next door followed right behind him. Their laughter did not make him smile, but somehow it seemed to protect him. He felt like if he could record that sound and play it back while he slept, it might keep the dreams away, the nightmares of suffocation.

"Babe?"

Melissa touched his arm and he blinked, turning to look at her.

"You look like you're in a trance," she said, smiling innocently, though her eyes were full of concern.

"I was. Still a little tired, that's all."

She kissed his cheek. "Dinner'll be ready in a little while. You should get Jake in here, get him into something dry."

Tommy nodded. He took a sip of beer and set the bottle down on the kitchen table, then went out into the backyard.

"Daddy!" Jake called, racing toward him.

Once, Tommy might have caught him and dangled the boy away from him to keep from getting wet. Not now. He let Jake jump up into his arms and hugged the boy to him. His son wrapped his legs around him, soaking his shirt. Tommy actually laughed.

"Sorry, Katie," he told the girl. "Jake's gotta come in for dinner now."

"Can he come out after?" she asked, all wide eyes.

"Sure," Tommy said. "Why don't you run on home and we'll see you in a bit. I think Jake's mom is gonna make brownies tonight."

Katie took off across the backyard toward her parents' deck, arms out as though she was playing airplane. Tommy set Jake down and shut off the sprinkler, then stood and looked again at his son.

"Mom wants you to put something dry on."

Jake smiled, pointing at him. "She's going to want you to put something dry on, too."

"No doubt," Tommy said. "C'mere, bud."

He hoisted the boy up again and went up to the screen door, letting them inside. Melissa had been watching from the kitchen window, a wistful look on her face.

"Dry clothes, Jakey," she said.

"I can do it! I'll get 'em!" the boy said, reaching to be put down.

Tommy let him down and Jake tore through into the living room and then they heard him bounding up the stairs. He'd kick his clothes off onto the carpet of his bedroom and put dry clothes on, but that was all right. They'd pick the dirty clothes up later.

Melissa slipped her arms around Tommy and pushed up close. He liked her there, where he could smell her hair and trace his hands along the small of her back.

"It's been so good for him, having you home for a while," she said, her breath warm on his neck. "It's been good for you, too."

"Yeah," he said. And that was all.

There were so many thoughts he might have shared with her, but Tommy had never been that kind of man. In that, he took after his father. He would have felt like a fool trying to explain to Melissa that the time he spent with Jake seemed to make it easier to deal with his father's death, and to make it harder as well. But he wanted every moment he could have with them, there at home, because the doctor had been clear about his prognosis. Another week, two at the most, and he'd have to go back to work.

He'd have to go back down into the mine.

Jake came down the stairs and pranced into the kitchen to show off the t-shirt and shorts he'd put on. The shirt was on backwards, but Tommy didn't mention it. The kid was so damned proud of himself.

The t-shirt had a bunch of trucks on it. Jake loved building things and even at five, thought the coolest job in the world had to be making bridges and skyscrapers. "I want to build a whole city," he'd said once, not long ago.

"Good job, buddy," Tommy said.

"Dinner!" Jake commanded, slipping into his seat at the table and picking up his fork and knife, ready to eat.

"Yes, your majesty. Coming right up," Melissa said, rolling her eyes with a soft chuckle.

"Then brownies!" Jakey cried.

"But of course."

Tommy had to control the temptation to talk about the trucks on Jake's shirt, one of which was a crane. Melissa had already pointed out how much he'd been harping the past couple of weeks on the construction thing. Jake was only five, she'd said. He'd change his mind almost daily about what he wanted to be when he grew up. Tommy had told her that all he wanted was to make sure Jake went to college. No one in his family had ever been to college.

College, somewhere away from West Virginia. Away from the mine.

He wanted his son to grow up to get a job doing something he loved, something that would make him happy. Hopefully. But if not, Tommy wanted Jake to do something he hated. Anything, really, except following in Daddy's footsteps. Anything except the mine.

But college cost a lot of money. Nobody in the Betts family had ever gotten that kind of education. Hell, Tommy was the first one to finish high school. They were a mining family, like so many others in the area. The odds were against them, and against Jake finding a different sort of life for himself.

And so tonight, before bed, Tommy would tell Jake the first of the stories. Oh, he'd been telling his son stories almost every night, the past couple of months. All kinds of stories. But as of tonight, he would from time to time include tales of the ghost of a lost miner named Ostergaard. He would tell them as best he could, make them as real as possible. It wouldn't be difficult. Jake loved ghost stories. But Tommy had to make absolutely certain that his son believed.

Just in case.

THE ART OF THE DEAL

Craig met the negotiator away from the office like it was some clandestine afternoon fuck, the really dirty kind when you can't even meet the eyes of people on the street because you think they'll be able to tell. There would be no torrid sex during his rendezvous, but someone was certainly going to get screwed. Eighty-seven someones, actually.

The Hotel Atheneum was a grand old dame, as they used to say in an age when the common man still understood what it meant to venerate beauty and high achievement. It stood a block from the Boston Public Library, just at the edge of Copley Square, some of the trendiest real estate in the city. To Craig it was nothing more than neutral territory. The negotiator from IllumiNet had wanted the meet to take place at their lawyers' office at One International Place. Craig's own attorney had suggested IllumiNet send their people out to Cambridge, thinking that they would benefit from home field advantage.

But that was impossible. Craig hadn't told his employees about the buyout yet. New England Electrical Safety Systems had been in his family for forty-two years. Half a dozen of his staff were second generation at NEESS and others had been there almost as long as Craig had been alive. His father had brought him into the offices as a kid and these folks had been his extended family.

So much for loyalty, he thought as he pushed through the revolving door and stepped into the hotel. He glanced around, taking it all in. The chandeliers, the polished wood and brass, the strategically placed plants. At the grand piano in the corner an attractive brunette woman played an old Billy Joel song.

He froze a moment. His face flushed warmly and bile rose in the back of his throat. *Turn around, Craig. Just turn around and walk out. You don't have to do this.*

But he did. NEESS had suffered its worst year ever. The industry was consolidating and he either had to let the company be merged into one of the bigger players or shut the doors completely. Craig had done everything he could, but they'd been hemorrhaging money for years. He had made a promise, once upon a time, that as CEO he would not take a salary higher than the best paid of his employees and he had kept that promise, no matter how much it had cost him.

His marriage, for instance.

Guilt and humiliation pinned him to the spot, there in the lobby of the Atheneum. The comparison to the covert assignations of a cheating spouse rose up in his mind again and nausea roiled in his gut. Hannah had been the one to cheat on him, not the other way around. She was the one engaging in sweaty hotel sex. Craig's reward for fidelity was obscenely high alimony.

Your Honor, the amount in question is fully three quarters of Mr. Spencer's annual after-tax earnings. Are you penalizing the one person in this marriage who respected the vows they both made?

Craig had just sat there with his mouth agape. The numbers were burned into his brain but he had been thinking he had misheard right up until the judge had fixed him with as disdainful a glance as Craig had ever witnessed.

Mrs. Spencer's counsel has made a convincing argument that as the owner and chief executive officer of his company, he is entitled to a far greater salary than he currently draws. Perhaps this is some outmoded sense of equity, but I'm inclined to believe the assertion that it is an attempt to elicit from this court an alimony payment far lower than Mrs. Spencer should rightfully expect.

That had done him in. Craig had kept the company afloat during very dark times, had somehow managed to make it all work. In the wake of Hannah's betrayal, he had given all his love to the job and used NEESS as his lifeline, putting all of his energies there. All his life he had tried to be a fair man, to provide for his family and his employees. Then the Commonwealth of Massachusetts had decreed that he was a sap. A sucker. Loyalty and equity were *outmoded*.

Craig Spencer had inherited some integrity and principal from his father, some sense of people's dignity. Somehow in the morass of cynicism the world had become, he'd held on to it. And they crucified him for it.

Enough was enough. He had done all he could. At least this way, some of his employees would retain their jobs after the merger. He had no choice. It was the right thing to do.

So what are you doing standing in the lobby looking like a fool, ready to puke on your shoes?

"Mr. Spencer?"

Somehow, in the buzz of voices and dinging of elevators that filled the lobby, the negotiator had managed to walk up on him unheard. The man had a name, but Craig never liked to use it, for it ascribed to him a humanity that he had clearly abandoned a very long time ago. He was a crusher of hope. A killer of dreams. All wrapped up in a mask of kindly concern and rationality.

"Hello," Craig said, voice sounding hollow even to himself. His hand felt numb as he held it out to shake. "Thank you for agreeing to meet here."

"Whatever you need to make you feel as comfortable as possible," said the negotiator. He showed his too-white teeth in a shark smile, eyes sparkling with amusement disguised as genuine sympathy. His hair had a scatter of silver in amongst the dark and was cut short. Very now. Yet his face was young and cut and handsome, so much so that if Craig didn't know any better—and really, he didn't, did he?—he would have suspected the negotiator of adding those little flecks of silver to his hair to earn some of the respect that came with age.

The man took him by the arm and propelled him toward the hotel bar. Like a somnambulist, Craig shuffled along. There were only a handful of people in the bar and for that he was grateful. Glasses clinked as the bartender racked clean ones behind the counter. The lights were low and the sunlight seemed disinclined to come very far into the bar, as though it hesitated to disrupt the gloom. The negotiator chose well, leading Craig to a corner table at the far end of the bar, the very spot he would have picked himself, hiding in shame.

What he had not expected was that they would not be alone. Already at the table was a woman in a red dress. She stood as they approached and Craig did his best to hide the instant reaction he had to her. It was all he could do not to mutter 'whoa' under his breath. Tall and thin, she had Asian features and shoulder-length, stylish black hair that shone like silk in the dim glow of the bar. Her smile was knowingly sultry and suddenly his cock had a pulse. All the fucking luck. He'd barely had any interest in sex since Hannah had emasculated him in court. Now wasn't the time.

"Craig, let me introduce you to my wife, Anita. Honey, Craig's the gentleman I was telling you about, from NEESS."

So interested, Anita nodded and held out a hand to shake. "Right. The family business. My husband's told me a lot about the deal you two have going on. What you've been able to do for your employees is pretty amazing, Craig. They don't make men like you anymore."

California girl, from the way she spoke. He ought to have been appalled by her presumptuousness. What was she doing talking about the deal anyway. As far as Craig knew she didn't even work for IllumiNet. The negotiator shouldn't even have been discussing the situation with her until the deal was done. That was how whispers started. And Craig didn't want any whispers. Not until it was over and then he would face the anger and disappointment from his people all on his own.

Sure, he *ought* to have been appalled. It was just the sort of bullshit sucking up that the negotiator always dropped into their conversations and that Craig despised. But Anita's eyes were so kind and her expression so genuine that he felt a swelling of righteous pride in his heart. His father had been a good man. The kind of man you just didn't find in the world anymore. An *outmoded* man. And Craig was happy to think even for a moment that he might measure up.

Whatever it had cost him.

After all, they didn't make men like him anymore. Ask Anita. He smiled at her.

"That's very kind of you, Anita," he said. "I've always tried to follow my father's example. To do my best for the people who work for me."

As the three of them sat down, the negotiator signalled to the waiter. Meanwhile, Anita's attention was on Craig. She gazed at him with those brown eyes, so filled with understanding.

"But the world is changing," she said, nodding sadly. "The way we do business is changing. No one man can do it all these days. It's all about alliances."

"That's it exactly, sweetheart," the negotiator said. He focused his shark smile on Craig. "She has a way of getting right to the heart of things, doesn't she? It's her magic."

Craig nodded out of courtesy but the moment the bastard had spoken up he felt uneasy again. Where was the small talk? Where was the polite, happy bullshit they were supposed to start with? Nothing about this meeting was turning out the way he had expected. He didn't want to be here. Not at all. Circumstances were forcing his hand. He had held fate off for as long as he could, and the negotiator and his employers knew that. But the least the fucking guy could do was let him work up to it slowly.

"Listen," Craig began.

But his train of thought was interrupted by the arrival of the waiter, asking what they would like to drink.

"I don't think I—"

"Go on, Craig. One won't kill you. Sometimes it helps to have a glass in your hand when you're hashing out the final details." The negotiator glanced at his wife.

"Well, while you boys decide, I'm going to have a Manhattan," Anita said, flashing a radiant smile at the waiter and tucking a lock of that silken hair behind her ear. "It's an old-fashioned drink, I know, but I'm an old-fashioned girl."

"Craig?" the negotiator prodded him, waiting to see what he would order.

"Seven and Seven," Craig said at last.

Anita gave him an approving smile. "There you go. You won't be sorry."

And that was the beginning. The negotiator took the departure of the waiter as his opening and the business began. No more preamble than that. Craig figured his idea of foreplay with Anita was a slap on the ass. The cosmic wrongness of it all was not lost on him. As the negotiator went over the points that still needed to be addressed—mainly having to do with how many NEESS employees would lose their jobs and how many shares of IllumiNet stock Craig would take away from the deal—he marvelled at how a woman of such obvious intelligence and integrity could be married to such a shark. The negotiator must have made her a hell of a pitch.

The waiter came with a second round and as Craig sipped his Seven and Seven, Anita seemed more and more to lure the two men off into conversational tangents that had nothing to do with business. NEESS was in Cambridge, and she wanted to talk about Harvard Square, and a quaint little restaurant she'd been to there. Somehow the talk shifted to art, and then she really came alive.

The negotiator kept pulling them back to business, but Craig would much rather listen to Anita talk about art. Her eyes lit up and she spoke with such fire that she made the subject fascinating, though his own interest in art was only a fraction of hers. The passion in her made her even more beautiful. He was aware during the conversation that Anita was another man's wife and so he tried to keep up a façade of detached curiosity. But more and more he watched her lips as she spoke and admired the curve of her neck, where he wanted desperately to kiss her.

"Look," he said, standing suddenly even as the waiter delivered his third drink, unasked. "I've got to go. I'm . . . I need a night to sleep on all of this. You're talking about less than a quarter of my employees keeping their jobs. I was led to believe the number would be much higher than that. These people are depending on me and . . . I just . . . I'll call you in the morning. I'll come to you."

The negotiator was startled and a flash of annoyance swept his face, revealing too-sharp teeth, completing the shark-allusion. "Hey, hey, Craig. What's the problem? You knew all of these deal points before you got here. We went over everything with your lawyer this morning. It's really a formality, now. I sent a messenger over to your lawyer's office with the paperwork. You're going to meet with him later, right?"

Craig understood the question. The meeting really had been just a formality, an opportunity for him to ask last-minute questions. He was supposed to go straight to his lawyer's office from here and sign the papers.

"I'll . . . look, I'll call you in the morning."

He turned to Anita. "I'm sorry to leave so abruptly. It was a pleasure meeting you."

"And you," she said, her eyes full of concern. "Don't worry. My husband has a job to do, but you have to do things in your own time."

The negotiator seared her with a look. Craig smiled at Anita, pleased that she had annoyed her husband on his behalf.

"Thank you."

That night as the clock ticked toward eight P.M., Craig sat at his desk staring out the window at the lights of Cambridge dotting the darkness. He could not bring himself to go home. The truth was that since his divorce, and perhaps even before it, this was home. This chair, this desk, this *place*. This company had raised him, in its way. In these halls he had grown from boy to man, with dozens of aunts and uncles to help guide him, from Sam Small in the mailroom to Debbie Tyll in the typing pool.

So strange to think of Debbie, dead now over a dozen years. What was truly bizarre was not her mortality, but the idea that he was old enough to remember when a company needed a typing pool . . . that such an antiquated occupation was not a relic from the twenties and thirties but as recent as 1990. Then again, the whole place was antiquated now, wasn't it? Even the occupation of CEO. Outmoded.

His father had kept a bottle of Wild Turkey in the desk and taken a single drink on Christmas Eve and one on his birthday. That was another tradition that Craig had kept up. He did not believe in drinking on the job. In his life outside of this office, what little of it there was, he rarely drank alcohol of any kind. But every year on Christmas Eve and on *his* birthday—Dad's, not his own—he had one drink.

Tonight that was yet another bit of his integrity that he had thrown away. The glass on his desk was half empty, but he had topped it off twice already. He had not bothered to turn on additional lights in the office as the night had fallen and so aside from a small lamp in one far corner of the room the only light was the glow of his computer screen. Open on the screen was Sam Small's human resources file. The others were all there as well, just a click away. Before him on the desk was a yellow legal pad and a pen. He had made a list of all of his employees, trying to figure out which would lose their jobs and which would remain, and whether or not he could save one or two more, making their positions seem more vital to IllumiNet than they probably were.

He wasn't having much luck, not because these weren't valuable people, but because IllumiNet didn't value much.

Also on his desk, in a thick manila folder, were all the documents for the finalization of the deal with IllumiNet. He'd had his lawyer send them over but so far had not been able to bring himself to look at them. Craig took another sip of Wild Turkey and the whiskey seared his throat, opening up his sinuses. He ran his tongue over his teeth, licking away the slick sugary film that covered them.

"Alcohol won't do it."

The voice was enough to startle him nearly out of his chair. He half-turned abruptly, his hand barely missing the chance to knock whiskey all over his computer keyboard. Anita stood in the open doorway, leaning against the jamb in that breathtaking red dress. For all that she had been stunning before, she was more so now that he saw her entirely. Her body was petite, though she was taller than he had imagined, and her legs were strikingly sculpted below the hem of the short dress.

"What's that?" he asked, confused by her arrival.

"Alcohol. If you're trying to distract yourself or soothe your soul, alcohol isn't the answer."

Through a slight whiskey haze it took him a moment to evaluate his reaction. She was a charming woman and as lovely as he had ever seen. But she was not supposed to be here.

"Anita." He frowned. "I don't mean to be rude, but how did you get in here?"

Her smile was almost shy. She shrugged her shoulders as much as her posture, leaning there in the doorway, would allow. "I can be pretty persuasive."

Craig could not help laughing at that. He had no idea what she had said to the security guards downstairs, but the mischief in her eyes was infectious. "I have no doubt of that."

Then his humour was gone. He reached out for his whiskey but hesitated with his fingers an inch from the glass as he glanced up at her.

"Don't stop on my account," she said. "Every man has his poison."

His throat was dry. He licked his teeth again and settled back into the chair without touching the whiskey glass. The bottle of Wild Turkey seemed an ominous presence there on his desk, out in the open, but he ignored it.

"What brings you here? Does . . . does your husband know where you are?"

Her gaze shifted away from him for a moment that was filled with doubt, and then she tried on a mask of a smile. "Of course he does."

A lie. Craig sat up a bit straighter in his chair, the whiskey haze clearing away now just enough for his interest to stir. What was she doing here late at night without her husband's knowledge?

"You still haven't said why you're here. What is it you want?"

Her eyes narrowed. No trace of a smile remained on her face. "To make a deal."

"I'm afraid I'm not following you."

"Oh, but I think you are."

Stunned as he was—this was, after all, the sort of lurid thing he would never have imagined himself involved in—Craig was not a stupid man. Anita had been kind to him at lunch, nothing more. A sweet, intelligent woman who apparently had a bit more in common with her negotiator-husband than it had seemed at first glance. Craig was relieved that she was managing to avoid falling into the role of some Humphrey Bogart movie femme fatale. Along with the mischief there was eagerness and desperation in her eyes, and more than a little sorrow as well.

But she wasn't going to bullshit him.

Anita entered the office at last, stepping away from the threshold and taking up a stance before him reminiscent of some errant schoolgirl called down to the headmaster's office. She had her hands behind her back and though her breasts were small this made them more prominent. Her back arched slightly.

Her eyes never left his. Those mischievous eyes. Awkward

though she might seem, something about her was amused by the scenario they were playing out.

"You know this deal is going to happen," Anita assured him. "IllumiNet is acquiring your company."

"Then why are you here?" The question was purposely blunt. No games.

"At lunch I got the distinct impression that you might turn your regret into the need to do something to make it difficult. To impede the process. My husband . . . has had enough impediments in his work lately. He's had a couple of big deals go sour. He needs this one to close smoothly. And, frankly, I think you do, too. From everything he's told me about your financial situation most of these people would lose their jobs even if you didn't sell. You can help some of them or none of them. I just wanted to talk to you . . . to make sure you do what's best for everyone. This thing should be easy, not ugly. But you could make it ugly."

A bitterness rose like bile in the back of his throat. She shifted her weight from one foot to the other and the dress seemed to caress her body. He had been becoming increasingly aroused by her presence, but now his cock went rigid.

"And you . . ." he said in a rasping voice, "you could make it beautiful."

At last her smile returned. "Something like that."

"No build-up to it, then?" he asked, amazed and entranced by her. "No talk about how you were attracted to me at lunch, no more bullshit about my integrity."

Her brow knitted and she winced as if hurt. A new boldness arose in her. "All right. If you want frankness, I don't find you especially attractive. But I wasn't playing you at lunch. I do admire your integrity, the way you've tried to take care of people here. There should be . . . there should be more of that in the world. And I could see how painful this all is for you. I'm not going to lie. I'm here selfishly. My husband needs this deal to keep his career afloat, and I can't afford for him to mess it up. But I thought you might benefit as well. I thought with all that's been happening in your life, you could use a . . . distraction."

Craig's chest rose and fell too quickly. He stared at her in disbelief. This place, this company that had been his home since his boyhood, seemed to hold its breath, wondering what he would do. It was on its deathbed, and his poor management had put it there. Yet it was still all he had in the world, and this woman's husband was the one orchestrating its removal from his hands. He was reminded of a book his father's secretary, Janine Wylie, had given him for his seventh birthday. *The Giving Tree*, it was called. It concerned a boy who loved to climb a particular tree, to swing from it and eat its fruit, and the way it offered him everything it had only to try to make him happy, no matter what, and in the end can only give a very old man a stump upon which to sit and rest. And yet at the man's advanced age, the stump is all he needs to be content, and both he and the tree are happy.

Craig had envisioned himself and NEESS as the boy and the tree. Growing old together. Himself knowing that wherever he went in the world and whatever he did, the company awaited him back home. But IllumiNet was taking that contentment from him, and the negotiator was the one making absolutely certain there wasn't even a crumb left behind for him, or the employees he had watched over for so long.

In his long silence, Anita had shifted anxiously several times and now her face flushed with embarrassment and she turned away from him. "Obviously it was a mistake even coming here. Forgive me for making such a fool of myself."

She was so damned beautiful, so delicate and perfect. He was even more aroused now at the sight of her vulnerability.

"Wait!"

With one hand on the doorframe she paused, head hung low, her hair a silken black curtain sweeping downward, but she did not turn to face him.

"It wasn't . . . it wasn't a mistake." His whole body trembled, his skin tingling. It seemed like eons since he had made love to a woman and if he was honest with himself he had never made love to a woman as fine as Anita.

"What . . ." he licked his lips now, but it wasn't from the whiskey. He felt embarrassed by the eagerness that rose in him, but his cock was so hard in his pants that it hurt. "What did you have in mind?"

"We talked about art," she whispered. Then she stood straighter and turned to face him, the mischief back in her eyes and her chest rising and falling in quick rhythm. "I thought I might show you my collection."

What are you doing, Craig? he thought, almost giddy. *You're complicating everything. You're going to make this whole thing even messier than it already is.*

But deep inside, a part of him he had sublimated for most of his life was waking up. He was through doing everything for others and not watching out for himself. This was where that had gotten him. A whoring wife, a failing company, and the public humiliation of losing both of them.

Yeah, he thought, grinning. *Yeah, I am.*

"Where?" he asked, surrendering to temptation. In the roiling chaos of his bitterness and resentment, he did not have the strength to overcome it, and deep down part of him was glad about it. "Where do we go to see your collection?"

Anita warmed to the role of seductress now. Her thin smile was knowing and sweet all at once. Here he was, this shattered man, and she was going to ease his pain. She seemed to like that idea, and he was not about to disabuse her of it.

"We don't have to go anywhere," she said. "You can see it all right here."

She moved toward his desk again, came around the side to stand only a few feet away. Her fingers came up and slipped the straps of her dress aside and she let it glide down her body, sliding to the floor to pool around her red heels.

Craig could not breathe. His chest hurt. She wore nothing beneath the dress. His heart beat like a hummingbird's wings and it was like the very first time he had seen a girl nude all over again. That had been Sara Dobler, two years older and two years wiser, after the freshman dance in the fall of his first year of high school. Sara had let him touch her all over. And back then, touching had been more than enough. He had stammered and held his breath and marvelled at the soft smoothness of her, at the hardness of her nipples and the way in which her body responded to his hands.

This was that awe of discovery all over again.

Anita's body was perfect, her skin a bronze Asian hue, her small breasts tipped with long nipples. Her belly was taut and her hips were round. Her legs were supple and between them, her pussy was completely shaved, the lips tucked away like the petals of a flower just about to blossom. He had heard that this was the style now, the trend, but had never been with a woman before who shaved.

And yet in spite of all of that perfection before him, all of that raw sensuality so powerful that it nearly stopped his heart, his eyes lingered only briefly on her breasts and her sex. There was so much else for him to look at, to admire.

There was her art.

Her skin was the canvas. From just above her breasts to her upper thighs she was nearly covered in illustration, tattoos in gold and black and red, in jade green and sky blue, the richest colours he had ever seen. The images ran together as though her torso was a Ming vase, and yet there were enormous stylistic differences, and some of the tattoos seemed fresher, more vibrant. Some of the illustrations on her flesh were beautiful and some terribly disturbing. Her left nipple was the eye of some Raven god in whose talons there were human beings, gored and bleeding and screaming. Her right nipple was the eye of a coyote that stood upright, a sly grin stretching his snout.

There were dozens of other figures on her skin, all of them

imposing. Some were sensual creatures, exposing themselves, while others wielded axes and bloody daggers and weapons of war. Some were wreathed in fire while others emerged from the ocean onto stony shore. He saw Egyptian influence and what he thought was Greek. There were oil-black gods in African headdress and a thing with many arms and shrunken heads dangling from its belt that he thought was some Indian deity, Kali or Shiva. There were simply too many for him to take them all in.

"My God," he whispered.

"That's almost funny," Anita replied.

Craig gazed up at her, eyes wide in astonishment, and he saw doubt in her eyes.

"Are you repulsed?" she asked.

"No," he said quickly, shaking his head. "No, it's . . . it's the most extraordinary thing I've ever seen. What made you do it? All of this?"

Her fingers caressed her stomach, showing off the figures there, presenting them to him as her pride and joy. "Ancient cultures from around the world all have their own gods. I've been fascinated by it all since I was a little girl. I started with the conventional ones. Roman. Norse. Egyptian. But the more I researched the more I wanted to know about others. Inca. Mayan. Etruscan. The gods of Sumeria and ancient Babylon. African. Mesopotamia. And from each culture I chose at least one god to keep with me permanently. It was what I studied in college, where I met my husband. He always encouraged my passion. Later, I received my Master's in myth and folklore. I wanted to know them all."

"I don't recognize most of them," he confessed, hypnotized by the gentle motion of her fingers moving across her own flesh. There was a scent coming off of her now, a strange combination of musk and damp copper and summer rainstorms. It was a rich, earthen odour and it quickened his pulse. He had to shift in his seat and pluck at his pants to relieve the ache of the hardness of his cock.

"The further I searched the more I wanted to find. The old gods. The forgotten ones. Every single tattoo has a story of its own, a myth. Its own history."

"And this one?" Craig asked, bending close to point to a small figure just above her navel. "This doesn't look like an ancient god. It looks . . . modern."

The moment his eyes had been able to focus, to pick apart the images and examine them for themselves, he had noticed that one illustration. The tattoo was finely detailed, much more so than most of the others. The god wore a black top hat with a bright red band that was dotted with tiny gleaming blades. His teeth were like two rows of shiny needles and he had knives for fingers. His clothes were leather and upon his feet were a pair of human heads.

"What is it? Aztec? But what about the hat?"

"Modern?" Anita asked, and when she laughed it was a hollow, rasping sound like the dry rattle of a smoker on his death bed. "Oh, no. It's one of the oldest of them all. There have been names for it in many cultures, but none of the scholars know where it originated or what its true name was."

Craig gazed up at her eyes at last, awed by her. "You're exquisite. Truly. I've never met a woman like you. Never imagined anyone like you existed. I always thought of tattoos as . . . as low . . . crass. But this—"

Anita beamed with pleasure, flattered by his words. She ran her hands over her breasts, over Raven and Coyote, and touched her nipples with just the tips of her fingers. "Thank you," she whispered. "They're meant to be seen. That way they won't be forgotten forever. Usually they're only for me . . . my husband doesn't really see them anymore. Doesn't even notice when I've added a new one."

"He's a fool, then. It really is art."

His hands hesitated, hovering in the air. He wanted to touch her, to have his hands follow the paths trailblazed by her own fingers, but he did not know where or how to begin. He was long out of practice and would have been awkward even with an ordinary woman. But Anita was far from ordinary.

There was magic here. Magic that tingled his skin and stole his breath and made him feel thirteen years old again. She was another man's wife and this moment was not born of genuine emotion but of need and desperation and surrender. And yet the magic swept such concerns away. He thought he would come just from the touch of his fingers upon her skin.

She took his hand and led his fingers between her legs. He felt the smoothness there, that unblossomed flower, and as she pressed his fingers into her he found her warm and glistening wet, and she sighed and leaned down to put her weight on him, sliding her red heels apart so that he could explore her properly.

Anita reached for his belt and hurriedly unbuckled him. She reached inside his pants and gripped him firmly in her hand and he groaned, a noise that came from so far down inside him that he did not recognize the sound as his own. He bent to her, tongue thrusting out, licking the Eye of the Raven, then taking it into his mouth. His free hand slid over her back and cupped the rounded flesh of her ass and he knew he had to trace every line of her art, to study her, to consume her.

He slid from the chair to the ground and pulled her down after him.

Craig had never been with a woman like Anita before. Not with anyone so beautiful, nor with anyone so debauched. She loved it all and he gave it to her willingly. Anything he could conceive of, she was eager to indulge him. And while he took her from behind, or lay her across the desk, or knelt in front of this exotic woman while she sat in his chair, he studied her illustrations, every single line. Every forgotten god.

Yet when at last he was completely spent and all the lust had been drained from him, guilt seeped in to replace it. It didn't bother him that he had just fucked another man's wife, though he felt that it should have. No, it was the company that shot tendrils of guilt through him, sent it racing through his veins. He lay there on the floor with his cheek resting on Anita's stomach and a sickly twist roiled in his gut. Yes, Anita was beautiful and her tattoos were exotic. She was alluring, unlike any woman he had ever made love to before.

But now it was over. His reason had been overwhelmed by lust, such a foolish, *man* thing. His principles were in the toilet. His loyalty to his employees was out the window. When his cock had gotten hard and she'd moved in close to him, nothing else had mattered.

"God," he whispered with a grimace, fighting despair.

Craig wondered if Anita felt any guilt but he did not want to look into her eyes, now, did not want to see her face. He knew he ought to just get up and dress, but felt as much a captive as if he'd put his foot in a bear trap. What to say to her now that his lust was gone and the rational Craig had returned? How to get her out of there as quickly as possible? And if he should try to fight any further for the jobs of his employees, what might Anita's husband bring into the conversation? What might his employees and his clients—former employees and former clients—what might they learn about this evening?

The more he thought about it the more paralyzed he felt. Anita touched his hair, gently caressing the back of his neck, as though she cared for him. As though there was something more than business going on here. But Craig knew better. Her belly felt warm beneath his cheek and the softness seemed all a part of the lie he had told himself to make it all right to do this . . . that it would be worth it . . . that there was no more room for negotiation anyway and this was just a bonus. He closed his eyes tightly and breathed in the scent of her.

It had been extraordinary. But worth it? He didn't think so. Not now. He'd compromised everything he had ever believed in, all of the values his father had instilled within him. He trembled to think of it. What was left of him now? Craig had thought IllumiNet and their negotiator had taken everything away from him but now he realized there had been that one last little bit. His conscience. And that hadn't been taken away. No. He had thrown it in the gutter himself.

His face twisted up again and he felt the despair overtaking him. *No one can know*, he thought. *No one.* And on the heels of that thought came anger. Pure, undiluted anger, at himself, for all of the bad choices he had made over the years, at the negotiator for being so fucking smug, and at Anita, for seeing his weakness and exploiting it, even as she pretended to admire him. For long minutes he lay there with his eyes closed and his pulse sped up, his breath came more slowly, more deliberately, and his jaw clenched. It was wrong. All of it, so completely wrong. All he had tried to do was take care of people and run an honest business, and it had all turned into a cosmic joke. And *he* was the punchline.

It was too late to save the company. Too late to stop the inevitable. It was far too late for him to save any jobs. The negotiator was full of shit. Craig was certain that only a handful of his people would keep their jobs.

His eyes opened to a splash of rich colours, his cheek pressed against the soft flesh of Anita's belly, laying upon the pantheon of ancient gods that were tattooed there. *What the hell have I done?*

Yet even as the question was posed, it left his mind. He blinked, studying Anita's belly. The flesh remained still and yet, on her skin, something moved. It was the figure with the top hat, the illustration of the ancient god with needle teeth and knives for fingers.

And it was moving.

The motion was barely perceptible, but Craig was sure the tattoo had turned toward him and it was inching closer to where his flesh touched Anita's. He held his breath. It was impossible, of course.

But he had not had enough to drink to hallucinate. He stared at the forgotten god with the razor fingers and the top hat, and it stared back at him. It grinned, but the result was terrifying, up close like that. He could see so many details that he had missed before.

Then it spoke to him. Softly.

It wanted to negotiate.

Morning had never taken so long to arrive for Sam Morelli, a.k.a. Salvatore, a.k.a The Negotiator. When midnight had come and gone with no sign of Anita returning home he had been unable to pretend to himself any longer. He knew where she had gone and what she had done. Self-loathing had taken root in him years earlier and now it blossomed fully. And yet there was gratitude mixed in there with it, a fact that repulsed him, though there was no escaping it. This was not the first time Anita had put herself on the line for the sake of Sam's career. Maybe if he had made a bigger deal out of it the first time, protested louder . . . but even that first time, when the truth of it had shocked him, he had been thankful.

That's how low you can go, Sam thought, standing at the window in his office at IllumiNet, looking out at the Boston skyline toward the harbour.

But that was bullshit. He could go lower, get dirtier. The true depths of his iniquity had yet to be explored. Other than Anita, Sam loved nothing but success. Victory. And victory, in business, meant money. The cash-out.

Where are you, baby?

The thought had echoed through his mind again and again since last night. Anita had never come home. Sam was sure he knew the reason. The deal wasn't sealed yet. His wife would do whatever she had to do to close the deal. He was a good negotiator, but she was the best. Absolutely tenacious. Whatever she was up to this morning—or whatever she had done to need to sleep so late—Sam knew it had been all for him, for them. So though *Where are you, baby?* kept coming back into his head over and over, he didn't really want to know the answer. She would call.

She would call.

She'd better. Sam winced at the coldness of the thought, but there it was. As stylish as he looked in his brown tailored suit and red tie, as immaculate as his grooming was, he might as well be working in the mailroom for all the pull he'd have at IllumiNet if he couldn't close this one smoothly. It was damned likely he'd lose his job. So if Anita wanted to continue living the lifestyle she had, she would have to come through for him.

His gaze shifted to the clock on the wall and he shifted anxiously. Going on nine thirty A.M. Time was running out. His boss had expected a final report on his desk by ten o'clock.

Hands shoved down into the pockets of his trousers, Sam stared at the phone on his desk. Miraculously, it rang.

He hurried to the desk and slipped on his headset even as he punched the button to pick up the line. "Sam Morelli."

"Good morning again, Sam." It was Martha at the front desk. He ought to have checked his caller I.D. "You didn't want to be interrupted, but there's a delivery for you out here. Also a manila envelope from NEESS."

Contracts? he thought, a hesitant relief awaiting confirmation in the back of his mind.

"Can you send them back with it?"

"Sure. Have a great day."

Sam smiled to himself, hopeful. "You too."

Half a minute later there was a rap on the door to his office. Sam hadn't even bothered to sit down at his desk and was instead staring out at the cityscape when the knock came.

"Come in," he said, turning around.

A pair of delivery men were carrying a large package whose size and shape—beneath brown paper wrapping and string— suggested a framed canvas. Some kind of art, Sam assumed.

What interested him far more was the manila envelope one of the deliverymen clutched in his right hand, pinned against the brown paper-wrapped gift.

Yes, he thought. *Here we go.*

"I'll take that," he said, snatching the envelope from the man's hands, nearly causing him to drop the big frame. He tore the envelope open and slid out a sheaf of documents—all the closing materials on IllumiNet's takeover of NEESS—then flipped a few pages to find the line where Craig should have signed them. And the signature was there.

Sam Morelli smiled. He riffled pages, rejoicing at the fact that there were no marginal changes stuck in by Craig's attorney. On the last page, however, there was a note on yellow sticky paper. Two words. *DONE DEAL.*

He let out a long sigh of relief. His job was safe.

So focused had he been on the documents that he had barely heard the delivery men tearing the paper and string from the large portrait. He could see the top of the frame and it was lovely, gilt with gold.

Anita, baby, you must have done something right, he thought, grinning at the gift Craig had sent. The delivery men tore the paper away from the front of the frame in one long rip.

The smile left him. The art was familiar. Each individual illustration was known to him. And why not. He had paid for them.

That large frame was filled with Anita's tattoos . . . with her skin, stretched tautly over the canvas. The delivery men were staring at it, trying to understand what it was they were seeing. Sam's mouth hung open and he tried to scream but no sound would come out. He only shook his head in denial and stared, staggering toward the frame against his will, unable to stop himself.

For despite the chaos in his mind, he had noticed something. Grief tore at him, gutted him. He whimpered something, but moved even nearer, and now he saw for certain. There was a clear place just above her navel . . . a place where her beautiful skin was unmarred by ink or tattoo needle. He could make out the shape of the missing tattoo, a hole in the tableau, a vacancy in the pantheon of forgotten gods.

And at last he could scream.

Done deal.

QUIET BULLETS

If Teddy had seen the cowboy's ghost at night, he probably would have wet his pants. When he thought about it later, he had to admit to himself that if he had been in his bedroom, or reading a book in the sitting room, and looked up to see the grey spectre of a gunfighter looming in the doorway or some dark corner—maybe even blocking his ma's view of the TV, as much as a guy you can see through could block anything—it would have scared him right out of his socks. As it happened, though, the worst he got was a serious case of the chills, and an even bigger dose of curiosity, mostly because, at first, he didn't even know he was looking at a ghost.

On that early October day, Teddy walked home from school the usual way. He knew from reading and from movies that October could be nice and cool in some parts of America, but in Tucson, Arizona, most days were still warm, like the heat from the long summer had been stored in the ground and didn't want to leave even when the days turned grey.

He walked with Mike Sedesky and Rachel Beddoes most days, except when Sedesky got in trouble and had to stay after school, which seemed to happen more and more often. The boy just didn't know how to keep quiet. One time Sedesky had told Teddy that his daddy drank some, and took the belt to him if a note came home from the teacher. Sedesky had taken to writing his own notes back and forging his father's signature. One of these days, Teddy figured his friend was in for a hiding like none he'd had before, but he did not say that to Sedesky. He could see that Mikey—which was what Rachel called Sedesky—knew exactly where all of it would lead.

Teddy and Sedesky were both ten years old and in the Fifth Grade at Iron Horse Elementary School. Rachel, a year older, had moved on to the upper school right next door, but never seemed to mind walking home with the boys despite the difference in status. Privately, though, the boys had debated whether or not the pleasure of walking home with Rachel—something that did make them stand a little straighter and lift their chins with pride—was worth the beatings it sometimes earned them from Artie Hanson and the goons with whom he palled around.

The older boys didn't like Rachel spending time with Teddy and Sedesky, and any time they crossed paths after school, Artie and the others would block their way, or worse. Sedesky made noises about giving those guys "the business," but Teddy had never been able to figure out what "the business" was, unless it included getting their books dumped in the shrubs, their noses bloodied, and their arms twisted behind their backs so hard they'd ache for days afterward.

There were Indian burns and wet willies and cries of "uncle," and those were the good days. On the worst day, Artie had tried to force Sedesky to promise never to speak to Rachel again, and when Mikey wouldn't promise, the goon had broken the pinky on his left hand.

Rachel had avoided them for a week after that. For their own good, she said.

After, when she started walking home with them again, none of them brought it up. Teddy assumed that Sedesky had persuaded her that he wasn't afraid, but he wished that the two of them had consulted with him before any decision had been made. He liked his pinky fingers just the way they were, thank you very much.

On the day he first saw the cowboy's ghost, they had walked home without encountering any sign of Artie Hanson. Teddy and Sedesky had said goodbye to Rachel at her gate, and then a block later Sedesky had taken off between houses, cutting through backyards on his way home.

Teddy and his mom lived in a small house on a quiet street, but it was neat and tidy and Mr. Graham and Mr. Hess—who lived on either side of them—had pitched in to paint the house just this past spring. They'd said it was the least they could do to help out, what with Teddy's daddy dying in Korea and his mom ailing. Teddy, who'd still been nine, had been their helper that day. He still remembered it with a smile.

But on the afternoon when he spotted the cowboy in front of his house, his thoughts weren't on painting or on his daddy. Instead, he mostly thought about Sedesky and Rachel, and how come Rachel seemed not even to see Teddy when Mikey was around. It made him feel bad—kind of small, really—and he didn't quite know why. Girls were a mystery, and not one he felt in much of a hurry to solve. They just didn't understand most of the things that were important to him, like cowboy stories and rockets.

With these thoughts in his head, he turned the corner onto Derby Street and noticed the cowboy walking up to his front gate. A smile blossomed on Teddy's face instantly. The cowboy looked like the real deal, from the hat to the long coat to the tips of his boots. If Sedesky had been there, Teddy would have bet him a quarter that the cowboy carried a Colt revolver. Maybe two of them. He picked up his pace, wanting to talk to the man, wondering why he seemed to be headed to Teddy's own house.

Two things happened at once. First, Teddy noticed that the sunlight passed through the cowboy—that he could see the fence right through him. Second, the man walked to the front door without opening the gate, just stepped right on up as though the gate did not exist.

Teddy stopped short and stared. The cowboy cast no shadow. The longer Teddy looked, the more transparent the man seemed. It scared him a little, knowing a ghost stood on his front stoop, but with the afternoon sun shining down, and the fact that there could be no denying this was an honest to goodness western gunfighter— maybe someone who'd been shot right here in Tucson—after a couple of minutes he felt a lot more *Wow* than spooked.

The cowboy turned, tipped him a wink, and gave a nod toward the door, as if he wanted Teddy to follow him inside. Then the gunfighter passed through the door and vanished within.

Teddy followed. What else could he do? It was his house.

The weirdest thing about opening the door and stepping into his house was how ordinary it seemed. Dust motes swirled in the shafts of light that came in through the windows and eddied along the floor on a breeze from the open door. Teddy stood on the threshold a few seconds, but nothing seemed amiss. The stairs leading up to the second floor were dark with shadow, the hallway vacant, and from the living room came the sound of the radio playing low.

With a frown, he peeked into the room. His mother lay on the sofa, hands resting on her chest, tuckered out after a long morning. She woke up early every day to fix his lunch and send him off to school and then sat down at her sewing machine. Teddy's ma did great work as a seamstress—everybody said so—and so her mornings and early afternoons were spent hard at work to earn enough money to buy them food. What little money the government gave her every month—she had explained that they paid the money because Teddy's daddy had died in the war—covered rent, but not food or clothes.

In the afternoons, she turned on the radio and took a nap, sleeping so deeply Teddy had to shake her awake at half past four so his ma could make dinner. The radio stayed on, then, until dinner was ready. His ma said she liked the voices. They kept her company. Most days, Teddy did his homework at the kitchen table while Ma made dinner, and sometimes she laughed softly at things he either hadn't heard or didn't understand. Radio things. Even when he had no idea what had made her laugh, he would smile. Ma had a beautiful laugh.

She looked pretty when she slept, but kind of sad, too, and he always wondered if she were dreaming of his daddy. They didn't talk much about him. Teddy wanted to, but he had the idea that maybe that would hurt too much for his ma.

So that afternoon after he followed the cowboy's ghost into the house, it surprised him to find nothing at all out of the ordinary. The radio voices talked and his ma slept on, the sound of her deep breathing filling the living room. A song started to play, one with lots of horns. Teddy always liked music with horns—trumpets, saxophones, anything. Confused, he looked back toward the hallway, but still saw no trace of the ghost. He might have thought he imagined the whole thing if not for the creak of a door opening.

Now Teddy's heart skipped a beat. He felt his face flush and his breath quickened. The sight of the ghost outside on the street had seemed weird and wonderful, but that creak of hinges made the hair on the back of his neck stand up.

With a glance back at the sofa to make sure his ma hadn't been disturbed, Teddy went to the doorway and peeked out into the hall. He had left the front door open and a light breeze swirled along the floor, gently swaying the door to the closet under the stairs so that the hinges creaked just a little.

Teddy frowned—he didn't recall ever seeing that door open before. Most of the time he forgot it was even there, but now he walked over and gave it a closer look. The top of the door had a diagonal slant that followed the angle of the stairs. At some point the door had been painted over, so that the iron handle and the deadbolt were thick with the same dark green as covered the wood. Even looking at it now, the deadbolt seemed stuck in place, like it would be hard to move. He doubted he could slide it to the right to lock it again, and wondered how it had come unlocked.

Well, he didn't wonder much. In fact, a smile spread across his face as he glanced around. It had to have been the cowboy's ghost. The only other person in the house was his ma, and he could hear her softly snoring in the next room.

"Excellent," Teddy said, nodding as he stared into the closet. "Totally, totally excellent."

A single bulb dangled from the ceiling in the closet. He pulled the chain, but the light didn't come on. Nobody had changed that bulb in forever. Still, enough light came down the hall that he could see inside well enough. There were old pantry shelves, mostly full of dingy coffee cans full of buttons and nails, shoe boxes, and faded old table cloths. Teddy could not remember his ma ever using a table cloth.

Somebody's moth-eaten sweater hung from a hook on the back of the door. There were other hooks in the closet, to either side of the shelves, and to the right hung the thing that he had focused on since first glancing inside. The gun belt looked worn by age and coated with the same dust that lay over everything else in the closet. The empty holster disappointed him, but he took the belt out anyway, putting it around his waist. His daddy had been a big man and even at ten years old, Teddy had some of his size, so when he cinched the belt as tight as it would go and cocked it at an angle, he just managed to keep it from sliding down over his hips.

Now he felt like a gunfighter. He opened his stance a little and imagined himself preparing for a shoot out at high noon. His hand dropped to the holster and he made a little face when it closed on nothing. *Right. No gun.*

Where had the belt come from? It must have been his daddy's, maybe the one he had worn in Korea. The thought sent a shiver through him, but the good kind. Curious, now, he investigated the closet shelves more closely and immediately noticed the triangular wooden box with its glass top. Teddy stopped breathing. He took it down from the shelf and looked through the glass at the American flag that had been draped over his daddy's casket.

Teddy's eyes felt hot. He didn't remember much about that day, but now that he saw the flag a memory surfaced of soldiers folding it up and one of them handing it to Ma and then saluting her. The soldier had saluted Ma. Boy, he had loved her that day. Through all the tears he had felt proud.

He slid the wooden triangle box back onto its shelf, sorry to have disturbed it. As he pushed it back into the shadows it knocked against something else. A frown creased his forehead and he moved the flag box aside, stood on his tiptoes, and reached into the back of the closet. His fingers closed on something round and metal and he drew it out, smiling when he discovered it was a Christmas cookie tin. Through the dust he saw the face of old Saint Nick, an antique-y sort of Santa Claus, and he remembered that Christmas was only a couple of months away. Maybe if he took the tin out and cleaned it up, his ma would make some cookies to put in it.

Only the tin felt pretty heavy already, and he wondered what was in it. He crouched and set it down on the floor of the hall with a clunk, and even as he pried off the lid, somehow Teddy knew what he would find inside.

The gun metal had a bluish-grey colour, which surprised him. He had expected it to be black. Teddy's heart beat loudly in his ears as he lifted the gun out of the cookie tin, glancing over his shoulder to make sure his ma hadn't gotten up from the sofa. He held the gun in both hands, barrel aimed at the floor, fingers away from the trigger. If there were bullets inside, he didn't want to fire the gun in the house. As tired as his ma always seemed to be, and even though she hardly ever got mad at him, he had a feeling he'd get whooped worse than Mikey Sedesky if that happened.

He whistled through his teeth, the only way he knew how. The cookie tin had a coating of dust, but the gun looked clean and almost new. Handling it like the snake charmer he'd seen down at the grange hall, he slid the gun into the holster on his daddy's belt, and it fit just fine. *Daddy's gun*, he thought. And he knew it had to be true. This was the gun his daddy had taken to war.

All serious now, no smiles, Teddy backed up from the closet, right hand hovering over the gun as if he were about to draw. Partly he wanted to be a gunfighter, and partly a soldier like his daddy. He turned toward the front door, ready to face off against an imaginary enemy.

The cowboy's ghost stood just inside the door, daylight streaming through him, not much more to him than if he were made of spiderwebs.

"Oh," Teddy said, in a very small voice. He stared, eyes wide, mouth open. He knew he had seen the ghost before, but they were up close now, maybe ten feet apart. "Are you . . . what are you doing here?"

The cowboy narrowed his eyes.

"Wait," Teddy said, realizing that he'd known all along. "You opened the closet."

The ghost nodded at him in grim approval, the way Mr. Graham next door always did. Then he turned, gestured for Teddy to follow, and walked out of the house, passing right through the screen door.

Teddy blinked a few times. Seeing it up close like that kind of made his eyes hurt. His lips felt dry and he wetted them with his tongue, unsure what to do next. The ghost wanted him to follow, and if he understood right, had something to show him. At least that was how it seemed. He knew he shouldn't go running off without telling Ma, especially after some ghost, but she wouldn't be waking up for at least half an hour or so. Not if today was like every other day. And if he didn't follow, gosh he would always wonder what it was the ghost had wanted to show him.

"Damn," he said, but only because nobody would hear.

Teddy swallowed hard, then hurriedly put the Christmas cookie tin back into the closet, grabbed the old sweater from its hook, shut the door tight, and rushed outside, careful not to let the screen door bang behind him.

It felt like the kind of thing you ought to keep secret, partly because it seemed special and Teddy wanted it all to himself, and partly because he didn't want anybody to think he'd lost his marbles. So as he followed the ghost around the side of his house and through the Mariottes' backyard, Teddy tried to look like nothing at all out of the ordinary had happened today. He pulled on the ratty old sweater, realized immediately it had to have belonged to his daddy, and smiled to himself. The mothball smell didn't bother him. The sweater hung low enough to cover the gun hanging in its holster. Combined with the sweater, it made him feel really grown up.

The ghost ambled sort of leisurely, like he wasn't in any hurry, but Teddy knew the cowboy was hanging back to make sure he could keep up. Every couple of minutes the spectre glanced over his shoulder, then sort of nodded to himself as he kept on, leading Teddy out onto Navarro Street and then onto the dirt road that led out to Hatton Ranch. When the ghost walked in sunlight and Teddy looked at him straight on, he could see right through the fella, like he was cowboy-coloured glass. But whenever the gunslinger passed into the shadow of a tree or a telephone pole, he seemed more *there* somehow, like in the dark he might fill in entirely.

Only one car went by on the dirt road, kicking up dust that swirled right through the ghost, obscuring him from sight for a few seconds. The car—a brand spanking new Thunderbird—kept on going. The old, jowly fella behind the wheel did not so much as glance at the cowboy, but he gave Teddy a good long look as he drove by. Teddy's face flushed all warm and the gun weighed real heavy on his hip, but the car kept on going and soon even the dust of its passing had settled again.

The cowboy had stopped up the road a piece, leaning against the split-rail fence that marked the boundaries all around the huge spread of the Hatton ranch. He waited while Teddy caught up.

"Where are we going?" Teddy asked, keeping his voice low and glancing around. If people like the porky old fella in the T-Bird couldn't see the ghost, anyone watching him would think he was talking to himself. He didn't want stories like that getting back to his ma.

The ghost didn't answer, though. Instead, he nodded in an appreciative way, wearing the kind of expression Teddy remembered on his daddy's face now and again. Then he cocked his head, indicating that Teddy should follow, and hopped the fence.

Teddy hesitated. He licked his lips. His whole body felt prickly, like his hands or arms sometimes did if he laid on them wrong. Ma would say his hand had fallen asleep, but Teddy knew it had to do with the blood inside him not flowing right 'cause of the position he'd been in. Rachel had told him that, and it was just the sort of thing the Beddoes girls had always been smart about.

It wasn't that he had suddenly become afraid of the ghost. Heck, that gunslinging spectre had to be the coolest thing he could ever have imagined—and it *had* occurred to him that he might be imagining it. But trespassing on the Hatton ranch, well, that could get him in trouble. Old man Hatton had run Teddy's daddy off his land dozens of times in the old days, at least according to Ma, and Teddy didn't like the idea of being run off.

The cowboy turned, cocking his head like a bird. This time when he beckoned, there was a little impatience in him, and suddenly none of this seemed as much of a lark as it had a few minutes ago. Something in the cowboy's face, what little Teddy could see of it, considering the sun passed right through it and all, told him they had serious business on the Hatton ranch.

Teddy swallowed hard, looked around to make sure no one was watching, and then threw one leg over the fence. Then he was on the other side and running like hell after that cowboy, toward a stand of trees fifty or sixty yards from the road, and a giddy ripple went through him. So what if old man Hatton ran him off? He'd run Daddy off, and Teddy liked the idea of being like his daddy. He liked that a lot.

Heck, the old guy hadn't killed his daddy. The Koreans had done that.

"What's your name?" he asked the cowboy, when they were on the other side of a tree-lined rise, walking across open graze land that looked more like scrub than field. No wonder there weren't any horses around when this part of the ranch gave them nothing to nibble on.

The ghost gave him a strange look, then, half-smile and half-frown. Teddy got that look a lot in town, especially from folks in McKelvie's store. Ma said people didn't know what to make of Teddy, but she didn't say it like it was a bad thing. She said it proud, like it mattered to her. She said he was smart and grown-up for his age, and folks weren't used to little boys who could speak for themselves. One time Mrs. McKelvie overheard Ma saying something like that, and said children ought to be seen and not heard, and Ma had said that someday the whole world was gonna hear from her Teddy.

He'd beamed for the rest of that day. She'd even bought him licorice.

They didn't get over to McKelvie's store much lately. Most of the time, his ma said she was too tired to walk that far. Teddy would have liked some of that licorice, but he never complained. With everything Ma did for him, he knew it would be ungrateful, and Mr. Graham always told him that was one thing he ought never to be.

The cowboy didn't talk at all. Teddy had sort of figured that out, but the questions kept coming out of him, like he had no control over his mouth at all. Finally he managed at least to turn his babbling into just plain talking. He told the ghost about all the books he'd read about gunslingers and whenever he played cowboys and Indians, he pretended he had a pair of Colts strapped to his hips. He even demonstrated his technique, drawing invisible guns and firing, making the *pa-kow* sound with his mouth. As soon as he heard himself, he stopped. Out there alone on the rough land of the Hatton ranch, it sounded kind of childish. And the gun—the real gun—banging against his hip seemed to get heavier.

Teddy hitched up the gun belt, and his pants, which had started to slide down from its weight.

"Are we almost wherever it is we're going?" he asked. "We're awful far from home and I oughta be there when Ma wakes up. Or at least home for dinner. I don't want her to worry."

That's when they came to the fence. Maybe the Hatton property kept going beyond it, and maybe it didn't. On the other side was a stretch of woods he couldn't see the end of from here, and there were empty beer bottles scattered on the ground on either side. Some pop bottles, too, but mostly beer. Teddy looked at them, wondering who would come all this way just to drink beer. Then he thought of Artie and the goons he palled around with, and he had a pretty good idea.

When the ghost picked up a couple of bottles, one in each hand, Teddy's jaw dropped. Ma would've said he was trying to catch flies, and he did feel like a dope just standing there like that, but he couldn't believe what he was seeing. The ghost—barely there at this angle, the sun bleaching him out like the yellow scrub grass—actually touched the bottles, picked them up and set them on the fence rail.

"How did you do that?" Teddy asked at last.

The ghost winked, but kept going, picking up more bottles and gesturing for Teddy to do the same. Between the two of them they set up more than two dozen empty beer and pop bottles, all along the rail, and by then Teddy had figured out just what they were up to out here.

Target practice.

The ghost led him a dozen paces back the way they'd come. Careful, nice and easy, not like some high noon gunfight, the cowboy took out his phantom pistol, cocked it, and pulled the trigger.

Teddy flinched, waiting for the gunshot, but it did not make a sound.

The last bottle on the left shattered, glass showering to the ground.

"Wow," Teddy whispered.

The cowboy gestured for him to try it. Teddy's hands shook as he took off his daddy's old sweater and drew the old Army pistol. He had seen enough movies and read enough books to understand the basics—which end the bullets came out of and how to pull the trigger—but aiming the thing took a bit of getting used to. For a few seconds he just tried to get used to holding the gun straight, realizing that if he supported his right wrist with his left hand, he could just about keep it steady.

He pulled the trigger.

Nothing happened. The gun did not kick in his hand the way the cowboy's had. No glass shattered. Disappointment flooded through him. All this way, standing there with a ghost, and he didn't have any bullets.

The cowboy held out his hand. Teddy flinched, afraid the ghost would touch him. It never would have occurred to him if he hadn't seen the cowboy pick up those bottles, but now the idea of being touched by a ghost—a dead man, though he felt sort of sad thinking of his new friend that way—gave him the shivers.

If the cowboy noticed Teddy's reaction, he didn't let on. Warily, Teddy handed him the gun. The moment when the ghost lifted its weight from his grasp made him catch his breath, smiling nervously.

"You're really here," he said.

The ghost shook his head with that same indulgent smile. Teddy missed his daddy something fierce when he saw that look, but still he was glad he had met the ghost and that they were out here having this adventure. He had already decided he would tell Sedesky about it, but not Rachel. A girl wouldn't understand. And he bet Rachel Beddoes didn't even believe in ghosts, but Sedesky did. Ghosts scared the crap out of Mikey Sedesky. Teddy would have to tell him there wasn't anything to be scared of.

The ghost opened up the gun—Teddy didn't really see how he'd done it—and slid out the cylinder where the bullets went. All of the chambers were empty. But the cowboy didn't seem at all surprised. He just lifted the gun up to his face, pursed his lips, and blew into the empty chambers, not like he was trying to clean dust out of the cylinder, but nice and easy, like breathing.

Then he snapped the cylinder shut, gave it a spin, and handed the gun back to Teddy.

The metal felt cold, the gun heavier than before.

And this time, when Teddy pulled the trigger, the gun kicked in his hands so hard that all the bones in his arms hurt. But like the cowboy's gun, his daddy's old pistol fired quiet bullets.

Of course, Teddy's shot didn't hit much more than a few leaves in the trees beyond the fence. But the cowboy demonstrated how he ought to stand and hold the gun, and sight along the barrel, and Teddy did his best to mimic the ghost.

It took over an hour, but he managed to shoot two of the bottles right off the fence, and all the while, the gun never ran out of bullets, and never made a sound.

When Teddy looked over and saw the sun sinking low, a little tremor of panic went through him. He slid the gun into its holster and tugged the ratty sweater back on to cover it.

"Tomorrow I'll do better," he said as he turned to bid the ghost farewell, but the cowboy had vanished in the twilight.

Teddy was alone.

Hitching his pants up, he ran all the way home.

That night, Teddy lay in his bed, staring at the ceiling without really seeing it. It seemed almost as if the images in his mind's eye were projected on that blank surface, and he played out the day's events over and over. A ghost? Thinking about it now, it amazed Teddy that he had not run away screaming, but in the moment, with the cowboy right there in front of him and so *real*, he had known he had nothing to fear. The gunslinger had kind eyes.

Now he couldn't sleep. It felt like Christmas. Not the excitement of Christmas Eve, knowing that Santa would be coming within hours, but the following night, after spending an entire day opening presents and celebrating and running over to Sedesky's so they could compare notes about what they'd gotten.

There had been no comparing notes with Sedesky tonight. He had to think about what he wanted to say about what had happened to him today. Maybe if he tried to arrange for Sedesky and Rachel to come over tomorrow, and the ghost came back, they would see him, too. If not, he knew they would never believe him. They might wish they could see a ghost themselves, but if they weren't going to get to see one, they weren't going to allow the possibility that Teddy had, either. Sedesky and Rachel were his friends, but fair was fair. He understood that.

Teddy yawned. His eyes burned, he was so tired. Really, it wasn't so much that he could not have gone to sleep, as that he did not want to. No matter how excited he might be, if he just closed his eyes and turned over, he knew he would drift off eventually. But the events of the day were crystal clear in his mind—fully real. And he worried that if he slept, when he woke in the morning the hours he spent with the ghost would have blurred some, and started to seem like maybe they were a dream. He hated that idea. Teddy wanted to hang onto the certainty of the memory as long as he could.

Yet amidst the nearly giddy aftermath of his day, something else lingered, niggling at the back of his mind, and that gave him another reason to stay awake. If he drifted off to sleep, he knew his thoughts would turn in that direction, and he did not like the troubling things that waited there.

After target practice at the Hatton ranch, Teddy had rushed home as fast as his legs could carry him. Twice he'd had to halt and drag up the gun belt before its weight pulled his pants down to his knees. In the gathering dusk he had raced along Navarro Street as lights came on inside some of the houses, families sitting down to dinner. He had cut through the Mariottes' backyard and into his own. Breathing hard, more than a little frantic at the idea of going in through his front door wearing his daddy's old ratty sweater and carrying his gun, Teddy had looked around for a hiding spot. He'd pulled off the sweater and wrapped up the gun and belt, then tucked the whole package behind the coiled up garden hose before rushing inside.

He needn't have worried. Ma had still been asleep. It had been a simple thing to retrieve the gun and return it to its rightful place, and all the while she hadn't stirred. It worried him.

The radio voices still filled the house, and there his ma lay, curled up on the sofa, snoring lightly. The last of the day's light filled the room with a blue gloom, and after he'd put the gun away, Teddy went and clicked on the floor lamp by the sofa. He knelt beside his ma and shook her gently awake.

"Ma, you're still sleeping," he told her, and the words sounded so dumb to him. "Sorry I'm so late. I was out with Mikey and we kinda lost track of time."

Such a weak excuse, and he hated to lie to her. It made him feel ashamed. But Ma had smiled sleepily and then, as she sat up and saw the darkening windows and realized the time, she had frowned deeply.

"Look at the time," she said. "You must be starving, and I haven't fixed anything for dinner."

"How about breakfast for dinner?" Teddy had suggested.

Sometimes, as a special treat or when they were in a hurry, his ma would make bacon and eggs for dinner. They always made a big deal out of it, like they were getting away with breaking the rules somehow.

Tonight, it had not seemed so special. His ma had barely touched her eggs and only had a couple of pieces of bacon. Teddy had been famished, but the weight of guilt slowed him down and when the eggs got cold he stopped eating. His ma had asked him to clean up the dishes, apologized, and then gone back to the couch, and when

Teddy asked if she was okay, all she would say was that she was a little under the weather.

"I'll be right as rain, tomorrow," she had promised.

By the time Teddy finished up with the dishes, she had fallen asleep again. He had left her with her radio voices and gone out back to retrieve the sweater and the gun belt, quickly returning everything to the painted-over closet in the front hall.

Now, lying in bed, he could still feel the weight of the gun tingling in his hands, and he could still hear the low murmur of radio voices drifting up to him from below. His ma had slept on the sofa before, but she had never been asleep when it was time for Teddy to go to bed, not even when she had the flu. Tonight he had brushed his teeth and put on his pajamas and gone down to say good night, but he had not wanted to wake her, so he had kissed her softly on the cheek and gone upstairs.

He didn't like sleeping upstairs all by himself, but if his ma had the flu again, he wanted her to get the rest she needed. She had promised she'd be right as rain come morning, and he hoped she was right. But deep down he doubted that, and it made him wonder if she doubted it, too.

Teddy opened his eyes slowly, only vaguely aware of the hiss of static from downstairs. The radio station had gone off the air for the night. As that bit of information formed in his mind, he realized with no little surprise that he had fallen asleep after all. Quickly he remembered the ghost, and almost as quickly he wanted to see the cowboy again. As he had feared, already the image had lost its sharpness in his mind, and he could not summon a complete picture of how the ghost had looked when he had first seen it, out on the street in front of his house.

He sighed with disappointment, but knew he could do nothing to get that moment back. His eyes were heavy and even now he had not come fully awake. Sleep called him to return, and though he knew the memory would retain little clarity come morning, he began to succumb.

A sound halted his eyelids at half-mast, and a slight frown creased his forehead. Tick-tock, tick-tock, but it wasn't a clock. Teddy listened with half an ear, trying to sort out the origin of that familiar sound. It grew louder, though still muffled, and he opened his eyes fully and stared at his bedroom window. He did know that sound. Not a tick-tock, but the clip-clop of a horse's hooves.

His bedroom lay draped in indigo darkness, enough light provided by the streetlamp in front of Mr. Graham's house to silhouette the furniture, but not enough for him to make out the time on the clock by his bed. Who rode a horse down his street in the middle of the night?

A terrible possibility rushed through him—*Mr. Hatton*. Had the rancher learned of his trespassing and come to confront him? Teddy's heart pounded in his chest for ten full seconds before the absurdity of that idea made it crumble apart. Mr. Hatton might be the only one living around here who kept horses, but the old man would not come riding up in the middle of the night just to scare a fifth-grader.

Don't be stupid, Teddy, he thought to himself, and smiled.

But the clip-clop sound began to slow, and curiosity dragged him out of bed. If not Mr. Hatton, then who could be out riding so late? It occurred to him as he went to the window that, since he didn't know anyone else who owned horses, maybe someone had stolen one from Mr. Hatton. Teddy might be able to get a look at the thief and tell the police. He might even get a reward!

On the book shelf next to the window was a little lamp, but Teddy didn't turn it on. If he managed to get a look at the horse thief, he didn't want to be spotted. Instead, he crouched beside the window and peered around the edge of the dusty curtain. A quarter moon hung low in the sky and the street lamp down in front of Mr. Graham's flickered a little, like maybe it would go out soon, but despite that illumination, for a few seconds he didn't see anyone out there at all.

Then movement caught his eye, and he heard the slow clip-clop of hooves again. Teddy narrowed his eyes as he saw the rider—all dressed in black and astride a black horse—and then he blinked and his eyes went very wide. With his black cowboy hat pulled low over his eyes and the long black coat he wore, the man on horseback looked even more like a gunfighter than the cowboy's ghost.

Holding the horse's reins loosely, the man in black sat up high in the saddle, and his coat fell open to reveal the moonlit gleam of black metal at his hip. He watched as the rider urged the horse forward at an achingly slow pace. The man in black studied the Grahams' house as he passed, and then glanced across the street at the Sullivans', like he might be searching for a certain house but didn't know the exact address.

The thought froze the breath in Teddy's throat. He stared, eyes widening further as the man passed through the dome of yellow light from the street lamp, and he realized he could see right through both horse and rider.

Shivers went up his spine and he bit his lip. From downstairs he could hear the hiss of the radio, the sound it made when the world had stopped broadcasting.

Clip-clop, clip-clop, the rider came on, more and more slowly. Right out in front of Teddy's house, he seemed to pause a moment and tilt his head slightly to the side, like he was listening for something.

"No," Teddy whispered, there alone in his darkened room. "Keep riding."

For another breath, the black rider hesitated and then, almost reluctantly, spurred the horse onward. The animal's hooves clacked on the pavement, and Teddy felt pretty sure it had picked up the pace a little. Still, he stared, watching as the black rider and his horse moved on, past the Hesses' house and then the Landrys'.

Teddy's lower lip trembled and his eyes began to fill. He slid down and leaned against the wall, taking long, steadying breaths, unable to put together even just in his own thoughts why such fear had gripped him. A single tear traced its way down his cheek and he sighed with relief.

"You should have been here," he whispered into the dark, thinking of the cowboy, and then realizing that the words had not been meant for that ghost, but for his father. His heart hurt his chest.

Then he froze once more.

Outside, the clip-clop had ceased. Teddy rose up to his knees and peered out the window, hoping for a moment that the black rider would have simply vanished, the way the cowboy's ghost had earlier in the day. But no, the figure remained. The rider had come to a halt in front of the Landry house, but wasn't looking at the Landrys' or at the Mansurs' across the street. The black rider hung his head, hat tilted almost straight down. He seemed almost to have fallen asleep in the saddle.

Then, without looking up, he tugged the reins and the black horse turned. Slowly, the rider raised his head, facing Teddy's house, and though the brim of his hat covered his eyes, Teddy knew the dark man was looking right at him, that the rider could see him despite the darkness in his bedroom.

With a tug on the reins, the black rider started back toward Teddy's house. Clip-clop, clip-clop. His coat hung wide open, and in the moonlight, the black metal of his gun seemed to wink.

"No," Teddy whispered. "I won't let you."

The rider snapped the reins and the horse leaped into a gallop, and then Teddy was up and running. His bare feet squeaked on the wood floor as he raced into the hallway and sprinted for the steps. The hiss of the radio grew loud in his ears as he gripped the banisters and half-ran, half-slid down the stairs. His face burned with the desperation of tears he refused to shed, and he tried to steady his heart the way that his hands had steadied his father's gun that day.

And he knew why the ghost had visited his house.

At the bottom of the steps he came face to face with the front door, and he heard the thunder of hooves right outside, could practically feel it shaking the floorboards as he turned from the door and ran down the front hall. In the room on the left, he could hear his mother coughing in her sleep. It was an awful sound, almost like choking, and the wheeze that went along with it seemed to match the static hiss of the radio.

Teddy grabbed the handle of the door under the stairs and yanked hard. Thick with old paint, it stuck.

The sound of hooves had stopped, but now he heard the tread of boots on the front stoop, and the doorknob rattled. The frame creaked as the rider tested its strength.

The little pantry door under the stairs gave a shriek of warped wood as he forced it open. Desperate, he snatched the old cookie tin off of its shelf, popped off the cover, and let the tin clatter to the ground as he hefted the weight of his daddy's gun.

As all fell silent at the front door, he twisted around to see the black rider step right through the door, just as easily as the ghost had passed through the screen earlier, his head still dipped, face half-hidden behind the brim of his hat. Hands shaking, Teddy nearly dropped the gun, but he managed to lift it and take trembling aim.

"I won't let you," he said, and somehow his voice did not quaver, and then his hands went still.

The rider lifted his head as though taking notice of him for the very first time, and Teddy nearly screamed. Where his face ought to have been there was only emptiness, darker than the darkest night and deep as forever.

The rider went for his gun, and Lord he was fast. Teddy pulled the trigger three times. His daddy's gun bucked in his hands but made not a sound. The rider staggered backward and fell through the door, like it wasn't even there.

Whispering silent prayers, and sometimes private thank-yous to a gunfighter whose days had passed, he stood with the gun aimed at the front door for as long as he could keep his arms raised. When he could no longer hold them up, he sat on the floor and leaned against the frame of the open pantry door, the gun cradled across his lap, listening to the hiss of nothing on the radio.

Ma woke him in the morning, flushed with colour, eyes bright with anger and confusion, wondering what he thought he was doing sleeping in the hallway.

Teddy caught hell for playing with his daddy's gun. Even got grounded for a week, which meant he had to spend every second he wasn't at school right there in the house with his ma.

He didn't mind at all.

THIN WALLS

Tim Graham woke slowly, the sounds of raucous sex drawing him up into the waking world. He frowned sleepily and looked around in the darkness of his hotel room as though he expected to find the perpetrators of the disturbance screwing acrobatically on one of the floral-patterned chairs near the balcony slider. He liked to keep a room as dark as possible for sleeping—something he'd picked up from Jenny—so the heavy curtains were drawn and the only light came from the ghostly glow of numbers on the alarm clock. If someone *had* been screwing in his room, he would barely have been able to see them.

But the sounds, he quickly realized, came from the room next door. The bed in there must have been head to head with his own, for he heard the lovers far too well, their grunts and moans and exhortations, the slap of flesh on flesh, the rhythmic tap of the headboard against the wall. Most hotel chains had long since learned to attach the headboards to the wall so they wouldn't knock against it when guests got busy, but apparently that bit of logic had been overlooked here.

At first, Tim smiled. Half asleep, he felt a mixture of envy and arousal.

"Yes, like that!" the woman said and sighed, repeating it several times, making it her mantra. Then she started to plead, almost whining, urging him on.

After several minutes of this, Tim's erection brought him fully awake. He closed his eyes and put a pillow over his head, trying to force himself back to sleep, but he could not drown out the sounds. His pulse quickened. He wondered how long they could go on. Unless the guy was young—or old and using Viagra to regain his youth—it shouldn't take that long.

He had heard people having sex in hotel rooms before. More

than once, he and Jenny had *been* the people making too much noise. One time an angry old woman had banged on the wall and shouted at them to keep it down and they had laughed and made love even more vocally. Tim had never banged on the wall himself. He didn't like the idea of interrupting, and he had always felt a little thrill at overhearing.

So he listened, his erection painfully in need of attention. Jenny had been gone for nearly a year. He was tempted to masturbate, but the image of a sad little pervert jerking off on the other side of the wall disturbed him, so instead he got up and went to the bathroom. With the light on, the bathroom fan drowned out most of the noise from next door. He splashed water on his face and looked in the mirror at the dark circles under his eyes. He had to wait for his erection to subside before he could aim for the toilet, but at last he managed to piss, then washed his hands and returned to bed.

The fucking continued.

"Christ," he muttered.

He wanted sleep more than cheap thrills. The voyeur inside him seemed to have given up and gone to sleep, because though his cock stirred and rose once more, it only achieved half mast, apparently tempered by his growing irritation.

He laid his head back on the pillow and stared up at the darkness of the ceiling. Had they heard him go to the bathroom? The sound of the fan and the flush of the toilet? If so, it had not troubled them at all. If anything, the lovers had gotten louder. The man started to call her filthy names, making her his slut, his whore, his bitch, and she rose to what she seemed to consider a challenge, agreeing with him at every turn. If he'd ever tried that with Jenny he would never have had sex again, but for these two it seemed a huge turn-on.

Long minutes passed. Tim's throat was dry, his breath coming a little quicker as his erection returned, more painful than ever. He could not help but start to imagine the scene taking place next door, picturing positions and stiletto heels. In his mind the guy was a blur, but the woman had a body sculpted by desire, with round, heavy, real breasts and hip bones perfect for gripping.

He rolled his eyes and shook his head, not daring to look at the clock, though he felt sure he had been awake at least half an hour by now, and had no idea how long they had been going at it before they had woken him.

And still they went on.

Tim lay on his side, listening closely. There was no alternative except leaving the room or hiding in the bathroom, and so he surrendered to eavesdropping, trying to pick out each word. Mostly it was repetition, dirty talk, and baby-oh-baby-come-on from him and give-it-to-me from her. *The classics*, he thought, chuckling tiredly. *Unoriginal but much beloved the world over.*

And then a break in the rhythm, a pause.

"Can I?" the man asked.

The answer, when it came, sounded clear and intimate and close, as if she had whispered the words into Tim's ear.

"You can put it anywhere you want."

Jesus, he thought, breath catching in his throat. It really had sounded like she was there in bed next to him. He listened as the sounds started up again, but soon the man lapsed into silence broken only by wordless grunts. His lover continued to urge him on—demanding, pleading for him not to stop.

Then the man let out an almost sorrowful groan and the woman cried out in triumphant pleasure and, at last, the thumping of the headboard subsided.

Tim's heart was still thudding in his chest and his face felt flushed, but he figured if he just lay there in bed, he would calm down enough to go back to sleep. He closed his eyes and took a breath.

And she spoke again, there on the other side of the wall.

"Thank you, baby," she said, and he heard it as though she was whispering it right into his ear. "That was exactly what I needed."

The hunger and the pleasure in her voice did him in. He threw back the sheets and went back into the bathroom, where it took only seconds for him to get himself off.

Afterward he lay in bed, ashamed and frustrated and missing Jenny so hard he felt ripped open inside.

Eventually, he slept.

Room service brought his breakfast at nine o'clock on the dot. Tim figured that most people who had their morning meal brought to their rooms were up and out of the hotel for meetings by 9 A.M., which explained them being so timely. He signed for his breakfast, giving the thin Mexican guy who'd delivered it a decent tip. In his visits to Los Angeles over the past few years, he had been consistently amazed by how much more effort Mexican immigrants seemed to put into their jobs than native born Los Angelenos. And not just more effort, but more hustle, and greater civility. There was a lesson to be learned in the great immigration battle, but he had lost too much sleep last night to give it very much thought.

Sunlight splashed into the room through the sliding glass door that led out onto the balcony. He liked to sleep in the dark, but during the day he wanted as much sunshine as he could get, and if there was any place in the world to find it, it was right here.

In light cotton shorts and a blue t-shirt Jenny had bought him two years back in Kennebunkport, Maine, he carried the tray out onto the balcony and set it onto a little round table. First order of business, he poured himself a cup of coffee—cream, no sugar—and sipped it as he looked down at the beach below, the waves crashing on the sand. The surf made a gentle shushing noise that comforted him.

The hotel backed right up to the ocean. From the balcony he could see the Santa Monica Pier. At night, the lights from the pier provided their own kind of beauty, but during the day the view was truly spectacular. Tim breathed in the salty ocean air and felt cleansed, refreshed. The coffee relit the pilot light in his brain and he started to feel awake for the first time this morning.

Jenny had loved the view. They had stayed here during both of their visits to L.A. together, the first time only months after they had started dating—it had been that weekend, Tim believed, that they had fallen in love—and the second as a special getaway for their fifth wedding anniversary. Not in the same room each time, of course. Jenny might have remembered the room numbers—he had never asked her—but guys just didn't pay attention to that sort of thing.

And, anyway, it was the view that she had loved, not the room.

With another deep breath, he sipped at his coffee and then set it down, settling into a chair beside the small table. He removed the metal cover over his breakfast plate to reveal a Western omelette accompanied by a small portion of breakfast potatoes and half a dozen slices of fresh melon. Sliding the table over in front of him, he tucked into his breakfast. The omelette was delicious, but halfway through, his appetite failed him and he wondered why he hadn't just ordered juice and toast. He ate the melon because it was sweet and good for him, and drank the small glass of OJ that had come alongside the coffee pot and then he settled back to digest.

Already the day had grown warmer. The weatherman had said it would reach the mid-80s by noon, and Tim had no trouble believing that. He planned to go to Universal Studios in the afternoon, just for a few hours—it was what he and Jenny had done the last time they were here together—but this morning he intended to take it easy. He got up and went into his room, fetching the James Lee Burke novel he'd bought to read on the plane. Then he shifted the chair to keep the sun out of his eyes, poured himself another cup of java, and sat reading and enjoying his coffee with the sound of the ocean enveloping him.

Twenty or so pages later, he was pulled from the book by the sound of a slider rattling open. He looked up to see a woman stepping out onto the balcony of the room next door. Instantly his mind went back to the night before and the sounds that had come from that room, and he felt both embarrassed and aroused at the same time. This had to be the same woman whose voice he had heard so clearly. It was too early for her to have checked out and a new guest to have arrived.

"Good morning," she said, raising a coffee mug in a toast to him.

Her smile was brilliant. His throat went dry just looking at her—five feet nine or ten, lean and limber like those Olympic volleyball girls, long blonde hair back in a ponytail, bright blue eyes—and the pictures he had painted in his mind of last night's acrobatics became that much more vivid. She wore a black and gold bikini that nearly gave him a heart attack.

"Morning," he said, wondering if she would notice the flush in his cheeks—was he actually blushing? God, he felt awkward.

He forced himself back to his book, desperate to look at anything but her. The words blurred on the page. The balconies were open-post style, and he had gotten a fantastic look at her stunning legs.

Just read, he thought, trying to focus. Should he get up and go into his room, or would that be even more awkward?

"I'm sorry," she said. "Am I disturbing you?"

God, he thought, *you have no idea.*

"Not at all. Just enjoying the morning."

"I know what you mean," she replied, sinking into a chair and stretching her legs out, propping her feet up on the railing of her balcony. "I don't have to be anywhere until after lunch and wanted to get a little sun while I have some downtime. It's quiet out here this morning."

She stretched out to maximize her body's exposure to the sun and, consequently, to Tim as well. He held his place in the book with one finger and turned to smile politely at her.

"It's a weekday. People are off at business meetings, I guess."

She shielded her eyes from the sun to look at him. Her lips were full and red and perfect. "No meetings for you?"

"Fortunately not."

He shifted uneasily, not sure he wanted to have this conversation but also not wanting to be rude. And God she was beautiful. The sounds from the previous night returned as he stared at her and he could not help imagining those lips saying those things, pleading, moaning, and then . . . *You can put it anywhere you want*. Shit, he'd almost forgotten about that, and now that he'd remembered he could barely even pay attention to what she was saying.

"I'm sorry," he said. "What was that?"

She smiled, a sparkle of mischief in her eyes, as if she knew exactly what had distracted him.

"I asked what brought you to Santa Monica, if not business."

Tim ran through possible answers in his mind, but they all came down to a choice between lying and telling the truth and he had given up lying years before. He and Jenny had been going through a rough patch, distance growing between them because he had been travelling for work so often, and he had been unfaithful. It had nearly ruined his life, nearly destroyed their life together when he confessed to her, but they had gotten through it. He had vowed that he would never stray again but it had taken years before she actually seemed to believe him. Forgiving him, though, was something else. She had said she did, but he had always wondered, and wondered even still.

"Honestly, it's sort of a sad story for such a beautiful morning," he said. "What about you?"

She cocked her head curiously, maybe intrigued by the tragic air about him. Tim had seen it before. Maybe someday he would take advantage of the way some women reacted to sad stories, but he had not yet reached a place where he could do that.

"Just sightseeing. A little California dreaming, you know? Started in Napa and made my way down with . . . well, Kirk's no longer with me."

So his name had been Kirk.

"Kirk?"

She arched her eyebrow suggestively. "I guess I was a little too much for him."

Tim could have taken that any number of ways, but the eyebrow made it clear what she meant. In his mind he could practically hear Kirk's voice even now, calling her every filthy thing he could think of. When he had imagined the woman on the receiving end of those words, she had been nothing like this lovely creature on the balcony. As beautiful as she was, she seemed sweet, even charming.

"I'm sorry to hear that," Tim said.

"It's a morning for sad stories, I guess," she said. "My name is Diana, by the way."

"Tim," he said.

"Sorry if we kept you up last night, Tim."

He grinned, feeling himself flush even more deeply, and glanced away. If he had seen the comment coming he could have prepared, pretended to have slept through it all, but her directness had snuck up on him.

"Nah, it's fine. I mean, not for long—"

Diana pouted. "I think I might be insulted."

"—no, no, that came out wrong," he stammered. Then he laughed at his own embarrassment. "I'm a pretty sound sleeper. And who hasn't been on the other side of thin walls at least once, right?"

Her eyes seemed to dance with merriment. "Exactly. That's so true."

She sat up to take a sip of her coffee, her breasts straining against the thin fabric of her bikini top, a single strand of her blonde hair—loose from the ponytail—hung across her face.

"So, are you going to tell me why you're in Santa Monica?"

Her boldness impressed and entranced him. As he thought about it, he could see this woman being the honest, passionate, carnal lover whose voice he had heard through the wall the night before. Yet Diana had many facets, and he saw one of them now, as a kind of sorrow filled her eyes.

"I don't mind sad stories. I've got a whole catalogue of them myself. Go ahead. I'm a big girl, I can take it."

Something in that last line made him wonder if she had said it to tease him, but he might have imagined it, added a pouty, sexy insouciance to it that was really only an echo of the night before.

"You might think it's a little strange," he ventured.

Diana turned her chair slightly, basking in the sun even as she transformed their two balconies into a strangely intimate confessional.

"I like strange."

Tim thought about Kirk, the idiot who had apparently left this woman after a night like they'd shared last night. What kind of fool must he be?

"All right," Tim said. He turned down the page in his book and laid it across his chest, staring out at the ocean for a moment before returning his focus to Diana's curious gaze. "I'm on a kind of tour, I guess. I've been to New Orleans and Montreal and to Martha's Vineyard, off Cape Cod. I even went down to this little village on the Gulf of Mexico. They're all places that were important to my wife, Jenny, and me during the years we had together."

The kindness in Diana's eyes broke his heart all over again. "She's gone?"

"Just over a year ago. Pancreatic cancer. It was agony for her, so it was probably good that she went quickly, but I didn't have time, you know? No time to get used to the idea of life without her. It's taken me this long to accept that I've got to live my life. I know she'd have wanted that for me. I'm only thirty-seven. There are a lot of days ahead, if I'm lucky. So I'm on vacation, but it's also kind of our farewell tour."

"Wow," Diana whispered, almost wistful. "That may be the most romantic thing I've ever heard. You're, like, the perfect husband."

A familiar guilt filled him. It had grown like rust on his heart over the years. After he had betrayed Jenny, he had spent every day trying to make it up to her. He doubted he would ever have been able to, really, no matter how much time they had been given together. But he had wanted more time to try.

"Far from perfect," Tim said, staring out at the Pacific.

"No, you're a good guy. I can sense those things," Diana said. "And you're lucky, too."

He frowned. "Lucky?"

The mischief returned to her eyes and she stood, adjusting the strap of her bikini top.

"You said you were a sound sleeper," she reminded him. With one hand on the handle of the slider, ready to go inside, she glanced over her shoulder at him in a pose so sexy it was painful to behold. "I always have trouble falling asleep. I need someone to tire me out. The only way I can really sleep well is if I'm so exhausted that I'm a quivering mass of jelly. And with Kirk gone . . ."

Diana glanced away, almost shyly, before looking back at him with renewed boldness. "I don't know what I'll do tonight."

Tim could not speak. He dared not move for fear that she would notice the effect she had had on him, if she hadn't already.

Obviously pleased by his speechlessness, Diana opened the sliding door into her room. "Enjoy your day, Timothy."

He managed to croak "you too" before her door slid shut.

Shaking his head in amazement, he went back to his book, the erection Diana had caused—the second in a very short time— slowly subsiding. After a few minutes he realized that his thoughts were straying and he had not understood a word he'd read, and he laughed softly at himself. Had that really been an invitation? Did she mean it?

Not that it mattered. As arousing as it was just being in the presence of this woman, Tim knew that any sexual trysts were still in the future for him. In another life he would have climbed mountains for an opportunity to sleep with a woman like Diana, and he knew that he would remember what he had overheard last night for years, maybe forever. Maybe someday he would even regret being faithful to a woman who was now only a memory, but this trip was about him and Jenny, and he would honour that, no matter what. He wanted to start a new life, but not quite yet.

He laughed again, thinking of Jenny. If she were alive for him to tell her the tale, she would have mocked him with love but without mercy. Men, she had often said, were pitifully simple and predictable creatures. Pavlov had used dogs to test his theories about programmed responses, but all he would have had to do was put a man in a room with Diana, and there would have been no need to experiment further.

This final stop on his farewell tour was by far the strangest.

How Jenny would have teased him. God, he missed her.

The phone woke him. In the darkness he searched for it, fingers scrabbling on the nightstand, and only managed to find it when it rang a second time. As he pressed the receiver to his ear, he saw the faint glow of the alarm clock.

12:17 A.M. After midnight. *Who the hell . . .*

"Hello?" he said, voice full of gravel.

"I can't sleep," she whispered.

It took him a moment, and when the pieces clicked together, his breath caught in his throat.

"Diana?"

"Hey," she said in a sleepy voice.

Tim had come back to the hotel around eight P.M. and eaten a late dinner alone in the restaurant downstairs. Afterward he had held his breath walking past her room, heart racing. Their conversation on the balcony that morning had stayed with him all day, and he had caught himself fantasizing about her, wondering if her thinly veiled invitation for tonight had been more than just flirting.

It hurt his heart. This whole strange vacation had been meant to be about Jenny, and his not being able to get Diana out of his mind seemed a dark stain on pure intentions. But, Christ, he was only human.

"Did you have a nice day?" she asked, when he hadn't replied.

"Yeah. I guess. Do you . . . do you know what time it is?"

Even her laugh had that soft, sleepy intimacy about it.

"I do. I'm sorry. I told you I have trouble falling asleep."

They both let that hang in the air for a bit. Lying in bed in the dark, hearing her voice in his ear, Tim found his memory of the previous night returning with perfect clarity. He could practically hear the thump of the headboard against the wall behind his head, and now that he knew what she looked like the images in his mind were more than imagination.

"Listen, Diana, I enjoyed talking to you this morning—"

"Can I come over there?"

Tim squeezed his eyes shut. How come this couldn't have happened to him before he met Jenny, or sometime in the future? Six months—hell, one month—from now, maybe his mind would have been in a different place.

"I'm sorry, I just . . ."

You can put it anywhere you want.

Holy God, how was he supposed to handle this? His heart slammed in his chest. His face felt flushed and once again this woman had given him a painful erection, this time with nothing but a whisper. He felt like a fool for having so little control of his body.

"Tim, hush," she said. "Think about this. You're trying to forget, right? I can give you that. We can help each other. I can make you forget, and you can help me get to sleep."

"It isn't that simple."

"But it is." She laughed that sweet, soft laugh again. "Honey, trust me, I'll make you forget your own name."

There in the dark, he felt himself grin. "I have no doubt you would. And you have no idea how tempting it is—or, actually, you probably do. But this isn't about forgetting Jenny. . . . I never want to forget her. It's about making peace with the fact that she's gone, and . . ."

He trailed off. The rest was too personal. He didn't know Diana.

"And?" she whispered.

Tim took a breath, turned onto his side, phone pressed between his cheek and the pillow.

"I betrayed her once. This would feel too much like doing that again."

"She's been dead over a year, you said."

"Not to me. I need to finish saying goodbye. Whatever life has in store for me after, I'll embrace it, but not here. This place was part of us."

"Please?" she said in a little girl sort of voice. "I can't sleep."

His words dried up in his throat as the reality of the conversation struck him hard. *Please*, she'd said, and now that he reminded himself what she was pleading for, what she wanted from him, he could barely think. It could be the night of his life.

But he would never be able to enjoy the memory of it.

"I'm sorry," he said. "Good night, Diana."

As he reached out to return the phone to its cradle, his hand hesitated involuntarily for just a moment. But if she said anything more, he did not hear it. He hung up and laid his head back down with a mixture of relief and regret.

His arousal subsided and a peaceful sort of contentment filled him. Though he half-expected the phone to ring, it did not. He closed his eyes and burrowed down into the bed. Sleep had fled, but only for a while, and soon enough it began to envelop him again.

"Tim."

He came half awake, lost somewhere in a dream.

"Tim."

Now he blinked and opened his eyes. In the darkness he reached out to search the rest of the huge hotel bed to make absolutely certain he was alone there. She sounded so close.

"Are you awake?"

She wasn't in the room; her voice came through the thin wall, a lover's whisper, though she must have been speaking up in order for him to hear her.

He considered replying but then thought better of it.

"Think of something you've always wanted to do, but never dared to ask of a woman," she said. *"You don't have to ask me. You could do whatever you want, and I won't stop you. I won't say no. Better than that, I'll ask for more."*

Scenarios played out in his mind instantly and once again she had him captivated.

"Please," she said. *"I need you."*

She began to tell him in great detail every little thing she would be willing to do, and have done to her, and how much she would enjoy it. How she would moan, even scream.

Then, at last, when he did not reply, she sighed.

"All right. I'll just have to call room service. But you're to blame for what happens."

You're to blame? What the hell was that supposed to mean?

Tim pulled a pillow over his head to block out her voice, but it seemed she had surrendered at last. Yet still her promises echoed inside his head. He lay curled on his side, unable to make his erection go away, unable to deny his arousal, and yet filled with more sorrow and missing Jenny more than he had since the day he had lost her.

At some point he drifted off, temptation still burning in him.

A sharp rap at the door snapped him awake. His eyes burned and his head felt full of cotton. What little sleep he'd had tonight had been shallow and restless. In the blackness of the room he threw back the covers and started to climb out of bed.

Gotta be her. Crazy woman, Tim thought. *I've got myself a stalker.*

"Who is it?" Diana called.

Tim froze, brow furrowed. Had the knock been at his door, or at hers? With the walls so thin, it was difficult to know.

A muffled voice replied. He heard Diana unlocking her door and, out of curiosity, pressed his ear to the wall again. The rattle of a room service cart was followed by a murmur of voices. Tim fancied he could smell food—a burger, maybe?

He glanced at the nightstand. In the pitch dark of his room he could barely make out the glow of the alarm clock, which he'd turned away from him. Now he felt his way onto the bed and crawled over to it, turning the clock round to read the time.

Room service at 2:13 A.M.? Did this hotel even have twenty-four hour room service? Or had Diana persuaded someone to break the rules for her? Tim had a feeling Diana had spent her entire life tempting and cajoling and getting exactly the result she desired.

A spark of irritation ignited within him. Though he felt a now-familiar stirring at the thought of her, his frustration at this long night of broken sleep trumped any lingering arousal.

From next door he heard the sound of a door closing and he assumed the room service guy had left. But a moment later the murmur of voices began again, both hers and a man's, and then they moved nearer and he heard the creak of weight upon the bed.

"Trust me," he heard Diana say, "this is going to be the best tip you've ever gotten."

Tim couldn't help himself. He laughed softly, falling back onto the bed. "You've got to be fucking kidding me."

But he should not have been surprised. Diana had told him that if he wouldn't come over and have sex with her that she would call room service. He supposed things like this must happen fairly often in the real world, but to him it seemed like something out of the *Penthouse* letters page or some porn film.

Already the noises had begun. How fast had she stripped the guy? Tim lay there staring at the ceiling in the dark and listened to the grunts and moans quickening. Diana urged the room service guy in words almost identical to those she had used with her lover of the previous night. Tim began to get an erection and he felt a ripple of anger at himself. Tired and frayed and amused, he should not find any of this arousing, but he could not help himself. Men were pitifully predictable creatures.

Not so predictable, he thought. *You didn't go over there.*

But he knew that meant little. Under other circumstances, he would have jumped at the chance to be with a woman like Diana and been just as grateful as, no doubt, the room service guy felt at that very moment.

The noises in the next room reached an initial crescendo, with Diana crying out in a throaty, shuddery orgasm followed almost immediately by the groan of a man stunned by his own good fortune. If last night was any indication, though, Diana would not let it go at that. As soon as the guy had a few minutes' rest . . .

The groan had not stopped. The man's voice began to rise and fall, perhaps with each spasm of his own orgasm. It sounded like he was still coming, like she had brought him to the height of ecstasy and somehow managed to keep him there. The guy cried out to God but even those words were barely more than grunts.

The headboard slammed the wall in quick rhythm, punctuating each spasm. Diana talked to him, urged him on, and Tim wondered what kind of woman this was, what tantric magic she had that could keep a man locked in ecstasy, and suddenly he knew that while he would always know he had done the right thing, he would also forever regret not having felt what the lucky son of a bitch next door was feeling in that moment.

And then the room service guy began to cry.

In the midst of his climactic groaning, he sobbed and began to say "please" every few seconds. The tone alone told Tim that the man wanted it to end. That he had had enough.

Diana laughed.

"Come on, baby," she said. "Fuck me harder."

Then it was her turn to moan, sounding the way some lovers did when they were locked in a deep kiss, or during oral sex. Tim's erection had returned full force even as he listened with growing unease. The room service guy's cries sounded full of pain, now, even fear.

Tim reached out and turned on the light. Sitting up in bed, he stared at the wall, trying to decide what exactly he was hearing.

You're to blame for what happens, Diana had said.

But what, exactly, was happening? This did not sound like sex anymore, not like ecstasy. And now that he thought about it, some of the groans the previous night had sounded full of pain to him as well. What the hell was the woman doing to this guy?

He picked up the phone and reached out to punch the button for the front desk, but hesitated. What the hell would he say? Instead, he put the phone back in its cradle and climbed from the bed. Tugging on the pants he had worn that day, he ran the whole thing over in his mind. He could bang on the wall or go out into the hall and knock on the door, but if he was wrong . . . if this was just extraordinary sex or some S&M thing he was too naïve to understand, he would feel foolish. And to Diana he would appear jealous and full of regret, and he did not want to give her that satisfaction.

Diana's muffled moaning grew louder. The headboard kept banging, although if he was correct the rhythm seemed to have slowed. But in the midst of the man's groaning he felt certain now that he heard sobs and weeping.

That's not pleasure.

Fully awake now, he went to the slider, unlocked it and drew it open as quietly as possible. Hesitating only a moment, he went to the railing that separated his balcony from Diana's and carefully threw his leg over, settling his weight on the railing a moment in order to shift his weight from one balcony to the next.

You'll be arrested, he thought. *Peeping Tom. Pervert. She'll think you just wanted to see.*

But such reservations did not stop him. Something was wrong.

He could feel it in the rising of the small hairs on the back of his neck and the icy dread that raced through him as he crept across Diana's balcony.

Her slider was open halfway. The crash of the surf on Santa Monica Beach, just behind him, covered any noise his bare feet might have made. He paused just outside the slider, hidden from within by the curtain hanging on the other side of the glass. But where the slider was open, the curtain had been drawn back to let moonlight into the room. Tim took a deep breath and held it, then carefully leaned in so that he could get a glimpse into the room.

Diana knelt astride an olive-skinned man, rocking herself back and forth on him, riding him hard enough to keep the headboard slamming the wall. The sensual curves of her body in the interplay between moonlight and shadows made Tim catch his breath. But then he noticed the way the man's body bucked beneath her, the way his hips seemed to come up off the bed with her, not as if he were thrusting into her but as though with each motion she dragged him up with her, as though her sex had clamped onto him and tugged again and again, milking him, attached in some unfathomable way.

So entranced was he by the strangeness of that, and by the swaying of breasts, that at first he did not notice the wrongness of the shadows around her face. The man continued to cry out, his eyes rolled back to the whites, his cheeks looking sunken—Jesus, he looked sickly, how old was this guy? Diana had her mouth against his chest and at first Tim thought she must be licking his nipples or his skin, but then Diana shifted in the moonlight, drew her head back a bit, and Tim's heart seized in his chest.

His mind tried to make sense of what he saw. He stared, breathless, as denial tried to fight back the horror and disgust and fear that filled him. Chills rippled across his body and his stomach churned. Bile roared up the back of his throat and he had to force himself not to vomit.

CHRISTOPHER GOLDEN

Diana's mouth was distended, stretched into a pale, blue-veined funnel attached to the man's chest, right above his heart. Her lips trembled with a quiet suction, the skin around them glistening wetly, but he could hardly tear his eyes away from the disgusting proboscis that her face had become.

The man's cheeks were streaked with tears.

As Tim watched in mounting horror, the man's face seemed to become thinner. His entire body had begun to wrinkle, even to wither, and Tim wondered what he had looked like before he had crawled into that bed. *Kirk's no longer with me*, Diana had said of her previous night's lover. So where the hell was Kirk now?

The room service guy's head tossed to one side and for just a second, his eyes were on Tim. That was enough.

He swept the screen open and burst into the room. Diana glanced up but did not slow the thrust of her hips, the slam of the headboard, the suction of her hideous mouth.

"Get off him!" Tim shouted.

He grabbed her with both hands, gripped her upper arms from behind, and used his momentum to drag her off the bed, straining with the effort. *Too heavy. What the . . .*

As Diana flopped to the carpet, Tim watched the room service guy dragged along with her, her pussy and that grotesque, distended mouth suctioned to his flesh. Her hips continued to piston onto him and he kept groaning, but his voice had become weaker now and his skin had begun to turn a hideous coal grey. Smoke rose from his open mouth, as if he were on fire inside.

"Jesus!" Tim cried. He wanted to bolt from the room, to pretend he'd never seen this thing, but he knew he would never erase it from his mind.

He reached down and tried to separate them but Diana flailed at him, fingernails furrowing his neck. She and her prey were on their sides on the carpet. The stretched funnel of her mouth still adhered to his chest, but now Tim saw the lips crawling caterpillar-

156

like trying to keep hold of the flesh.

"No. No way," he said.

Clutching at his bleeding neck, he stomped a bare foot onto that thin, pale flesh. Her mouth came free with a pop and he saw a black tongue, needle-thin and long—so long—slip from the man's chest before she sucked it back between her lips and spun on Tim.

"What the hell *are* you?" Tim rasped.

Diana hissed, tore herself from the man, and leaped up at Tim. She attacked with her fingers hooked into claws and now panic raced like poison through his veins. What the hell had he done? Why had he intervened? He grabbed her by the wrists but she was strong. She spun him around and slammed him into the wall and that long mouth thrust at him, long black tongue darting out, and now Tim saw it had a glistening stinger on the tip. He shoved her backward, clenched his fist, and struck her in the temple. He punched her again and again, drove her against the mirrored closet door, which shattered into hundreds of shards that cut their feet as they grappled.

Tim caught only a glimpse of the room service guy out of the corner of his eye before the guy smashed him in the head with the telephone. He spun backward and crashed into the wall, sliding to the carpet even as blood trickled down into his right eye and pain clutched vise-like at his skull. Darkness danced around the edges of his vision and for several seconds he blacked out.

He opened his eyes again to the room service guy's voice. Full of desperation, pitiful and withered, half the life already leeched from him, the poor bastard's cock was still hard.

"Please. Finish," he pleaded.

The hideously disfigured mouth on the creature Tim knew as Diana twitched, and then smiled. She reached out and took the lost soul's hand and led him back to bed, mounting him again, reattaching her lamprey mouth to his heart and her sex to his.

Amidst the tortured music of the headboard and their moans,

Tim managed to stagger to his bloodied feet. He nearly tripped over the guy's uniform as he shoved the room service cart out of the way. Through the wreckage of the closet door he saw a body laid out on the floor inside. The shrivelled thing between its legs had once been a penis. The skin was like shrunken leather, split in several places to reveal dry, pink meat inside, and the cheeks had been torn badly enough to show bone. It looked as though all of the moisture had been sucked out of him, along with all of his youth and vigour, and his life.

Kirk. And now this guy.

Tim had tried. Whatever Diana had done to Kirk, and who knew how many guys before him, she was now doing to the room service guy, and like some kind of junkie, he needed it now, needed her to finish the job. The hook was in deep. The things that made him *him* had already been taken away.

Kirk's no longer with me.

I guess I was a little too much for him.

Tim opened the door and staggered out of the room and down the corridor on bloodied feet. He banged the elevator call button and then ran on to the stairwell door and slammed it open. Ever since Jenny's death, the people who loved him had told him that she would be watching over him. He had never quite believed it— she had gone from this world, a wall thrown up between them— but after this night he was not so sure. It seemed that even those walls could be thin at times.

As he raced down the steps to the lobby, he wondered again if Jenny had ever forgiven him for what he had done. Yet for the first time, it was an idle curiosity. He had loved her as well as he was able and knew she had loved him in return, but she was gone now, and would never be able to give him the forgiveness he sought. He would have to claim it for himself. And he would. Tim had done his penance.

Tonight most of all.

MECHANISMS
(WITH MIKE MIGNOLA)

On that particular October morning—a lovely fall day, a Wednesday—the autumn light fell across the rooftops of Oxford with a hint of gold sufficient to transform the view from mundane to wondrous. Colin Radford, a young man of serious scholarship, found himself so taken by the panorama visible from the classroom window that he had difficulty following the threads of Professor Sidgwick's lecture on Suetonius. This was especially troubling when Colin considered that the biographies which comprised the Roman historian's *De Vita Caesarum* had been amongst the most compelling reading that the young man had encountered in his time at Oxford, second only to the comedic plays of Aristophanes.

Colin Radford adored university—all of the thinking, the constant discourse over questions of philosophy, scholarship, and theology. At times he felt as though he had been waiting all of his life to escape dreary Norwich, with its forbidding cathedral and the chill wind that swept across the Channel all the way from the Russian Steppes. He had found in Oxford a truer home, where men put their minds to work upon the mechanisms of intellect. There were kindred spirits here, competitive though they might be.

So for Colin to allow his mind to wander required a vista of unparallelled beauty. And yet on certain mornings, Oxford glistened in such a way as to have earned the lyrical nickname that romantics had bestowed upon it.

The City of Dreaming Spires, they called it.

Had he known on that morning that he would never see it again, Colin would have been filled with such grief as to make him weep. And yet there was much more grief to come.

A Mods student named Chisholm hurried into the room the moment the lecture concluded, earning a disapproving glare from Professor Sidgwick, even as he handed a folded sheet of cream parchment to the bespectacled old man. Colin watched Sidgwick dismiss the lad with a sniff and then glance at the note, which could only have come from the Headmaster's office. Somehow, even before it happened, he knew what would come next. Sidgwick lifted his gaze, glanced around the room, and they locked eyes.

"Mr. Radford, come here, if you please."

Colin felt a strange heat prickle his face. He did not fear Sidgwick the way he knew some others did, though if he thought the professor had caught him drifting during the lecture he might have done well to be afraid of his wrath. Yet the look on the old man's face, the way he stroked his pointed beard, and the almost militaristic manner in which he held that crisp letter still half-raised in his right hand, made the young scholar cringe.

"Yes, sir," Colin said, and as the other students departed, he made for the lectern.

Sidgwick looked at him over the tops of his spectacles. "You're from Norwich, lad? I'd never have thought it."

The significance of this—whether it contained compliment or insult—escaped Colin, so he did not reply.

"Instructions from the Headmaster," Sidgwick said, proffering the note in his right hand, fingers bent as if in a claw, half-crushing the parchment. "You're to return home at once. You've a train leaving in less than two hours, so you'd best be on your way."

Poison twisted in Colin's gut. Expelled? How could it be? He'd done nothing.

"But, sir—" he began.

Sidgwick must have read the reaction in his face, for the old man instantly waved a hand in the air as though to erase such thoughts.

"It's not expulsion, boy. You've been summoned."

Reluctantly—as if by not doing so he might avert his fate—Colin took the note.

"But why?" he asked as he unfolded it and began to read.

Sidgwick did not wait for him to discover it on his own. "It appears," the professor said, "that your father has disappeared."

The Radford ancestral home rested on a hill in the city of Norwich, on the eastern coast of England. The 17th-century manse neither perched nor loomed upon its hill, and though there were many trees on the sprawling grounds, neither could it rightly be said to nestle there. Even to say the old house 'stood' on that slope, with its distant view of the blue-grey waters of the English Channel, would have been a kindness. No, Colin had always thought of the house as resting there, after more than two hundred years providing hearth and shelter for the Radford family, its halls echoing with the shouts and laughter of Radford children.

Now, as the carriage which had awaited him at the train station climbed the long drive up to the front door, Colin stared at the house and considered another interpretation for his insistence upon the lazy imagery that accompanied the house's personification in his mind. Absent his father's inhabitance, the house seemed a body without its soul, a still husk of a thing, awaiting burial. Whether his own arrival might breathe some new life into the stones and beams of the place he quite doubted, as he had no intention of remaining forever, or even for very long, once his father's whereabouts had been ascertained.

For all the golden, autumnal beauty he had cherished in Oxford, here in Norwich there was only grey. The sky, the stones, the prematurely bare trees, the pallor of its citizens, and the wind-chopped water of the Channel, all grey.

The carriage came to a halt and it was not until he had climbed down and retrieved his single case that he realized he had taken for granted the comfort afforded him by the familiar clip-clop of horses' hooves on the road and the rattle of the conveyance itself. Without it, here on the hill, the only sound remaining was the wind, which, when it gusted through the hollows and eaves of the old house, moaned with the grief of a forlorn spirit or a heartbroken widow.

Fortunately, Colin Radford did not believe in ghosts. Prior to university, he had lived all of his life in this house and he knew it as a lonely place, but not haunted.

Still, he hesitated as the carriage driver snapped his reins and the carriage began to roll away. The sound that had been a comfort receded; soon not even its promise would remain and the wind would rule. Better to be inside. The timbers and stones still moaned, but sorrowful as they were—grey sounds in a grey house in a grey city—they were familiar sounds.

As he started toward the door, it swung inward. Colin looked up, expecting Filgate or one of the other servants, but the silhouette that greeted him—stepping forward, bent and defeated—belonged to the nearest thing the estate did have to a ghost: his grandmother, Abigail.

"Took your time about it, didn't you?" she said.

Trouble on the rails had delayed his arrival in London until after the last train had left for Norwich for the day, so he had been forced to spend the night in the capital and board the rescheduled train this morning. But the old woman's disapproving tone and baleful gaze discouraged any explanation. Let her think what she wished.

"I came as quickly as possible," he said, carrying his case into the foyer, where he set it down as Grandmother Abigail closed the door.

They faced one another in the elaborate foyer, surrounded by the odd religious icons that had been his father's passion and then peculiarity over the years.

"I suppose it's too much to hope that he's turned up," Colin said.

Grandmother Abigail shook her head, her lips quivering slightly, a tiny yet startling concession to her fear for her son.

"Not a trace, Collie. Not a trace," the old woman said, and then the familiar, hard mask he knew so well returned. "Word has spread throughout the city for people to be on the lookout for him, but there's been no word. The grounds have been searched and every room in the house, from attic to cellar, but the only thing down there is Edgar's mechanism."

Colin frowned. "Mechanism?"

His grandmother fluttered her hand in a way that revealed a new delicacy in her, one that he had never seen before, brought on now by fear or advancing age or some combination of the two.

"A strange contraption of metal and wood, with no purpose I ever saw or he ever shared," she said, her disdain obvious despite her concern for her son.

"I never imagined Father as much of an inventor," Colin said, mystified.

"He began building it last year, not long after an argument he had with that ugly Irish spiritualist."

Colin shivered. Finnegan had been a charlatan, no doubt, but his father had always seemed somehow to enjoy the man's company. The birdlike man with his small eyes and misshapen nose had always tried to get Colin to call him 'Uncle Charlie,' but as a boy he had only managed it once or twice, and as a young man, Colin had wanted nothing to do with him.

But he'd been away at university for more than a year, home only for brief visits in the summer and at Christmas, and had never thought to enquire about Finnegan. He had not even been aware that his father and the ugly Irishman had had a falling out.

Perhaps Sir Edgar Radford had finally realized that no matter what he claimed or what sort of show he put on, Finnegan's mediumship was a sham. The Irishman had been trying to help the man contact his dead wife for more than a decade.

"Do you want to see it?" Grandmother Abigail asked.

Colin frowned. "See what?"

"Why, your father's mechanism. The very thing we were just discussing."

"I'd think my time better spent in joining the search, wouldn't you?"

Grandmother Abigail dropped her eyes, as though worried what he might see in them. "Perhaps."

"And yet?" Colin prodded.

The old woman lifted her gaze. "The infernal thing troubles me, that's all. In the past few weeks your father spent so much of his time down there, and he grew increasingly irritated at any intrusion. Fervent in his efforts and . . . hostile, yes, toward anyone who might question them. But you see I had no desire to linger in the cellar. The thing makes me uneasy, even if it doesn't . . ."

Dread climbed his spine on skittery spider legs. "Doesn't what?"

Again she glanced downward. "It doesn't work, of course."

"What is it you're keeping from me, Grandmother?"

With that, she shook her head and waved him toward the stairs. "Go on. Put your things away. Martha has seen to your room, and I'll have a meal prepared for you. I imagine you'll wish to speak to Thomas Church, who is organizing the search."

Grandmother Abigail turned away, bent with age, and began to retreat along the corridor that led to the kitchens. "Perhaps it's better you keep away from the thing after all."

Befuddled, Colin watched her go. The old woman had never treated him with the kind of warmth many associated with the role of grandmother, nor did she exhibit the witch-like sort of behaviour often portrayed in stories. Neither kindly matron nor wizened crone, Abigail Radford kept mostly to herself and had a fondness for coffee over tea and biscuits rather than scones. When not knitting or strolling the grounds on watch for 'pests,' she had forever seemed to lurk just over young Colin's shoulder, ready to tut-tut at any seemingly imminent infraction. If he attempted to slip into the kitchen for an early taste of dinner or to snatch a cooling scone from a baking sheet, she would be there. If he jumped on his father's bed, slid on the banister, or tried to climb up onto the roof of the house, Grandmother Abigail seemed ever present, and able to dissuade him with a clucking of her tongue and the knitting of her brow.

A grey, joyless woman. And yet he knew she believed her efforts were all to keep him safe, and that in her way she loved him, a vital bit of knowledge for a boy who had grown to manhood without the benefit of a mother.

As a child he had been told that his mother had gone off with the fairies and that one day she might return. A million fantasies had been born of this lie, and he had often imagined himself wandering into the woods in pursuit of his beautiful mother, joining her in the kingdom of the fairies, living with sprites and brownies and other creatures of magic and mischief. By the age of eight he had begun to realize that this was mere fancy, but it was not until he turned twelve that his father had told him of his mother's drowning.

Now, with his father having also 'vanished,' he could not help but remember the lies about her death. Had Edgar Radford also gone 'off with the fairies'? Had the old man wandered off in the grip of some dementia, been killed by brigands, or suffered some fatal misadventure?

Colin meant to find him, no matter the answer. The idea that his father's behaviour had altered so radically over the past year with Colin completely unaware of the changes unnerved him. He would join in the search. If necessary, he would begin it again and conduct it himself.

Yet even as he made this silent vow—climbing the stairs and striding down the corridor toward his childhood bedroom—he realized just how impossible a task he had set for himself. Norwich was no tiny hamlet, but a city, with thousands of dark nooks and shadowed corners, not to mention the woods and hills, and the ocean that had claimed Colin's mother. And if Sir Edgar had left Norwich somehow . . . well, he would be found only if he wished to be found, or if some unfortunate happened upon his corpse.

The quiet emptiness of the house—despite the presence of his grandmother and the servants—closed around him, suffocating, as he stepped into the bedroom. A fire had been laid in the fireplace and logs crackled and popped, low flames dancing. The room had been decorated in shades of blue and rich cream and it ought to have been filled with warmth—if not of the fire then at least of memory.

Yet it was cold.

He did take a look that afternoon at what his grandmother had called Edgar's mechanism, once he had searched his father's study and found no note or journal or other document which might indicate the man's state of mind prior to his vanishing. Sir Edgar had left only the mechanism behind.

Though its intended use confounded him, Colin did not find himself unsettled by the machine the way the old woman seemed to be. Concerned, yes, even troubled—its seeming lack of purpose made him worry for the state of his father's mind—but nothing more than that. If anything, the madness inherent in the contraption's design made him hopeful that his father remained alive somewhere, that dementia had crept into his life and he had subsequently wandered off somewhere, forgotten the way home, and would eventually be found and returned to his family.

Dementia seemed horrid, but Colin told himself he would prefer that to learning of his father's death. Sir Edgar might be experiencing a certain amount of mental slippage, but at least Colin would be able to see him again, to provide him some comfort as he faded from the world. The man deserved that. For all of his eccentricities, Sir Edgar had been a proud, loving, and patient father.

Colin had left him behind without a single reservation, presuming that he would always be there, that there would forever be a home to which he might return, and the strange wisdom of Sir Edgar Radford to draw upon.

The air in the cellar was close and damp, warm even though the October days were chilly in Norwich and the nights even more so. Filgate had seen to it that there were lamps burning in the cellar before Colin descended, but as he examined the machine he wished he had arranged for more light, or less. A single lamp would have done the job almost as well. With several, the light shifted and shadows played tricks upon his eyes, so that he had to use the lamp in his hand to take a closer look at the various gauges and turns and vents to ascertain their true shape and attempt to determine their purpose.

No matter how much light he shed upon the mechanism, however, he could not divine its use. During its construction the cellar had been separated into three distinct spaces, one a wine cellar, one for cold storage, and one built around the base of a chimney, so that goods could be stored there in winter without freezing. Subsequent additions to the house had included expansions of the cellar, and it was in one of those that Sir Edgar had built his mechanism.

To Colin, it looked like discarded pieces of other machines, a tangle of pipes and flues, enormous cogs and gears, wooden joists and shelves and pulleys. He pulled levers and turned cranks, but his experiments with the thing yielded no result save for a clattering here and a grinding there. The machine, whatever its ambition, did not work. It did not run.

What puzzled him most were the thick iron pipes—perhaps four inches in diameter—that led off from the apparatus and directly into the stone walls in half a dozen places. They seemed intended to carry water or steam, but the mechanism worked not at all and so Colin could not determine which.

After half an hour wasted in the gloom, he doused the lights and ascended the stairs, to find Thomas Church awaiting him in the parlour. The ruddy-faced man had the paunch and thinning white hair of a friar, but his strong, scarred hands spoke of his youth as a mason, before circumstances conspired to raise him to a life in the magistrate. As a child, Colin had always found himself impressed by the air of authority Church carried with him, in spite of his meagre beginnings as a tradesman.

He spoke with that authority as he spoke of the search effort's utter failure.

"We've peered into every hole in Norwich and combed the hills and fields," Church said grimly, running his fingers through his shaggy beard. "If Sir Edgar isn't hiding, or being hid, he'll turn up at some point. The lads I've got out looking aren't ready to give up quite yet, but in a couple of days I'll have to call it off. They've got lives to return to, y'see. Jobs and families."

"I understand, Mr. Church," Colin said. "And I hope you'll pass along my gratitude to each of them."

It was obvious Church wanted to say more, that he felt gravely dissatisfied with his own performance, but Colin could think of no words he might have spoken that would have provided solace and so he offered none. He watched Church withdraw and then depart, allowing himself no outward expression of the despair that had begun to gnaw at his heart.

That night, in the darkness of his bedroom, he felt sure he heard the walls whisper his dead mother's name.

At first he thought it might be the moan of the October wind through the gap he had left in his window. He had surfaced from a deeper sleep into a state of disorientation, that drowsy, floating limbo that always waited on either side of wakefulness. Now his thoughts began to clear and he listened more carefully, ascribing any sound to the wind, the creak of old houses, or the rustle of curtains.

And then, now fully awake, he heard it clearly. "Deirdre?"

Not a cry or a shout, or even a moan as he had first believed, but a calling, as if the name were spoken by a blind man, lost and wandering, reaching out for the touch of the familiar. Colin did not recognize the voice, but it had a parched, weakened quality that might have masked its true timbre.

He sat up in bed to listen and, sure enough, the voice came again, calling his dead mother's name. "Deirdre?"

"Father?" Colin said, his own voice equally thin and reedy in the dark. Though the voice did not sound precisely like his father's, who else would be calling for long-dead Deirdre Radford in the middle of the night?

Colin sat and listened closely, but long minutes ticked past without any further occurrence. Over time, however, he slowly became aware of another sound, a low thrum or vibration, so minimal as to be almost unnoticeable. Had he not been listening so keenly, he never would have heard it, and the sound would have remained part of the shush of the world's quiet noise; the voice of a distant river, the wind on the grass, the soft breath of a slumbering lover.

Alighting from his bed, he went to the fireplace, at first believing it to be the source of the thrum. It did seem louder there, but when he bent to listen more closely, he realized the tone did not emanate from within.

As he cocked his head, trying to ascertain its origin, he placed his hand upon the mantel, then pulled it abruptly away as though he'd been burned. Thoughtfully, he put his hand once more upon the wooden mantel and felt the vibration there. With a glance around the room, wondering if the thrum was more pronounced in some corners than in others, he traced his hand along the mantel and then pressed his palm against the wall beside the fireplace.

That contact was rewarded with a shift in tone. The vibration became louder and turned, for just a moment, into a grinding noise, followed quickly by the clank of metal, like gears turning over, and then a sigh as though of steam, before it finally diminished once more to its original volume and tenor.

Somewhere in the midst of that noise, he might have heard the voice again, calling for Deirdre, but he could not be sure.

Barely aware that he was holding his breath, Colin pressed an ear to the wall. Beneath the continuous thrum he could hear a soft clicking, as of cogs turning. Abruptly he pulled away from the wall, fetched his robe, and slipped it on. Tracing his fingers along the wall to be sure the thrum did not subside or diminish, he went out into the corridor.

Colin kept his hand on the wall and then on the banister as he descended the stairs, but he already knew his destination. Only one new mechanism had been installed in the house during his time at university, and he had no doubt that his father's mysterious invention must be the source of these unfamiliar sounds.

No one else stirred as he made his way through the foyer and then along the hall to the cellar door. He thought that one or more of the servants might also be roused by the noise, though perhaps they had all grown accustomed to it over time. His grandmother had not been awakened, but she was an old woman and he presumed her hearing had deteriorated with age.

Constantly alert to any change in the sound, afraid with each creak of a floorboard beneath his feet that it might cease, Colin fumbled to light the lamp that hung by the cellar door. Its soft glow cast strange shadows as he lifted it down from its hook, so that he turned quickly, thinking that Filgate or Grandmother Alicia had heard him wandering the house and come to investigate, secretly sure in the back of his mind that his father had appeared from some hiding place to explain all.

But Colin was alone there, in front of the cellar door. And suddenly it seemed to him a dreadful idea to be up by himself in the middle of the night, about to descend into the cold and the dark and the queer depth of his father's obsession. As a boy, he had always feared the cellar, and somehow in the burgeoning confidence of his time at university he had forgotten that fear.

Now it returned.

But that mechanical hum still vibrated in the air, and when he touched the cellar door he felt it far more strongly than before.

"There'll be no jumping at shadows," he promised himself, and so doing, he opened the door and started down.

The cellar looked much as it had earlier. Colin took the time to light several of the lamps that Filgate had arranged for him, though it now occurred to him that some of them had likely been put in place by his father, when Sir Edgar had been working on the contraption.

Whatever he had been expecting upon his descent, however, his imagination proved far more active than the mechanism itself. The sound had gained in volume with every step and as he approached the room wherein the thing had been constructed, but when he stepped inside he had to stop and stare in surprise. No levers moved. No steam escaped the valves. Cogs did not turn. The machine was absolutely still.

Holding the single lamp in his hand, he manoeuvred around the mechanism just as he had earlier in the day, his robe catching on a hinge and tearing slightly. Colin swore and continued his examination. He reached out to touch one of the bars of the mechanism with a hesitation akin to petting a stranger's dog, but only the dullest vibration could be felt in the machine itself, less so than in the wood of the cellar door.

Yet there could be no denying that the sound had grown louder as he entered this room. Colin began to walk the perimeter of the room to see if there were places where the volume rose or fell, and when he stepped over one of the pipes that jutted from the mechanism into the wall, he paused and looked back at the metal cylinder where it entered the stone foundation.

Crouching, he grasped the pipe. His whole arm trembled with the vibration travelling through it, and he pulled away. Glancing back at the machine, he saw that nothing had changed. It remained still as ever. But here, where the pipe entered the wall, its extremities thrummed with the workings of some other machine or some unknown engine to which this one was attached, off beyond the cellar wall.

Colin rose, staring at the wall. He turned in a circle, trying to figure where the pipes might lead. One by one he walked to each of the seven pipes extending from his father's mechanism, checking to be sure, and he found that each of them vibrated just as urgently as the first. As he checked, he fancied he could hear more subtle noises now, his ears adjusting to the thrum. There were clicks and whirs, hisses and clanks. Machines.

But two of the pipes led into a wall that separated this room from another cellar chamber, and when he checked he confirmed that they did not exit on the other side of that wall. One led into a wall that bordered nothing but stone, and must have run far under the remainder of the house, although how his father had managed to install it without excavating down through the floor of the parlour Colin could not imagine.

This chamber sat at the southeast corner of the house, and of the remaining four pipes, two each had been pushed through holes in the south and the east walls, respectively. Colin wondered about those pipes. The two that led into the adjoining room did not emerge in that room, but what of these, which could run under the grounds outside?

He knew of only one way to find out.

With one last look at Sir Edgar's mechanism, Colin doused the lamps and retreated up the stairs. He did not bother returning to his room. Rather, he fixed a pot of tea and nibbled on a leftover apple tart in the kitchen as he waited for the sun to rise, so that he could pay a visit to Mr. Church.

"There's nothing wrong with my hearing," Grandmother Abigail insisted.

The old woman frowned at him, arms sternly crossed. When Colin had returned from town with Mr. Church and half a dozen of his workers, Grandmother Abigail had demanded to know what he thought he was doing, ordering them to dig holes in the grounds around the house.

Reluctantly, he had told her the story of his experience the previous night, including his amazement that the sounds he heard in the walls did not rouse any of the house's other residents from their beds. He had long suspected Filgate of relying heavily upon brandy to carry him off to sleep, which would explain the man's sound slumber, but his suggestion that perhaps age had diminished his grandmother's hearing brought this angry protest.

"I intended no offense," Colin said, his tone as much apology as he could muster. "I simply cannot imagine how you managed to sleep through the noise. Granted, it wasn't especially loud, but so consistent that the irritation alone would be enough to drive one mad if it persisted long enough."

Grandmother Abigail's expression faltered, and she shrank slightly. It lasted only a moment, but long enough for Colin to realize that her pique had been a mask behind which she hid some other, more subtle, response to his enquiries.

"What is it you aren't telling me?" he asked.

She shook her head and looked away, gazing out the window at two of the workers, who even now plunged shovels into soft brown earth, piling rich soil high beside the waist-deep hole they'd dug.

"I don't know what you mean," his grandmother said.

"You did hear it," Colin guessed. "You know precisely what I'm talking about."

Her jaw seemed set, as though she might never utter another word as long as she lived. She took a deep breath and released it before turning to him.

"I hear nothing of the kind," she said. "But your father heard . . . something."

Colin straightened up. "Tell me everything."

"He said almost exactly the same thing, about the sound being enough to drive one mad, given time enough. He heard . . . vibrations, yes, but he said whatever those machines were that he heard, they had a rhythm."

Colin nodded. Though it had not occurred to him in those precise terms, he understood what his father had meant. "Was that when he began to build his own mechanism?"

Grandmother Abigail seemed pale in the sunlight shining through the window. "He thought if he could match his own machine to the rhythm, find a way to get the two in harmony, he could make his mechanism function on its own, without his—"

She'd cut herself off.

Colin stared at her. "Without his what?"

She shook her head, willing to go no further.

"Without his what?" he shouted. "Grandmother, please, there must be some connection to this mechanism and his disappearance. If there is, the only way I will be able to discover it is if I understand what he was thinking while he built it."

Grandmother Abigail regarded him coolly, as if she had separated herself from him somehow.

"He managed to make it work in some rudimentary way by placing himself within the machine. Those shelves are seats, the levers and valves meant to be operated by hand."

"But Father left no designs—"

The old woman narrowed her eyes as if daring him to challenge her. "I burned them."

"Why would you do that?"

Her mouth quivered a bit, and then she lowered her gaze. "I was afraid for you, Collie. Your father thought . . . he . . ." She steadied herself, raised her eyes, and looked at him with the clearest warning he had ever seen. "You know that ever since your mother's death your father has been obsessed with the idea that the connection they had could not be severed, that there must be some way for him to speak to her, even beyond death. Beyond life."

Colin nodded. "All of those séances with Finnegan—"

Grandmother Abigail's expression turned to stone. "He educated himself, talked to spiritualists and scholars alike. If he heard even a whisper of some method he had not yet attempted, he experimented with it. Finnegan indulged him all along, let poor Edgar think his wish might one day be granted, and lined his own pockets with your father's money. But when your father began to talk of the sounds he heard in the walls, and when he began to build that mechanism in the cellar, Finnegan urged him to stop. No, *more* than stop. Finnegan wanted him to break it into pieces, threatened to have nothing more to do with Edgar if he refused."

Fingers of dread crept up Colin's spine. "What happened?"

"Your father had Filgate throw Finnegan out of the house and told him never to return," Grandmother Abigail said. "He kept working, building, testing that infernal machine, and less than three weeks later, Edgar vanished."

Colin turned and stared out at the hall that would lead him to the cellar door.

"Whatever you hear in the walls, lad, you mustn't listen," the old woman said.

"And if that means we never find him?" Colin asked.

Grandmother Abigail lifted her chin, trembling slightly. "Better that than risk losing you along with him."

Colin thought on that for several long minutes, alternately looking out the window at the diggers and back into the house in the direction of the cellar. When, at length, he finally met his grandmother's gaze, she must have seen his decision in his eyes, for her shoulders slumped with sadness and surrender.

The old woman turned from him without another word and left the room, as if he had already disappeared.

Church's men dug all around the foundation of the house at that rear corner, where Sir Edgar's mechanism filled the cellar room, but they found nothing. The pipes that penetrated the walls in that chamber did not emerge on the other side. Church had no explanation, nor had Colin expected one. The pipes must simply have stopped several inches into the wall.

Colin did not believe that, of course. He had jostled one of the pipes enough to know that it did not end after a few inches. And then there was the matter of the nocturnal thrum, the vibration, of the machine. Where did that come from? Colin supposed that his grandmother might be right, that he might have imagined it just as his father had done, but if that was so, then where *was* his father?

An answer to that question had begun to coalesce in the back of Colin's mind once Grandmother Abigail had told him of his father's falling out with Finnegan, but he tried not to dwell upon it, for it seemed impossible. Felt impossible.

All that day, as Church's excavations revealed more and more of nothing and Grandmother Abigail's words resonated deeper and deeper in his mind, Colin felt a growing anxiety. With the onset of evening, emotional tremors passed through him, a queer combination of unease and anticipation. There could be no doubt what his next course of action must be, and over the dinner table he saw in his grandmother's eyes that she knew it as well. They barely spoke during the meal, and when it had concluded she excused herself, claiming a headache, and retired for the night.

Soon enough, Colin found himself alone in the parlour with a glass of brandy and a crackling fire, all of the servants having withdrawn.

He did not even pretend to retire for the night. Instead, he waited there in the parlour, listening for the hum and staring at a shelf of his father's old books without even the smallest temptation to pluck one down to read. He sipped brandy and felt himself grow heavy with the influence of the alcohol and the warmth of the fire, but as drowsy as he became he would not allow himself to doze.

He felt his father nearby, as if, were he to close his eyes and reach out, he might grasp Sir Edgar's hand or tug his sleeve. The feeling chilled and warmed him in equal measure, and it occurred to him that this must be how his father had felt for so many years about his late mother. He had always talked of feeling her nearness, of his confidence that her spirit lingered, awaiting him, attempting to contact him, if only he could find the means to receive that communication.

Enough brandy, and the walls Colin had built inside his mind to prevent him thinking about his more outlandish theories regarding his father's disappearance began to break down. A little more, and he stopped denying to himself the certainty that had formed in the back of his mind. Somehow, in attempting to contact his mother, his father had succeeded in breaking down a wall, tearing away the curtain between what Colin knew as tangible reality and some other existence. Whether his father was alive or dead, he did not know, but he felt sure that in matching the rhythm of the vibration in the walls, he had slipped out of the world.

Yet he felt just as certain that his father was still in the house—still down there in the cellar—and if he could match that same rhythm, as his father had done, it might be possible to draw the curtain back one more time and let Sir Edgar return.

A loud, sobering voice spoke up at the back of his mind, warning him that he might share his father's fate, but he took another sip of brandy and pushed it away. If his father had stepped onto another plane of existence, joining him there was far from the worst thing Colin could imagine. And *not* attempting to save his father was inconceivable.

Sometime after midnight, his vigilance was rewarded with a whisper.

"Deirdre," said the walls. But now he felt sure the voice belonged to his father.

The thrum began moments later, and Colin set aside his brandy snifter, rose from his chair, and walked from the parlour, swaying only slightly.

Intuition guided him—at least that was what he told himself at first. From the moment he hoisted himself up onto the wooden shelf that functioned as a seat, and settled his arms onto the two smaller shelves that were angled downward toward the levers, he felt in tune with the machine. The support behind his arms gave him leverage, the seat taking his weight left his legs mostly free. Some of what had seemed to be levers were actually pedals.

But it wasn't enough simply to work those levers and pedals. One valve protruded from a metal arm which, when swung in front of his face, behaved more like the mouthpiece of a trumpet. When he breathed into it, the valve seemed to draw greedily from the air in his lungs until he found the perfect rhythm of inhale and exhale.

His breath powered the machine, as did his arms and legs. He listened so carefully to the rhythm in the walls, the clank and grind, the thrum and vibration, and worked his body—his own mechanism—to match it. Somehow, he knew, he had to find a way to meld himself to his father's machine, to turn the two mechanisms into one, acting in concert, and then extend that unification to the other machines beyond the walls, wherever they were, and to the mechanism that was his father. He could feel Sir Edgar there with him, breathing with him, moving with him, as if the man's body had been scattered into tiny particles that filled the air of the chamber.

The brandy had numbed him at first, blurred his thoughts, but soon it seemed to help crystallize them instead. Inhale. Exhale. Left hand, right foot, left foot, right hand, both feet, twist of the neck, inhale, exhale, inhale-exhale, as though playing a tune, a one-man orchestra, his body, the mechanism, a symphony.

Hours passed. His body did not require rest, did not crave food or even water. The machine was enough, feeding him, breathing through him. His limbs began to move of their own accord, instructed not by his own conscious thoughts but by the necessity of the machine.

"Deirdre," a voice whispered, so close it might have been breathing in his ear.

The rhythm, perfectly matched.

Elated, he opened his eyes, unaware that he had ever closed them, and saw that the curtain had at last been drawn aside. There were no walls any longer, only the machine, only mechanisms as far as his eyes could see in every direction.

Close by, perhaps twenty feet away, Sir Edgar Radford moved in unison with the machine, in perpetual motion. Arms and legs, inhale exhale. Pulling his mouth away to whisper and then darting forward again to place his lips on the valve. Pipes passed into his flesh and out the other side. Some seemed made of bone. Cables of sinew ran around pulleys, moving his limbs like the strings of a marionette.

The man's eyes gazed into the awful distance where cogs turned and pulleys rattled and levers rose and fell, and he never blinked.

"Father?" Colin said, his voice a new part of the rhythm between inhale and exhale.

His father did not seem to hear. He only stared deeper into the machine, far off across the joined mechanisms of this place behind the curtain.

"Deirdre?" Sir Edgar whispered.

Then Colin heard it, from far off. A reply. "Edgar?"

He watched as his father bent to his labours, working the mechanism feverishly, that one whisper of his name enough to drive him on with the promise that he had almost succeeded in his goal, that if he could draw back one more curtain, he might be with her at last.

"Deirdre?" Sir Edgar said again.

But this time, the voice that replied did not speak his father's name.

"Colin?" it said, so close he could feel her there, just out of reach.

He tried to scream but the valve stole his breath, requiring it to maintain the rhythm of the machine.

Inhale.

Exhale.

THE SECRET BACKS OF THINGS

In winter, the Pickthall estate was deathly silent save for the occasional comings and goings of the staff and the cry of birds foolish enough not to have sought warmer climes. Mrs. Pickthall— Helen—never made that mistake. As soon as December came round it was off to Ibiza on the coast of Spain. The children were grown but often visited her there with their own urchins, and she had acquired friends as she did antiques, populating the winter residence with both. James Pickthall joined his wife in Ibiza for at least two weeks of every winter month; as little as he could manage without her pique evolving into fury.

Despite the desolation of his ancestral home during the coldest months, Mr. Pickthall relished the days and weeks he spent there, alone save for the staff, who knew by intuition that he preferred them to be as ghosts when the Missus was away. They flitted like shades from room to room, laying a fire, setting out his meals, turning down the bed, but tried to keep clear of him at all other times.

They haunted the estate, but only as the most helpful of spirits.

Mr. Pickthall knew that he could have retired by now, passed control of the Norwich Rail Company to his son, Martin. The boy already took care of much of the day to day business. But if Mr. Pickthall did that, he would have no excuse to allow him to avoid spending four months a year in Ibiza, listening to his wife chatter and enduring all of her friends and their constant stream of social events. That would simply kill him.

The silence was blissful.

He was the man in charge and he liked it that way, was used to being catered and deferred to. Mrs. Pickthall was too busy dragging him about to have noticed or cared. He was no ordinary man, James Pickthall, yet his wife always made him feel ordinary, or even less than.

The winter was his respite. His own time. He was a man who valued his routine and scorned spontaneity. Thus, on that particular Sunday, Mr. Pickthall was most put out that his routine was interrupted. He had attended church as always and had Clarence, his driver, stop at the bakery on the way back to the estate. Mr. Pickthall shopped at the bakery himself rather than ask Clarence to go in for him. There had been those, including Mrs. Pickthall, who had suggested he did this in an effort to connect with the common folk. Mr. Pickthall allowed, even perpetuated, this misconception, though the truth was simply that he trusted no one else to choose the bread.

Upon returning home from church services with his fresh bread—a loaf of rye and a bag of pumpernickel rolls—he retired to his study where a fire had been stoked. It blazed and crackled in anticipation of his arrival. He packed himself a pipe and then sat, ruminating, staring into the flames.

That was his disposition come Sunday noon, when the front bell rang, its chimes breaking the silence, a shrill call and answer that seemed a conversation in and of itself, dull-voiced bells dinging at one another in a ripple of echoes through the house.

Mr. Pickthall was not a curious man. He didn't care who was at the door, only that the arrival had disrupted his meditations. So it was with no small amount of aggravation that he awaited word of his visitor, tapping his pipe upon the arm of his chair. A full minute passed by with no further interruption and he had begun to think that perhaps his man Lowestoft had succeeded in sending away whomever had intruded upon the peace of the house.

Then there came a hesitant rap upon the door.

"Come!" he called.

Lowestoft poked his head in, silver hair cut short but elegantly coiffed, clothing immaculate. His expression revealed his regret at the intrusion.

"Mr. Pickthall, so sorry to trouble you, sir, but there's a gentleman here from the railroad. A Mr. Whipple, sir. Says he needs to speak to you on urgent business. I tried to persuade him to leave a message with me, but he wouldn't hear of it."

With a sigh, Mr. Pickthall waved a hand. "All right, Lowestoft. If it's that urgent, we shouldn't keep the man waiting. Whatever's so bloody important, you'd think they'd ring me rather than send a messenger."

But the old man wasn't a fool. He had an idea his visitor might have something else in mind. Perhaps a process server or some other legal minion, delivering a summons of some kind. Such were the travails of a man of wealth and power that the proceedings of the law often produced entanglements that were unavoidable.

"Yes, sir," Lowestoft said with a nod.

He withdrew, and after a count of perhaps ten seconds there came another soft rap and then the door was drawn open. Mr. Pickthall was in the process of relighting his pipe and he took a long tug on it, relishing the flavour and the heat in his chest, even as Lowestoft introduced the visitor.

"Mr. Graham Whipple, sir."

Mr. Pickthall did not stand to greet his guest. Instead he raised an eyebrow to regard the new arrival. He was an exceedingly average man. Average height, average face, average build. Mr. Whipple wore eyeglasses and a grey suit with a blue tie, clothes he might as well be buried in. He certainly looked the part of a clerk or some other unremarkable employee. His hair was snow white, as white as December, and he wore a bushy moustache that was, without doubt, the only facet of his appearance with any character.

"Well, Whipple. Your visit is urgent. Have at it, then."

The man wrung his hands a moment like a worried grandmother. Regret gave him pause, that much was clear in his face. But there was something else there as well. Something Mr. Pickthall wished he had noticed right off. Mr. Graham Whipple was angry. The man reached up and smoothed his moustache and there was the air about him of a man in dire need of a drink.

Just as Mr. Pickthall was about to prod him again, Mr. Whipple knitted his brow and spoke.

"Have you ever ridden on a train, sir?"

Mr. Pickthall was drawing another inhalation of pungent heat from his pipe and now he let it stream in coils of smoke from his nostrils. One corner of his mouth turned upward in what he hoped was a sardonic smirk.

"I own the lion's share of a railway company, Mr. Whipple. I should hope I'd ridden on a train."

But Mr. Whipple was not discouraged. No, now that he'd mustered the courage to speak at all there was more than a glint of defiance in his eyes. "Not often, though, I'd wager."

Mr. Pickthall found the man tiresome. "If you've got a message for me, Whipple, I suggest you find your way to delivering it by a less circuitous route."

"Where the rails pass through the countryside, there's beauty beyond the glass, isn't there, sir? All the beauty of God's earth. Sunrise and sunset, flowers and streams. Little villages that look as though they've not changed since George was King."

With a low grunt of annoyance, Mr. Pickthall set his pipe in its stand on the small table beside his chair. The crackle of the blaze in the fireplace had pleased him before, but now he felt flush with unwelcome heat and the air seemed too close. Winter or no, he wanted to open a window. But he had an unwelcome visitor to tend to first.

"See here, sir. If you've something to say, get on with it. Otherwise, you will simply give me the name of your supervisor and then leave the premises, and I'll see to it that your impertinence is dealt with the moment you arrive at the office tomorrow morning."

Mr. Whipple's eyes seemed moist and red, stung by the heat and smoke of the fire, but now they grew distant a moment. "Never worked in an office. Not a day."

A shiver went through Mr. Pickthall. There was something not quite right about this man. The wealthy gentleman was about to rise and call to Lowestoft when Mr. Whipple smiled and his eyes focused once more on his unwilling host.

"I'm a trainman, sir. Have been all my life. Forty-four years on the rails, and I've worn the uniform of Norwich Rail from the day it was born."

Mr. Pickthall felt his grip tighten on the arms of his chair. This was not right. The man was not here to serve a summons and he most certainly had not brought a message from the office.

"You're a conductor? What in God's name do you think you're doing, Whipple, coming into my home like this?" he demanded, and at last he pushed himself to his feet.

Mr. Pickthall gave his visitor a wide berth but he started for the study door, a sneer curling his lip. Mr. Whipple made no move to stop him. It was only as Mr. Pickthall reached for the knob that the other man spoke again.

"I know about your whores."

A tiny gasp escaped Mr. Pickthall's lips as he froze by the door to the study. His fingers were inches from the knob. A chill unlike anything he had ever felt swept over him, a deeper cold that spider-walked up his spine with an icy prickle. The wave of menace that emanated from Mr. Whipple in that moment was as real and as unseen as the stink of raw sewage. He felt it touch him and knew he was its object.

For the first time in his adult life, James Pickthall was afraid.

When he turned to face Graham Whipple again he was rigid with dread. He half expected to see the devil in the man's eyes, but instead Mr. Whipple seemed oddly regretful, unable to meet his gaze.

"What did you say?" Mr. Pickthall asked. A foolish question. He had heard quite clearly, but he wanted elaboration.

Mr. Whipple nodded slowly, then once more looked into Mr. Pickthall's eyes. He seemed to be searching for something there and it unnerved Mr. Pickthall, felt to him as though he were being undressed, as though the image he had worked all of his life to build was a pitiful mask that fooled his visitor not at all.

How could he not have felt exposed, given the man's declaration?

With a shudder, Mr. Whipple waved his hand in the air as though he wished to erase something from the world. "I'm . . . I'm truly sorry, sir." He winced with pain from some spiritual wound. "This is quite unlike me. Never been one to talk such filth. But I've no other way to make my point, have I?"

What the bloody hell is your point? Mr. Pickthall wanted to shout. But he didn't dare. Not until he discovered what his visitor truly knew, and what he planned to do with such knowledge.

"I'm afraid I have no idea what you're talking about," Mr. Pickthall offered, a weak gambit.

Mr. Whipple seemed almost disappointed. "Please, sir. Must I go on? It really is unpleasant for me."

But when Mr. Pickthall replied only with a stony glare, Mr. Whipple sighed.

"All right," the trainman said, nodding slowly. "As I said, I know about them. Could tell you some of their names, though I suspect most of them don't use their real names."

His gaze darkened.

"Kit used her real name, though, didn't she? When you whispered that you loved her and made her with child. When you paid her to have the child in her belly destroyed? And why not? It was a bastard child, wasn't it? Son of a whore. Leastways that's what you thought at the time.

"But it haunts you now, Mr. Pickthall, sir. It's a spectre that's there every time you look over your shoulder."

As the man spoke, that fear had crept over Mr. Pickthall's flesh and made him shiver. But as the man fell silent, he forced himself to be calm. There was a bit of business to be conducted here, that was all. And Mr. Pickthall was nothing if not a businessman.

Mr. Whipple's small, damp eyes followed him as he returned to his chair by the fire. He tugged up on the knees of his trousers and sat, then rubbed thoughtfully at the back of his neck. At last he drew a deep, ragged breath.

"You her father, then? Kit's? That what this is about?"

The trainman blinked in confusion. "Sorry? No. No, why would you . . ." Understanding dawned, but he shook his head. "You've misunderstood. I'm no relation to the girl."

Mr. Pickthall gritted his teeth. He pushed up his sleeve and looked at his watch. By now his staff would be waiting for his visitor to leave, or else any moment there would come a rap and someone would enquire if Whipple was to stay for lunch. The idea brought a chuckle up in the back of Mr. Pickthall's throat, followed by a stream of bitter bile he had to choke back down.

"All right, then," he said through his teeth. "Enough of this. Speak plainly."

As though the question baffled him, Mr. Whipple gave a tiny shrug and then reached up to position his spectacles more firmly on the bridge of his nose. "Well, as I said, sir, I've spent my whole life as a trainman. There isn't anything else I know how to do. Only I've been sacked, haven't I? Oh, they find a dozen ways to say it. Early retirement is my favourite. Retire to what?"

His laugh was bitter, and it gnawed at what confidence Mr. Pickthall had been able to muster. The devilish chill he'd felt moments before had passed quickly. Yet now his recollection of it was refreshed. There was a hint of madness in that laugh, and in the trainman's eyes.

"I only want my job, is all, sir. Just want to be back on the trains."

Mr. Pickthall sniffed. "That really isn't my area, I'm afraid. I've no idea what you think you know about me, but it will hardly do you any good. I haven't anything to do with staffing."

It was as though all of the muscles in Mr. Whipple's face simply died.

Mr. Pickthall shivered beneath his gaze. "I mean to say, I *could* put in a word for you," he added tentatively.

Whipple shook his head. His eyes grew moist with tears and

he reached up to smooth his thick moustache again. There was an almost childlike petulance in him now, but the rage that fuelled it was poorly disguised beneath.

"You don't understand," he insisted. His nose crinkled and he began to pace, reaching up to lace his hands behind his head, muttering to himself. It lasted only a moment before he took a long breath and paused before an antique French corner chair. His expression was meek again, and strangely hopeful.

"Perhaps what you should ask, sir . . . yes, I should think so. Perhaps what you should ask is how I've come to know such a thing."

Mr. Pickthall's throat was dry. He wetted his lips with his tongue and remembered the tortured sobs of the girl, Kit, on the day they rid her of the child she carried. The memory had no room for a man like Whipple. How had he come into possession of such knowledge?

"Go on," Mr. Pickthall said.

Mr. Whipple sat on the chair. His gaze drifted once more, as though his eyes saw into some other place in time, and what he saw there filled him with strange contentment.

"I'm quite certain it didn't happen all at once. Only sensible to think something like this comes over time. Passengers, especially those in first class, as you might imagine, don't look out the window much unless there's something pretty to see. But there isn't always, is there? Most of the time the view is rubbish."

He laughed softly, a private joke.

"But a trainman sees something else. Oh, I performed my duties, sir. Never shirked. I punched tickets and greeted passengers with a pleasant word. Helped the ladies and the older gents with their bags. Knew every inch of track from London to Norwich, the way the cars would jerk a bit going round that last curve before the run into Colchester.

"There was time, though, a few minutes when all the tickets had been punched and the next stop was still a ways off, and I'd steal those minutes on the platform between cars and look out the glass set into the doors, watch the land as we passed by. It's mostly ugly, sir. Passengers only notice the lovely views, but trainmen notice it all. Running east out of London and through Ipswich and so many other cities, it's nothing but brick walls scrawled with filthy graffiti, metal fencing, drab bunkers, the rear of some warehouse or another. It's the homes that are the most interesting, though. Villages and neighbourhoods. The train runs through their yards, and through the windows you peer into their lives, see? Laundry out on the line, children's playthings scattered about, old tires, cars on blocks, bicycles rusted and abandoned. It's all back there. Gardens left untended and swings left behind and forgotten by children grown up and departed. All of the things people hide away from their neighbours and themselves."

Mr. Pickthall stared at the man, who seemed breathless with memory, and for a moment he thought that he could see images flickering across the man's eyes, as though they were windows that looked out at an ugly backyard world passing by.

When Whipple did not immediately go on, Mr. Pickthall cleared his throat and wetted his lips once again. "I . . . I fail to see what this has to do with—"

Mr. Whipple snorted derisively, giving a twist to his features that was anything but ordinary. "Yes, you do, don't you? Your sort always does. Fail to see, I mean."

And then Whipple merely looked at him, and Mr. Pickthall felt as though something pushed past his eyes, like insects digging in through the orbits. He clapped both hands to his face, covering them, and squeezed them tightly shut against the pain, hissing through his teeth. Cursing at God and the Devil alike.

It passed. He was breathing heavily and when he swallowed his throat was raw and sore. The fire was not burning nearly as hot, but sweat had begun to form upon his brow. There in the dead of winter, Mr. Pickthall was sweating. It was only with great reluctance that he looked up at Mr. Whipple again, his confidence eroded almost to nothing. He had to tell himself over and over that there was business to be conducted here.

"Get to the point, damn you!" he cried, hating the infantile shrillness of his voice, and the way his hands trembled.

"You can stare for hours at the branches of a tree and never see the birds amongst the leaves until they begin to stir," Mr. Whipple said. "It's all about what we want to see, isn't it? And what we want others to see. The faces we paint on. Eleanor Rigby knew. Had that face in a jar by her door, yeah?" He smiled softly. "Love that song."

For a moment he was lost, humming. Then his eyes refocused. Mr. Pickthall, afraid now of those eyes, looked away. He'd say whatever he had to say, now, just to get Whipple out of the house. If he'd just get to the bloody business of his blackmail, Mr. Pickthall would even give the man a downpayment. If all he really wanted was his sodding job back, he'd promise that. But only until he could have the police pick the bastard up. Without Kit, the filthy whore, Whipple hadn't a chance of convincing anyone of his claims. And even if he had the girl to back up his story, without a baby, there'd be no proof.

Yet there was no swagger in these thoughts. No arrogance. Only a kind of desperation. Anything to get Mr. Whipple out of his house.

"All those years," the trainman said, gazing back across time, or so it seemed. "And one day I was helping this elderly lady and her scarecrow of a daughter carry their bags up from the platform at Manningtree station, and I looked the frail daughter in the eye and I saw the venom she had for the old woman, and I saw the poison she put into her own food because she hadn't the courage to give it to her mother. Killing her own self slowly instead."

All the breath went out of Mr. Pickthall. He wrung his hands and when he realized Whipple had been doing it earlier he forced himself to stop.

"You . . . you expect me to believe that, do you? That you're some kind of mind reader?"

Mr. Whipple shook his head. "It isn't like that. Not at all. I couldn't say what you'd had for breakfast this morning, or what number you were thinking of, or whether you fancied the maid.

"It's the secret backs of things, Mr. Pickthall. I spent so many years on the trains, spying into the places people wanted to hide or forget, it got so I can see the secret backs of things. I look at you, sir, and I can see what you most want to hide. Your fears and your sins. The sorts of things you'd never share with another soul. Eleanor Rigby wore that face, and so do you, Mr. Pickthall. So do we all. But I . . ."

He whimpered, and tears came to his eyes, and his face was contorted with torment.

"I can see it all. The worst in all of us. It takes an effort *not* to see, though I manage most of the time. It's better on the trains. When I can look out the windows at the backs of walls and the rust and the rubbish. It soothes me. It's all I know. But now you've taken it from me, haven't you?"

Mr. Pickthall was paralyzed. His gaze shifted toward the study door and for once he found himself hoping for interruption, sent up a prayer that one of his staff would come and enquire about Whipple staying for lunch. But they were trained too well. Trained to fear reprisal. He could only imagine several of them commiserating at that very moment as they attempted to decide how to handle this breach in both schedule and protocol.

Ridiculous. That was what it was. Absurd.

But when he tried to meet Mr. Whipple's gaze, he turned his eyes away. The intrusion of the man's attention was too much. The violation. He could feel traces of Whipple's presence inside of him like muddy footprints tracked across his mind. The pain in his eyes had been real. The anger and malice flowing from Mr. Whipple . . . he had felt it.

And really, how else could the man know?

It was the black secret of Mr. Pickthall's heart.

"That's . . ." he rasped, coughing to clear his throat. "That's truly all you want? Your job?"

Hope flickered pitifully in Whipple's eyes. Slowly, he nodded.

"And if it's out of my hands? If I can't do what you ask? You'll tell what you think you know?"

Mr. Whipple's eyes went dark again and ice ran through Mr. Pickthall. He was convinced then that there really was a kind of devil behind the trainman's eyes, even if Mr. Whipple himself was not quite aware of it.

"You don't ride the trains much, Mr. Pickthall. But Mrs. Pickthall does. As do your children. Your son, Martin, in particular. Fancies himself a man of the people, rides the train to the office every day. I've seen them all, though of course they don't notice me. Just taking their tickets is all. Who'd see me?"

Mr. Pickthall took a long, ragged breath. "So you'll tell them my secrets, is that it?"

A sickening, brutal smile blossomed upon Mr. Whipple's face. A cruel thing, scarred with all of the private sins he had never wished to see. "Oh, no, sir," he said. "Who'd believe me, after all? I've no proof, have I?"

He paused and the smile went away. Mr. Whipple smoothed his moustache and narrowed the flickering windows of his eyes. "But you believe me, Mr. Pickthall. I see that you do."

Mr. Pickthall gave the tiniest of nods.

Mr. Whipple perched on the edge of the antique chair in the corner, firelight throwing shadows on his face.

"I'd like my old job back. On the trains. But no, sir, I'm not going to tell anyone what you're hiding. Not at all. I've looked into the eyes of your wife and your children, Mr. Pickthall. If you don't help me, I'm going to tell you *their* secrets. Each and every dark, wriggling worm that eats away inside of them.

"Ugly stuff, indeed."

NESTING

The weather man had predicted rain, but those guys would be right just as often by flipping a coin. That warm May evening, the sky was a clear, star-filled indigo, and even downtown Covington smelled like springtime. Whittier Street ran parallel to Washington, the main drag along the Merrimack River, which was lined with restaurants and boutiques. But if Washington Avenue presented the tight facelift of the old factory town's gentrification, Whittier's cafés and art galleries were the Bohemian, liberal heart of the place.

Mike Shaughnessy had dropped his wife, Cori, at the door of the Papillon Gallery and parked halfway down the block. Cori had balked, insisting that at six months' pregnant she was perfectly capable of walking a hundred yards, but Mike wouldn't hear of it. He liked taking care of her, indulging her. Until she'd gotten pregnant, he'd sort of forgotten just how much.

A trio of well-dressed women approached the gallery from the opposite direction, coming toward him along the sidewalk, and Mike slowed down to allow them to reach the door first. They were the perfect soccer moms, a species perfected in suburban Massachusetts. Mike and Cori had moved to Covington—just a few miles from the New Hampshire border—from blue collar Melrose, Massachusetts. They'd both commuted into Boston for work, and were used to a different breed of mothers in the neighbourhood, either working women or the stay-at-home wives of men who worked with their hands and spent their spring weekends with beer and fishing, and the fall with beer and football. Mike had felt torn between the two, a lawyer with a father who'd painted houses for a living for forty years. He felt just as comfortable with either extreme.

But he had no idea what to make of the Covington women, college-educated stay-home mothers who doted on their children while organizing charity events, book clubs, and artist receptions. They had perfect hair, perfect nails, perfect teeth, and every third woman had the same aquiline nose, the product of a small surgery necessary because of a "deviated septum." There were a lot of deviated septums in Covington.

There were other neighbourhoods in the city with a real cross section of race, age, and average income. But Mike and Cori had bought a house on a street loaded with other transplants who'd come north to find a neighbourhood where their kids could ride bikes without getting run over or shot, where they could afford a decent-sized yard as well as the landscaping service to groom it every week. There were women who still worked. Many of them, in fact. But a great many of these couples had moved specifically so they could afford for the new mother to stay home and raise their children. The New Feminism at work.

Mike had come to like Covington, with its half dozen home-made ice cream shops and funky restaurants, little book stores and music events at the library. The soccer moms were just a bonus. Some of them were nice to look at, some of them drove him nuts, but he had to give them points for sincerity. He doubted these women knew much more about art than he did—and he knew for sure that their husbands, whom they dragged off to various events when the guys got home from jobs in Boston, didn't—but they certainly *cared* an awful lot about it.

And they'd adopted Covington as their home town with great enthusiasm, though most of the couples in his neighbourhood hadn't grown up anywhere near the city.

Hence tonight's Local Artists' Spring Gala Exhibition at Papillon Gallery. A lot of words to express a simple concept, but as a lawyer Mike understood that approach all too well; why use two words when you can say it with twelve?

The women preceded him into the gallery. He spotted two couples walking down Whittier from the parking lot in Railroad Square, and realized that the gallery was going to be packed, tonight. He only hoped the fruit and cheese table had not already been ransacked. He'd gotten home late, so the free nibbles the Papillon provided would be his dinner tonight, along with a glass of whatever they were pouring.

"Mike, hello!" a happy blonde woman said as he stepped through the door. Her sharp features tugged into a grin and her long earrings swung like chimes as she turned to gesture toward the crowd jammed into the gallery. "Quite a turnout, don't you think? I saw your lovely bride a second ago. God, I wish I'd looked half that good when I was pregnant."

He smiled. Cynical as he liked to pretend to be, Mike really liked living in Covington. He liked his neighbourhood and most of his neighbours, and he especially liked Whittier Street's self-proclaimed Covington Arts District. If he could get Cori to like the city as much as he did, he'd be overjoyed. At first, adjusting had been hard for her. But now that she'd met some people, made a few friends, and been adopted by the Covington Arts District Council as a potential member, she was coming around.

"I've always thought pregnant women were sexy, Ellen," he told the blonde.

She arched an eyebrow. "Liar."

"Seriously. I'm sure you were a smokin' hot mama-to-be."

Ellen laughed and then turned to greet the two couples coming in behind him. Mike took a breath to get his courage up, then immersed himself into the crowd, working his way through the shifting labyrinth of people. He glanced at various paintings as he walked through, wondering if any of them were by Theo Bowden, the one local artist he was actually curious about.

A familiar laugh turned his head, and he spotted Cori talking with a couple he vaguely recognized—people from their neighbourhood, but what were their names? Mike had always been terrible that way. If he hadn't spent any significant time with someone, they floated to the bottom of his brain like pennies in a wishing well.

A waiter passed by and Mike gratefully accepted a glass of white wine from his tray. He took a sip as he walked over to Cori and the neighbours. His wife looked radiant, her auburn hair in ringlets and her mischievous eyes sparkling. Her nose crinkled when she smiled, drawing attention to the spray of freckles across her cheeks and the bridge of her nose.

"Hi, honey," she said.

"Hey." He slid an arm around her and bent to kiss her hello, and he felt the muscles in her back tense, saw the way she stiffened.

With the wine and the company and the whole atmosphere of the place, maybe she'd forgotten for a moment the tension between them. Mike hadn't forgotten. He couldn't forget even for a moment, and now he was sorry that he had reminded Cori. She'd been enjoying herself and now he'd tainted that.

"Mike, you know Doug and Jane Morgan from around the corner, right?"

"Of course," he lied, shaking their hands. "Though I don't get to spend as much time in the neighbourhood as I'd like. Nice to see you guys."

"You, too," Jane said. "Have you looked at any of this art? It's amazing we have this kind of talent in Covington."

Mike nodded, glancing around. "We were hoping to get a look at Theo Bowden's stuff."

"Right, right," Doug said. "You live in his house."

"Well, it's our house," Cori corrected. "He just lived there once."

"It's right over here," Jane said, leading the way into a rear corner of the gallery. "I don't know if they put the dead artists' work at the back because they don't think anyone's going to care, or because they think people will care and it'll make them walk past all of the other paintings to get back here."

Doug and Jane walked together, slipping through the crowd. Mike took Cori's hand as they followed. He thought she might pull away, but she did not.

"You didn't get a glass of water or something?" he asked.

195

Her smile had a bit of sadness in it. "You could give me your wine."

"You're not supposed to drink wine."

"Just a sip."

He handed it to her, then bent to kiss her temple. The discovery of Whittier Street had given Mike Shaughnessy hope that his marriage would survive. He and Cori had endured a great deal of change lately. Work and commute time had kept them apart much of the time, building lives away from each other, creating whole existences and other relationships that had nothing to do with who they were together. She had started to ask him awkward questions about one of the women at the office, and his denials had been just as awkward.

It was an old story. Typical. But when they were going through it, nothing about it felt typical. It just sucked.

Massive life surgery had been necessary to save their marriage, but he doubted either one of them would have taken drastic measures if not for the baby. He—or she—had changed everything. One day, perhaps, when the baby wasn't a baby any more, they would be able to tell him or her how the arrival of their first child had saved them.

Mike hoped for that. Wished for it.

Now the best he could do was take back the wine glass and give her growing belly a little Buddha-rub, and hope that when the baby arrived, it would make them a family again.

Cori slid between a couple of red-faced, white-haired guys who had to be local politicians, just by the look of their stiff collars and buttoned jackets. Mike had to actually go around them. Cori might be pregnant, but she was still small enough to slip through.

He caught up with her and the Morgans in a corner, where they were all admiring a series of small paintings, each seemingly tinier than the last. Theo Bowden had been known for the detail of his work and for working on small canvases. There were several larger paintings, but none more than eighteen inches wide or tall. Small town artists, people who painted for themselves and not in the hope of having their work hung in galleries like this one, could afford to be eccentric.

Bowden's paintings were mostly street scenes: Covington after a snowfall, children at the lake, a lone car driving down Washington Street, back when there had still been a Woolworth's on the corner and people still used the word "apothecary." A bicycle leaning against a lamp post. Men fishing from the bridge over the Merrimack River.

The artist had done a series of odd paintings of enormous stones, partially buried in the ground. *Standing stones*, Mike thought. They were more common in England, but there were examples of them all over northern New England, even a place in New Hampshire that marketed itself as "America's Stonehenge." Bowden might have done these still life studies up there, or elsewhere, but it was obvious he'd had a particular fascination for the things.

"Now it makes sense," he muttered to himself. They were having a swimming pool put into their backyard, and when the crew was clearing part of the woods behind the house they had come upon one of those stones and asked his permission to remove it. It was still lying around somewhere on the property, but looking at it, Mike realized he probably should have donated it to the historical society or something.

As for Bowden's paintings of the stones . . . well, they were paintings of stones. The images were so dull, he was surprised they hadn't bored the paint right off the canvas.

Fortunately, there were other Bowden paintings on display, without the serenity and charm of the street scenes or the cold boredom of the standing stones. The artist had painted various old houses in town, a series of them, and it seemed architecture fascinated him.

"Look at this, Cori," Jane Morgan said, beckoning them. "It's your house."

And it was, complete with the turret room they had just restored. Sometime in the 1960s, one of the previous owners had been stupid enough to tear it down. It had been a trend at the time, perhaps, or there had been damage. But when Mike and Cori had bought the house, its absence had been obvious. The rest of the design matched Victorian homes of the same era. There would have been a turret. Sure enough, when they searched the town records, they found old photos. There it was.

The neighbourhood association had tried to prevent them from putting up a new turret, but Cori had had the brilliant idea of enlisting the help of the Covington Historical Society, who argued in their favour because they wanted to restore the house to its original condition. The city found in their favour, and now the turret was up.

Mike and Cori both loved that room, and the view it provided. It had fast become their favourite room in the house, a tiny thing full of windows and benches and cushions. A room for thinking, or for not thinking at all.

"Wow," Cori said.

Doug and Jane Morgan had moved on to other paintings, leaving them to themselves for the moment.

Mike stepped up beside his wife. "What's 'wow'?"

"Take a look."

She pointed to a quintet of small paintings. They were oddly angled scenes, some of woods and others of old houses, but from above, as though looking down. Only when he looked at the fifth one, with its obvious lattice lines, did he realize that each one was the view out a window. That fifth painting, Bowden had painted in the crosshatch, so the view was through four panes of glass, complete with a bit of the warping that antique glass always created. It really was brilliant.

Now he went back and looked more closely at the other four. In two, the outer edges of the frame were clearly visible, but they were all of the view through a single pane of window glass.

"Don't you see it?" Cori asked.

"They're windows. It's a cool effect."

Cori smiled indulgently, all sins forgotten at the moment. She pointed to the paintings. "They're *our* windows, doofus. Fifty years ago, anyway."

Mike looked again. He stepped back and sipped his wine, studying each picture. He recognized the Beauregards' house, and then others started to fall in place. He imagined himself looking out the windows of his second floor, and saw that one of the houses in the second painting had been torn down and a pair of Colonials thrown up in the '80s. But the others—the landscaping was different, even the road was different, and the trees were either much taller or simply gone, but it was their neighbourhood, all right.

"Holy shit. This is very cool."

Cori kissed his cheek. "Eloquent as ever, honey."

They both studied the paintings more closely now, trying to figure out which windows would provide each of those views. As they did, Mike glanced to the right, and paused. A sixth painting seemed to go with the group. They'd nearly missed it because its shape didn't seem to be part of the set. It was wide, but not tall, and showed a view down upon thick woods, and a white church steeple in the distance.

"That's the view from the turret," Cori said, coming over beside him.

Mike nodded. He'd been thinking exactly the same thing. It had taken a minute to see it, because the contractors had cleared some of the woods to make room for the pool, but the angle, and that church steeple in the distance—at the centre of town—must be the view Theo Bowden had had from the turret room fifty years before. The turret had been torn down ten years later, so no one could have matched the images up until now.

After studying it a moment, Cori moved on, perhaps in pursuit of the Morgans or someone else to socialize with. That was all right. Mike had brought her here to socialize. Events like this gallery exhibit would be the saving grace of having to live so far from Boston. They could survive as long as Cori could manage not to feel too isolated. In time, Mike hoped, she might even come to think of Covington as home. They both could.

He was about to turn away when something about that one painting drew him back. Something seemed out of place. Sure, the trees weren't as tall, then, but it wasn't just that. He stepped back, trying to get a new perspective, and then he saw it. A brown structure, squared off at the top, which couldn't possibly be a tree. A blur that he'd assumed was from the warped glass now looked like smoke.

A chimney stuck up from the trees behind Mike and Cori's house.

What the hell? he thought, moving closer. Under scrutiny, the painting revealed edges and lines amongst the trees that might have been a roof.

Fifty years ago, there had been a house in the woods back there, on their property. Nobody had ever mentioned it to them—no realtor, no neighbour, nobody. The trees would have grown up to cover any trace of it now, even with the turret restored. But he had to wonder if the house itself remained.

Mike and Cori spent Saturday morning in the room they were slowly converting into a nursery. He'd put a fresh coat of paint in there the previous week—yellow, which was nicely neutral, given they'd chosen not to find out the baby's sex. They had gone through catalogues and picked out the crib and other furniture for the room, including one of those glider-rockers that Mike thought would always have a place in the house, even after their baby had grown up. But they hadn't ordered any of the furniture yet. Cori insisted it was bad luck.

Proceed with caution had always been her wisdom, and more and more, Mike had adopted it as his own. Several friends from her work had given her a mobile as a kind of quitting-to-have-a-baby present, but it sat in a box in a closet.

Somehow, though, the walls and ceiling were immune to this superstition. The paint had been acceptable, since a fresh coat of paint was welcome in almost any room. But today they were putting up the Winnie the Pooh border they had picked out while browsing at The Baby Carriage, and there could be no pretending that it served any other purpose than to make the room more pleasant for a child.

Mike had made the mistake of asking Cori why the border was an exception to her otherwise rigid caution. Her response had been a narrowing of the eyes that always seemed to put a thousand miles between them.

"We can't wait until the baby's *here* for this, Michael."

Yeah, Michael. That was never good.

He ought to have known better than to question the wishes of a pregnant woman; it was throwing himself into a maelstrom of hormones. He had agreed, reassured her that he loved the border, and she had deigned to allow him to kiss her. Minutes later she had been laughing and tickling him, and he loved her so hard it hurt his heart.

Mike didn't mind the mood swings that pregnancy had brought out in his wife. Seeing her revelling in impending motherhood made up for any snappishness on her part. It would pass. And it was far preferable to the months after she had first suspected he had been having an affair. During that time there had been long periods when she would answer him in monotone or pretend he wasn't even in the room with her.

This house and the baby were their new beginning, and whatever rules she wanted to put in place to define that were fine by him.

They put Cori's iPod dock in the nursery. She dipped four-foot lengths of the border into a plastic basin of water and handed it up to Mike, who balanced on an old, wooden chair. As he carefully aligned each piece and then ran a sponge over the surface to make sure all the air bubbles were out of it, they sang along to Maia Sharp and Sara Bareilles. They took breaks to rock out to the

Dropkick Murphys and the Frames, the music blasting out the open windows. And when Madeleine Peyroux came on, they danced, and they kissed.

Foreheads pressed together, grinning, Cori said, "I think Baby Shaughnessy's going to love this room."

Mike knew she meant the tall windows and the cross-breeze that brought in the spring air, but he also understood that she meant something else, too. Something about love and family, and the happiness it gave them to be preparing this place for her. Her. Mike thought their child would be a daughter. He just had a feeling.

As he put the last piece of the border in place, he could see out the window down into the backyard. From here he could only see the very tip of the church steeple in the centre of town. The swimming pool in the backyard was basically complete, but they were putting in a patio around it, and some fencing, and an outside grill that ran off natural gas that would be piped underground from the house. A little backyard paradise.

But he kept looking at the trees beyond the pool.

"I've got some chicken leftover from last night," Cori said from the doorway, where she surveyed the job they'd done with an approving smile. "I thought I'd make some chicken salad."

"One of the many reasons I love you." Mike dropped down from the chair. "I'm going to take a walk out back. We'll rendezvous in the kitchen?"

Cori arched an eyebrow and suggestively cocked a hip. "Why Michael, it's been ages since we rendezvoused in a kitchen."

He grinned. Maybe it wasn't always a bad thing when she called him Michael.

"And that's another of the many reasons," he said, going to her. He kissed her and ran a hand along the arc of her ever-growing belly. "Chicken salad or rendezvous first?"

"Depends on what you're hungrier for," she said, then initiated a wholly different sort of kiss.

They made love on the hardwood floor, gently because of her condition, a warm spring breeze caressing them, and found a kind of contentment that had been gone from their relationship for a very long time.

"I know I've been kind of freaked about the move, and staying home to take care of the baby, and everything," Cori said afterward, running her fingers through the short scruff of his hair. "But I think it's going to be good for us."

Mike kissed her nose. "I know it is."

He glanced back at the house only once. Cori would be in the kitchen, making chicken salad. His knees hurt from the wood floor in the nursery, but he wasn't about to complain. His nostrils were still full of the musky smell of sex and it gave him a kind of high, a bit of swaggering elation. A walk in the woods seemed to fit right in with that feeling. He'd always loved to go exploring as a child, and that hadn't changed just because he'd grown up.

He scanned the pool area, trying to imagine what it would look like when the contractors were finished. They needed to clean up the yard still. There were some tree stumps that had to be removed and he'd have to have some serious landscaping done back here. But he would keep these woods otherwise untouched. He and Cori hoped for two or three children, and someday there might be paths through these woods, worn down by Shaughnessy feet. One of the things he'd loved about this property from the beginning was the amount of land that came with the house. The realtor had thought they wouldn't want it because the city wouldn't allow development on the rest of the property due to open space regulations or something. But to Mike, that had been a wonderful thing. He didn't want other houses back there.

And yet, once upon a time, there had been at least one.

He set off into the woods, at first picking his way over fallen birch and lightning-split oak, but then finding the terrain easy to manage, despite thick roots and rocks that jutted from the earth. Off to his right, Mike spotted something that piqued his curiosity, and walked over to find a rough-hewn standing stone, almost identical to the one the pool contractors had removed when clearing his backyard.

What it meant, he had no idea. Someone had placed these things back here, based on some pagan belief or archaic science. He promised himself that he'd do some research starting Monday. Bowden's fascination notwithstanding, they still seemed boring things to paint, but their presence intrigued him.

Mike started off again, cutting back toward the angle he'd started out on. Just when he started to think he'd gone too far in that direction, he came upon another of those stones, sitting by itself in a circle of old oaks. Maybe he had overshot after all.

After a pause to get his bearings, he headed off in what he thought was a direct line between his house and where the church steeple scraped the sky at the centre of town. A slight incline brought him to what must once have been a path, though only the suggestion of it remained. Still, he had no doubt where the path would lead. He was on the right track.

Another minute or two of walking and he came upon the house, or what remained of it. A partially collapsed chimney stood in a clearing full of tall grass and weeds. Mike walked across the clearing, grass shushing around him. Some of the bricks had tumbled into a pile beside the ruin of the chimney and they were black from fire. He stumbled over something in the grass and looked down to see that he'd nearly tripped over a charred timber.

Walking around the chimney, he realized that more remained of the old house than he'd thought. There were bricks and rotten wood sunk partially into the ground, slowly being claimed by earth and vegetation. At some point, at least a decade past but possibly much longer than that, the house had burned down.

He turned in a circle, studying the trees at the edge of the clearing. The fire hadn't gotten far, otherwise none of those towering old pines would still be there, never mind the old growth birch and oak. He paused and narrowed his eyes. At the back of the clearing he spotted another of those standing stones, this one taller than the others he'd seen. And now that he looked, he saw several others, spaced about equally, creating a semi-circle behind the ruins of the house.

Brow furrowed in thought, he gazed into the woods on either side, suddenly sure that if he looked he would find others, extending the circle out into a long oval that must have ended at the outer edge of the woods behind his own home.

Mike smiled to himself. A genuine mystery in his own backyard. Cori would love this.

Investigating further, he stepped over a pile of stones that had once been part of the house's foundation, careful not to lodge his ankle amongst rotting timber. Hands on his hips, he stood looking around. Something was missing, and it took him a moment to put his finger on exactly what. Then he had it.

"Where are the empties?"

Local kids must know about this place. He figured that was how it had burned down in the first place. That was the first explanation that came into his head anyway, an old abandoned building, teenagers partying inside, a dropped match or a cigarette left burning. But, then, why weren't there any beer cans or bottles? He didn't see any. Not one.

Weird.

The old fireplace remained, a beautifully built hearth, its face blackened. He went over and crouched in front of it. Leaves layered the floor, now. Picking up a stick, Mike poked around in the fireplace, stirring up the rotting leaves and the damp ashes beneath, a black smear of ancient char.

The stick hit something and he moved closer. Batting it back and forth a bit, he saw the object looked like a strange stone or—odd that he should think this—a piece of coral. But when he reached in with his hand and pulled it out, blowing and rubbing the old ash and dirt off of it, he realized what he held was a fragment of bone.

A shudder went through him and he tossed the bone shard back into the fireplace—

—which ignited.

"What the hell?" he said, jerking back from the fireplace. He caught his heel and fell on his ass—

—then twisted around, gripped by panic. The light from the fireplace flickered off walls and old, dusty curtains. Beneath him the floor was rough wood and above the roof beams were heavy timber. Outside the windows, night had fallen. Snow accumulated on the sills and ice rimed each pane.

"You're not here. You're not really here," a cracking, frightened voice muttered.

Mike leaped to his feet, backing away from the voice. He blinked, shook his head, trying to clear his vision. Just at the edge of the light thrown by the fireplace, a stooped, white-haired woman sat in a sturdy rocker, a heavy shawl drawn around her shoulders. She did not rock. Rather, she leaned forward in the chair with her hands over her ears and her eyes pressed tightly shut.

She hadn't been there a moment ago.

"You're not here," she said again, voice rising in desperation.

"I don't *want* to be here!" Mike snapped, hating the desperate edge in his own voice.

The old woman didn't react at all. Mike glanced around, trying to force himself to accept what he was seeing. He could feel the cold of the winter and the warmth of the fire. Hell, he could smell the wood burning in the fireplace. His skin prickled and his heart slammed in his chest and he wanted to scream. So he did.

"What the *fuck* is this?"

Hysteria. Mike knew he was losing his shit, but he didn't mind at all. Losing his shit seemed very much the right thing to do.

"You can't be here. You aren't allowed."

He pressed the heels of his hands to the sides of his head, as though he needed to keep it from breaking open. And maybe he did.

The old lady started rocking. "Not here, not here, not here." She sounded almost like a little girl, teasing some other kid on the playground.

The ceiling beams creaked worryingly. Loudly. The rocking stopped and she opened her eyes and stared at the ceiling with milky-white, unseeing eyes. Mike held his breath, looking from her blind eyes to the ceiling. The storm hadn't made that noise. It sounded like an elephant shifting its weight in the attic, but this house had no attic.

"You're. Not. Here." The old woman spoke each word with furious defiance.

The floorboards creaked over by the door.

Mike and the old lady both spun toward the sound. Blind, she strained to listen more closely. But Mike stared in confusion, for there was nothing there to see.

A rap came at the window behind him and he jumped, shouting, turned expecting to see a face at the window, but there was only the night and the snow. His throat tightened and he couldn't even shout, now. His pulse sped so fast that his whole body felt flushed, warmer than the fire could ever have made him.

"Stop," the old woman whispered, and it sounded like a kind of surrender. An admission.

Rapid-fire, there came more rapping at the windows.

"Oh, Jesus. Holy shit," Mike whispered.

The floor groaned again by the door, creaking in increments as whatever had entered the house moved closer to the fireplace—to the old woman in her rocking chair.

Shaking her head, she pushed up from her rocker. "No, no," she said. "No, no, no. You won't. Not me."

Fierce and grim, she stepped backward toward the fireplace, one hand reaching behind her for the mantel. Mike sucked in air, breathing again, gaze shifting back and forth between the old woman and the place where the floor creaked, where something moved nearer to her.

"Leave her alone!" he shouted.

And he moved. He thought of Cori, and of their baby, but he couldn't stop himself. He went toward the old woman, but his focus was mostly on that empty-but-not-empty spot in the room.

So he only saw out of the corner of his eye as she peeled off her shawl and thrust it into the fireplace.

Mike turned. "Lady, what are you—"

The shawl caught, flames spreading with a rush of air.

He reached for her, and his hands passed right through as though she wasn't really there. Or he wasn't. Mike could only watch as she held the burning shawl out before her, both hands wreathed in fire. She knew this place, her home. Blind or not, she must have been able to see it inside her head. She went to the window, quickly touching the burning shawl to the dusty curtains.

The fire roared as the curtains began to burn, flames jumping up toward the ceiling, dancing as though in celebration. The rapping on the windows ceased. The floorboards shook. Beneath Mike's feet, one of them cracked.

He heard whispers, angry little bits of wind that whipped past him.

The woman reached the next window, and those curtains billowed with fire. She held her fists in front of her and Mike could see that the flames had spread to her dress. When her hair lit on fire, she started to scream.

As she reached for the next set of windows, something struck her from behind, lifting her off her feet and knocking her across the room. She hit the wall, and fell to the ground, where fire began to spread from the burning woman's broken body.

Dead. She had to be dead. But she'd finished the job she started. There would be no stopping this fire. It licked up the walls and raced across the dry timber beams overhead.

Mike ran for the door. The floor groaned and the ceiling beams creaked, but he couldn't tell now if it was the fire that caused the house to shift or whatever unseen thing had come inside. On either side of the door, the walls were starting to burn, smoke furling up from the wood.

Those whispers continued in his ears like the shushing of a theatre audience as the curtain went up. They seemed to chase him to the door. He grabbed the knob and twisted it, flung the door open, and the winter wind gusted in, feeding the flames.

He lunged out the door—

—and tripped on thick weeds, falling headlong into the tall grass.

The sun shone down upon him, the spring breeze rustling the grass and the trees around the clearing. Far off he could hear a truck's engine. Mike flipped onto his back and scrabbled backward a few feet, staring at the half-tumbled chimney, which was all that remained of that house. His breath came in quick gasps and he looked around one more time before leaping to his feet.

Eyes wide, he stared at the rubble of the old woman's house.

Something shifted in the ruins. An old length of charred timber cracked.

Mike shook his head. "No way."

The upper portion of the remaining chimney gave way, bricks and mortar tumbling and sifting down into the grass and weeds.

Mike took three quick steps backward, still staring, still slowly shaking his head. He didn't understand any of it, what he had seen and heard and felt. Where he had been. But as he stared at the jagged remnant of chimney, his eyes refocused on something beyond it, at the far side of the clearing. One of the standing stones.

They made a kind of oval around the area, like some kind of

property marker. *No trespassing,* he thought. And that old woman had been so sure that whatever unseen things had come for her, they shouldn't be there. Couldn't get in.

But she didn't mean the house.

Something shifted in his peripheral vision and he twisted, stared, waited. For a moment nothing moved, and then the tall grass parted as something he couldn't see moved nearer. The grass rustled to his left, and then it began to ripple in a dozen different places, parting as the unseen approached.

They'd entered the house twenty or thirty years ago, and they'd remained there, undisturbed. He'd stirred the ashes, he'd done something—that shard of bone, something he shouldn't have done. Did it matter what?

Whispering filled the clearing.

Like a starter pistol, it shocked him to action. He bolted, racing along the unused path. His legs pistoned beneath him and his heart clenched. He watched his footing, careful for roots and stones, and for a few seconds he thought they had not pursued. But then the leaves rustled and there was no breeze, and he heard the whispers again off to the right and then the left, and he knew.

He muttered things that were part prayer and part apology and he held in his mind an image of Cori's face, and he ran.

Mike burst from the woods into his backyard and by then his chest burned with exertion. He staggered to a stop, turning to face the woods, hands on his knees, and his mind worked feverishly. Whatever they were, they'd gotten past her markers, gotten in. But maybe the reason they had stayed so long was that they couldn't get out.

A spark of hope ignited. Breathing hard, he stood up and surveyed the woods. Young leaves rustled a bit, but only with the breeze. Just the breeze. He smiled, nodding to himself, convincing himself.

But he had to get back to Cori. Get her out of here for a while, think about this, talk it over. Have someone else come and take a look to make sure he wasn't out of his mind.

He started up to the house, looking over his shoulder, watching the woods. He had to go around the empty swimming pool, between two of the stumps the contractors had pulled up.

It lay there on the ground, bottom third caked with dirt—three feet of grey, rough-hewn stone, carved with crude symbols.

Mike froze, looked up at the house, and then broke into a run.

"Cori!" he shouted as he banged through the back door, running through the mud-room into the kitchen. A half-full glass of strawberry lemonade sat on the counter beside a small bowl of freshly made chicken salad.

He ran out into the corridor. "Cori!"

Up the stairs, images flashing in his mind of things that had been and things he hoped would be. Cori and her rounded belly. Laughter by the pool. A little girl on a swing set.

"Cori, honey?" he called as he reached the top of the stairs.

Then, her voice. "Mike? What's wrong?"

He darted down the hall to the door of the nursery, and relief flooded through him, a giddy love that made him hate himself for the wrongs he'd done her and renew promises he'd silently made to both of them about the future.

Cori was just getting up, pieces of the baby's mobile spread on the floor around her. Butterflies and rainbow hot air balloons and fairies and birds. She held the main body of the thing in one hand. It hung lopsided because she'd only half-finished attaching the items that would spin from it.

"You're okay," he said, catching his breath, leaning against the door frame.

"Of course I'm okay. What's wrong? You were gone a while."

Mike went to her and pulled her into his arms. He pressed his face into her curls, kissed her head, then moved down to kiss the spray of freckles across the bridge of her nose.

"God, you're shaking."

"What are you doing in here, Mrs. Shaughnessy?" he asked.

She looked at him oddly, but smiled. "It's only a mobile. I'm not that superstitious. What harm could it do? Besides, we're nesting today."

He let out another long breath and held her until his heart finally stopped pounding.

From the corner of the room came the creak of old wood.

THE MOURNFUL CRY OF OWLS

On a warm, late summer's night, Donika Ristani sat on the roof outside her open window—fat-bellied acoustic guitar in her hands—and searched for the chords that would bring life to the music she knew lay within her. The shingles were warm from the sun, though an hour had passed since dusk, and the smell of tar and cut grass filled her with a pleasant summery feeling that kept her normally flighty spirit from drifting into fancy.

The radio played in her room, competing with the music of the woods around the house—the crickets and owls and rustling things—which grew to a crescendo as though attempting to draw her down amongst the trees. Her fingers plucked and strummed, for she despised the use of a pick, and she created a third melody that created a kind of balance between the radio and the woods, the inside and outside.

Joe Jackson sang "Is She Really Going Out With Him?" Donika liked the song well enough, but her thoughts were elsewhere, thinking about inside and outside—about the person she was for her mother's sake, and the person that all of her instincts told her she ought to be. She found herself strumming Harry Chapin's "Taxi," lost in her head, and singing along to the weird bridge in the middle of the tune.

I've been letting my outside tide me over 'til my time runs out.

The truth frustrated the hell out of her and she brought her right hand down on the strings to stop herself playing another note of that song. Her gaze drifted down her driveway to the darkened ribbon of Blackberry Lane, searching for headlights, for some sign of her mother's return. Without so much as a glimmer from the road, she looked out across the dark, thick woods north of the house, impatient to be down there, following the path to Josh Orton's house. He'd be waiting already, and she could practically feel his arms around her, his face nuzzling her throat.

Donika laughed softly at herself; or perhaps she sighed. She couldn't tell the difference sometimes.

The DJ did his cool voice and introduced the next tune. Donika smiled and started playing the first notes on her acoustic before it even started on the radio. Bad Company. "Rock and Roll Fantasy." Good song. Her bedroom walls were covered with posters of Pink Floyd, Zeppelin, and Sabbath, but she liked a little bit of everything. Most of her girlfriends would have laughed at some of the stuff she sang along to on the radio. Or maybe not. Hell, most of them thought Donna Summer the pinnacle of musical achievement.

Now she wished she'd listened more closely to the Joe Jackson tune. She might have to break into her babysitting stash to buy that album.

Her fingers moved up and down the frets, playing Bad Company by ear. She'd never played the song before, but the guitar was like an extension of herself and picking out the notes presented no greater difficulty than singing along. The crickets had gotten louder, but she managed not to hear them. The radio crackled a bit; some kind of interference, maybe the weather or a passing jet. She didn't understand such things very well. Turn on the box, the music came out. What else did she need to know?

The heat of the day still lingered in her skin the same way it did in the shingles. No more sticky humidity, so that was nice. She felt comfortably warm up there in her spaghetti strap tank top and cutoff jeans, as if the sun had gotten down inside her instead of setting over the horizon, and it would hide there until morning.

Owls cried out in the woods, and Donika glanced up, searching the trees as though she might spot one, the strings of her guitar momentarily forgotten. Other people thought they were funny birds, but she had always heard something else in their hooting, a terrible sadness that she always wanted to answer with her own frustrations.

A flash of light came from the road. She watched the headlights move along Blackberry Lane and her breath caught as she thought of Josh again. When the car drove by without slowing down, she sighed and lay back against the slanted roof, the shingles rough and hot against her back. She hugged the guitar and wondered if Josh was sitting outside, waiting for her, or if he was up in his room listening to music on his bed. Both images had their appeal.

Somehow she missed the sound of an approaching engine, and looked up only as light washed across the trees and she heard tires rolling up the driveway. Donika sat forward as her mother's ancient Dodge Dart putted up to the house. When she turned off the engine, it ticked and popped, and then the door creaked open.

"Get off that roof, 'Nika!"

The girl laughed. The woman had eyes like a hawk, even in the dark.

She slipped in through her bedroom window and put away her guitar before going downstairs. Her mother stood in the kitchen, looking through the day's mail. Qendressa Ristani had lush black hair like her daughter, but streaked with grey. She wore it pulled back tightly. Though her mother was nearly fifty, Donika thought her hairstyle too severe, more appropriate for a grandmother. Her clothes reflected the same sensibility, which probably explained why she never dated. Though she'd given up wearing black a decade or so back, Donika's mother still saw herself as a widow. Men might flirt with her—she was prettier than most women her age—but Qendressa would not encourage them. She'd been widowed young, and had no desire to replace the only man she had ever loved.

Her life was the seamstress shop where she worked in downtown Jameson, and the home she'd made for herself and her daughter upon coming to America a dozen years before. But her old world upbringing still persisted in many ways, not the least of which was her insistence on using herbs and oils as homegrown remedies for all sorts of ills, both physical and spiritual.

"How was your day, Mom?"

"Eh," the woman said, "is the same."

Donika grabbed her sandals and sat down at the table, slipping one on. Her mother dropped the mail on the table. As she fastened the straps on her sandals, she looked up to find her mother staring at her.

"Where you going?"

"Josh's. Sue and Carrie and a couple of Josh's friends are there already, waiting for me. We're going to walk into town for pizza."

"You going to hang around those boys dressed like that?"

Donika flushed with anger and stood up, the chair scraping backward on the floor.

"Look, Ma, you need to get off this stuff. This is 1979, not 1950, and we're in Massachusetts, not Albania. You want me to be home when you get back from work so you won't worry about me? Okay, I sort of understand that. I don't like it, but I get it. But look around. I don't dress differently from other girls. Turn on the TV once in a while—"

"TV," her mother muttered in disgust, averting her eyes.

"I'm going to be sixteen tomorrow," Donika protested.

Qendressa Ristani sniffed. "This is supposed to make me less worried? This is *why* I worry!"

"Well don't! I'm fine. Just let me enjoy being sixteen, okay?"

The woman hesitated, taking a long breath, and then she nodded slowly and waved her daughter away. "Go. Be a good girl, 'Nika. Don't make me shamed."

"Have I ever?"

Finally, her mother smiled. "No. Never." Her expression turned serious. "Tomorrow, we celebrate, though. Yes? Just the two of us, all the things you love for dinner. You can have your friends over on Friday and we have a cake. But, tomorrow, just us girls."

Donika smiled. "Just us girls."

The path emerged from the woods in the backyard of an older

couple who were known to shout at trespassers from their screened-in back porch. Donika had never experienced their wrath and wondered if they didn't mind so much when a girl crossed their yard—maybe thinking girls didn't cause as much trouble as boys— or if they simply didn't see her. As she left the comfortable quiet of the woods and strolled across the back lawn and then alongside the house, she watched the windows, wondering if either of the old folks were looking out. Nothing stirred inside there. It hadn't been dark for long, but she wondered if they were already asleep, and thought how sad it must be to get old.

When she reached the street, she saw Josh sitting on the granite curb at the corner, smoking a cigarette. Her sandals slapped the pavement as she walked and he looked up at the sound. One corner of his mouth lifted in a little smile that made her heart flutter. He flicked his cigarette away and stood to meet her, cool as hell in his faded jeans and Jimi Hendrix t-shirt.

"Hey," he said.

Donika smiled, feeling strangely shy. "Hey."

Josh pushed his shoulder-length blond hair away from his eyes. "Your mom kept you waiting."

"Sorry. Sometimes I think she stays late on purpose. Maybe she figures if she keeps me waiting long enough, I won't go out."

"So much for that plan."

"I'm glad you didn't give up on me," Donika said.

They'd been standing a couple of feet apart, just feeling the static energy of the distance between them. Now Josh reached out and touched her face.

"Never happen."

A shiver went through her. Josh did that to her, just by standing there, and the way he looked at her.

His hand slipped around to the back of her neck and he bent to kiss her. Donika tilted her head back and closed her eyes, letting the details of the moment wash over her, the feel of him so near, the softness of his lips, the strange, burnt taste of nicotine as his tongue sought hers.

Only when they broke apart, a giddy little thrill rushing through her, did she look around and remember where they were. Lights were on in some of the houses along Rolling Lane, and anyone could be watching them.

She felt pleasantly buzzed, as though she'd had a few beers, but she slid her hand along his arm and tangled her fingers in his.

"We shouldn't be doing this out here. I told my mother Sue and Carrie and those guys were gonna be here and we were going to get pizza. If anyone ever saw us and told her, she'd have a fit."

"She doesn't think you've ever kissed me?"

"I don't know, and I don't plan to ask," Donika said. "God, she already thinks I'm slutty just for wearing cutoffs and hanging around with boys."

Josh arched an eyebrow and took out another cigarette. "Boys? Are there others?"

She hit him. "You know what I mean."

"Your mom's pretty old world."

Donika rolled her eyes. "You have *no* idea. She burns candles for me and puts little bunches of dried herbs and stuff under my bed, tied in little ribbons. Pretty sure they're supposed to ward off boys."

"How's that going?"

Donika only smiled.

Josh kissed her forehead. "So, do you want to go get pizza?"

"Only if you're hungry."

Josh laughed softly, unlit cigarette in his hand. His blue eyes were almost grey in the night time. "I could eat. I could always eat. But I'm good. We could just hang out. Why don't we walk downtown, get an ice cream or something."

"Or we could just go for a walk in the woods. I love those paths. Especially at night."

"You're not afraid?" Josh asked as he thumbed his lighter, the little flame igniting the tip of his cigarette. He drew a lungful of smoke and stared at her.

"Why would I be?" Donika said. "I've got you with me."

She led him by the hand back across the street and through the yard of the belligerent old couple. Josh's cigarette glowed orange in the dark. The moon and stars were bright, but as they passed alongside the house and into the backyard of that old split-level house, with the canopy of the woods reaching out above them, the darkness thickened and little of the celestial light filtered through.

"Goddamn you kids!" a screechy voice shouted from the porch. "You're gonna burn the whole damn forest down with those cigarettes!"

Donika started and looked at the darkened porch anxiously. Josh put a hand up to try to keep himself from laughing, and that started Donika grinning as well. The voice was faintly ridiculous, like something out of a cartoon or a movie. On the porch, in the dark, another pinprick of burning orange glowed. The old man was smoking, too.

Josh paused to drop the butt and grind it out with his heel. Then, laughing, they ran into the trees, following the path that had been worn there by generations.

Hand in hand, they followed the gently curving path through the woods and talked about their friends and families, and about music.

"I love talking about music with you," Josh told her. "The way your eyes light up . . . I don't know, it's like you feel it inside you more than most people because you can make music with your guitar."

Donika shuddered at that. No one had ever understood that part of her the way that Josh did. He liked the sad songs best, the tragic ones, just as she did. Their conversation meandered, but she didn't mind. All she wanted was his company.

Mostly, they just walked.

The paths had been there forever, or so it seemed. There were low stone walls, centuries-old property markers that had been built up by hand and ran for miles. Old, thick roots crossed the path and small animals rustled in the branches above them and in the underbrush on either side. An entire system of paths ran through the woods. They reached a fork and followed the right-hand path. The left would have taken them up the hill toward her house, and that was the last place she wanted to go.

"You seem far away," Josh said as they passed through a small clearing where someone had built a firepit. Charred logs lay in the pit and the stones around it had been blackened by flames.

Donika squeezed his hand and looked up at him. "Nope. Just happy. I love the woods. Being out here . . . it's so peaceful. So far away from other people. I walk through here all the time, but having you here with me makes it so much better."

Josh stopped walking and gazed down at her. The moon and stars illuminated the clearing, and she saw the mischief in his eyes.

"Better how?" he asked.

She gave him a shy little shrug. "Just feels right."

He kissed her again and she could hear music in her head. Or maybe it was her heart. His hands slid down her back, pulling her close, so that their bodies pressed together. She liked the feel of him against her, his strong arms wrapped around her. Through his jeans she could feel his hardness pressing into her, and she liked that very much. Just knowing that she had that effect on him made her catch her breath.

His hands roamed, fingers tracing along her arms, and then he stepped back just slightly so that he could reach up and touch her breasts through the thin cotton of her tank top.

"Josh," she rasped, enjoying it far too much.

"Yeah."

Donika took his hands in hers and kissed him quickly. "I think maybe I want ice cream after all."

"But it's beautiful right here."

He grinned and ducked his head, kissing her again. Their fingers were still intertwined and he made no attempt to pull his hands away, to touch her again. Donika felt her body yearning toward him, missing the weight and warmth of him.

This is it, she thought. *This is what frightens Ma so much.*

Donika pulled her hands from his and slid her arms around him, breaking off the kiss. She lay her head on his chest and just held herself against him, nuzzling there. Josh stroked her hair.

Deep in the woods, she heard an owl hoot sadly, and then another joined in. A chorus.

"I *am* far away," she confessed. "But you're with me. I wish we could be even farther away, together. I love feeling lost in the woods, like something wild. When I'm out here alone, I like to just run. You'll laugh, but sometimes I imagine I'm running naked through the forest, like I'm some kind of fairy queen or something."

Josh didn't laugh. "Hmm. I like the sound of that," he said. "What's stopping you?"

She blushed deeply and stepped back, trying not to smile. One hip outthrust, she pointed at him.

"You are bad."

"Only in good ways. Seriously, I dare you."

Donika's breath came in shallow sips as she regarded him, lips pressed together, corners of her mouth upturned. The mischief in his eyes seemed to have gotten inside of her somehow. Her skin tingled all over. Nodding her head, she crossed her arms.

"You first."

Without hesitation, he stripped off his t-shirt and dropped it at the edge of the path. He arched an eyebrow and looked at her expectantly.

A rush went through her, a kind of freedom she'd never felt before. It was as though she had just woken from some strange slumber. She grabbed the bottom hem of her tank top and slid it up over her head, then unhooked her bra and let it drop to the ground. The night breeze brushed warmly against her, but she shivered.

Josh stared at her, all the mischief and archness gone from his face, replaced by sheer wonderment. He'd never seen her breasts before—Donika didn't know if he'd ever seen this much of *any* girl.

She didn't wait for him to make the next move. Their gazes locked as she kicked her sandals off and then moved her hand down, unbuttoning her cutoffs. She slid them and her panties down together and stepped out of them, tossing them on top of her tank.

"Jesus, you're beautiful," he whispered.

The breeze picked up, rustling leaves. Somewhere close by, the owls cried again. For once, the sound did not seem sad. Josh stepped toward her and she knew how badly he wanted to touch her. She could already imagine his hands on her, the way she had so many times at home in her bed.

She shook her head, smiling, and stepped backward. "Uh uh. Not so fast, mister. We're going to run, remember. And you're not quite ready."

For a moment he only stared at her, his mouth hanging open. Donika laughed at how silly he looked, but thrilled to know that she'd beguiled him so completely.

Staggering around, hopping on one foot, Josh pulled off one sneaker and then the other. He shucked his jeans and then paused for a second before slipping off his underwear.

Donika trembled at the sight of him. She'd seen an older boy from the neighbourhood skinny-dipping in Bowditch Pond one time, but this was something else entirely.

"Oh," she said.

Josh walked toward her. Donika backed up and then turned, giggling, and began to run as swiftly as she dared, watching the roots and rocks and fallen branches in her path. Josh pursued her, laughing even as he called for her to wait for him. As she ran the thrill of it all rushed through her—her nakedness, his nakedness and nearness, and the forest around them. In her whole life, she had never felt as wonderful as she did there in the woods, running wild, full of passion and laughter.

The heat rose from deep inside her, desire unlike anything she'd ever known. Flush with abandon, she slowed her pace, and let Josh catch up. He nearly crashed into her and they slid together on the path. His lips were on hers and their tongues met. His hands were rough and caressing in equal turns, touching her everywhere, and she let him.

A small part of her—the part that remained her mother's daughter—knew that she would not let him make love to her. But, oh, how she wanted to. Anything else he wished would be his, only not that.

In the branches above them, the owls sighed.

Tangled in her sheets, drifting in that limbo between sleep and wakefulness, Donika knew morning had come. She loved how long the summer days lasted; she just wished they didn't start so damned early. Dimly aware of the bedroom around her, she squeezed her eyes tightly closed and admonished herself for not having drawn the shades the night before. She rolled over to face the other direction, twisting the sheets even more. For a moment she remembered her walk in the woods with Josh the night before and the way his hands had felt on her. A contented moan escaped her lips as she slipped back into blissful oblivion.

Drifting.

Somewhere, lost in sleep, she sensed a presence enter the room and began to stir. Then someone started to sing, loudly and horribly, and Donika sat up in bed, drawing a sharp breath, eyes wide.

Her mother sang "Happy Birthday" in a silly, overly dramatic fashion, gesturing with her hands as though on stage. She wore an enormous grin and Donika couldn't help laughing. Her mother always seemed so grim, and seeing her like this gave the girl such pleasure.

When the song finished, Qendressa bowed deeply. Donika

applauded, shaking her head. During her childhood, it had not been quite so uncommon for her mother to clown around for Donika's amusement. They'd shared so many wonderful times together. Now that she was older and their desires and morals clashed so often, it had become hard for Donika to remember those times.

Not this morning, however. This morning, all the laughter came back to her. Her mother would be off to work in moments, decked out in her usual sensible skirt and blouse and dark shoes, and her hair was tied back severely, but for a few minutes, it felt like Donika was a little girl again.

"Thank you, thank you," Qendressa said, her accent almost unnoticeable as she mimicked performers she had seen on television. "And for my next trick, I leave work early to come home and make all your favourites."

She ticked the parts of the birthday meal off on her fingers. "Tavë kosi, Tirana furghes with peppers, and kadaif for dessert. With candles and more bad singing."

Donika's stomach rumbled just thinking about dinner. The main course was baked lamb and yoghurt, which she'd always loved. But the dessert—she could practically taste the walnuts and cinnamon of the kadaif now.

"Can we have dinner for breakfast instead?" she asked, stretching, extricating herself from her sheets.

Her mother shook a finger at her. "The birthday girl gets what she wants, but not until tonight. Breakfast, you make your own. Toast, I bet. You going out today?"

"Maybe to the mall, if Gina can borrow her mom's car."

"All right. Back by three o'clock, please. We'll cook together?"

Donika smiled. "Wouldn't miss it."

That was the truth, too. There were times her mother drove her crazy with all her old world stodginess, but on her birthday and on holidays, she loved nothing better than to spend hours in the kitchen, cooking with her mom. She could practically smell all the wonderful aromas that would fill the house later.

"What about the girls? You talk to them?" Qendressa asked.

"Tomorrow night. They're going to come by to celebrate. We can just have pizza, though."

"Pizza, again?" her mother said. "You going to turn into pizza."

Donika didn't argue. She wasn't about to confess that she and Josh had never gotten around to having pizza last night. Maybe that was the reason she felt so hungry this morning. Her belly growled and she felt a gnawing there, as if she hadn't eaten in weeks instead of half a day.

"We love pizza," she said, shrugging.

"I promised birthday cake tomorrow night, too. And if you are lucky, maybe some good singing."

"Chocolate cake?" Donika asked, propping herself up on one arm, head still muzzy with sleep.

"Of course," her mother replied, as though any other kind would be unthinkable.

"Excellent!"

A flutter of wings came from the open window and a scratching upon the screen. Mother and daughter turned together to see a dark-eyed owl perched on the ledge outside the window, imperious and wise. Brown and white feathers cloaked the owl and it tucked its wings behind it.

"What the . . . ? That's freaky," Donika said, sitting up in bed. "I hear them in the woods all the time, but I've never seen one during the day. Do you think it's sick or some—"

"Away!" her mother shouted. She rushed at the window and banged her open palm against the screen. A string of curses in her native tongue followed.

The owl cocked its head as if to let them know it wasn't troubled by Qendressa's attack, then spread its wings and took flight again. Through the window, Donika caught a glimpse of it gliding back toward the woods.

She stared at her mother. The woman had completely wigged out and now she stood by the window, arms around herself as though a frigid wind had just blown through the room. She had her back to her daughter.

"Ma?"

Qendressa turned, a wan smile on her face. Donika studied her mother and realized that the birthday morning silliness was over. A strange sadness had come over her, as though the bird's arrival had forced her to drop some happy mask she'd been wearing.

"I should go to work," she said, but she seemed torn.

"What is it, Ma?"

"Nothing," she said with a wave of her hand, averting her gaze. "Just . . . sixteen. You're not a girl anymore, 'Nika. Soon, you leave me."

Donika kicked aside the sheet that still covered the bottom of her legs and climbed out of bed. She went to her mother. Even with no shoes on, she was the taller of the Ristani women.

"I'm not going anywhere, Ma."

It didn't sound true, even when she said it. There had been many days when Donika had dreamed of nothing but leaving Jameson, finding a life of her own, making her own decisions and not having to live in the shadow of the old country anymore. Her body still weighted down by some secret sadness, Qendressa reached out and brushed Donika's unruly hair away from her eyes.

"Tonight, we talk about the future. And the past."

Donika blinked. What did that mean? She would have asked but saw her mother stiffen. The woman's eyes narrowed as she stared at her daughter's bed.

"What is that?"

The girl turned. Specks of dirt, a small leaf, and a few pine needles were scattered at the foot of the bed, revealed when Donika had whipped the sheet off of her. A shiver went through her, some terrible combination of elation and guilt. She tried to stifle it as best she could.

"We cut through the woods to get downtown. I always go that

way. I took off my sandals. I like going barefoot out there. It's nice. It's all . . . it's wild."

Donika couldn't read the look on her mother's face. If the woman suspected anything, she would have been angry or disappointed. Maybe those emotions were there—maybe Donika read her expression wrong—but the look in her eyes and the way she took a harsh little breath seemed like something else. Weird as it was, in that moment, Donika thought her mother seemed afraid.

The woman turned, all grim seriousness now. At Donika's bedroom door she paused and looked back at her daughter, taking in the whole room—the guitar, the stereo, the records and posters, and the clothes she would never approve of that were hung from the back of her chair and over the end of her bed.

"No boys here while I'm gone. No boys, 'Nika."

"I know, Ma. You think I'm stupid?"

"No," her mother said, shaking her head, the sadness returning to her gaze. "No, you my baby girl, 'Nika. I don't think you are stupid."

With that, Qendressa left. Donika stood and listened to her go down the stairs and out the door. She heard the car start up outside and the sound of tires on the driveway, and then all was silent again except for the birds singing outside the window and the drone of a plane flying somewhere high above the house.

She wasn't sure what her mother suspected or feared, didn't know what had caused her to behave so oddly or why she'd freaked out so completely at the sight of the owl. But Donika had the feeling it was going to be a very weird birthday.

Gina couldn't get the car, so the trip to the mall was off. Donika knew that she ought to have been bummed out, but she couldn't muster up much disappointment. She'd be seeing her friends tomorrow night, and today she wasn't in the mood to window shop at the mall. The idea of wandering around Jordan Marsh or going to Orange Julius for a nasty cheese dog for lunch didn't have much appeal. If it had been raining, maybe she would have felt differently. But the day was beautiful, and in truth, she wanted to be on her own for a while.

All kinds of different thoughts were swirling in her head, and she wanted to make sense of them, if she could. Her mother's strange behaviour that morning troubled her, but she was still looking forward to the afternoon of them cooking together. The lamb in the fridge was fresh, not frozen. It had come from the butcher the day before. They'd put some music on—something her mother liked, the Carpenters, maybe, or Neil Diamond—and work side by side at the counter. Normally, that kind of music made Donika want to stick pencils in her eyes, but somehow with her mother whipping up the yoghurt sauce for the lamb or slicing peppers as she hummed along, it seemed perfect.

At lunch time she sat on the front porch with a glass of iced tea and a salami sandwich. A fly buzzed around the plate and then sat on the lip of her glass. Donika ignored it, more interested in the droplets of moisture that slid down the sides of the cup. She stared at them as she strummed her acoustic, singing a Harry Chapin song. Harry was one of the only musicians she and her mother could agree on.

"All my life's a circle," she sang softly, "sunrise and sundown."

Her fingers kept playing, but she faltered with the words and then stopped singing altogether. Despite her concerns about her mother, she could not focus on anything for very long without her thoughts returning to the previous night.

Pausing for a moment in the song, she leaned over to pick up the iced tea, pressing the glass against the back of her neck. The icy condensation felt wonderful on her skin. Donika took a long sip, liking the sound the melting ice made as it clinked together. Then she set the glass down and grabbed half of the salami sandwich. All morning she had been ravenously hungry, yet when she'd eaten breakfast—Trix cereal, an indulgence left over from when she'd been very small—it hadn't filled her at all. Later in the morning she'd had a nectarine and some grapes, and that hadn't done anything for her either.

Now, even though she still felt as hungry as before—hungrier, in fact, if that was possible—the idea of eating her sandwich held very little appeal. She took an experimental bite, and then another. The salami tasted just as good as it always did, salty and a little spicy. But for some reason she simply did not want it.

She set the sandwich down and took another swig of iced tea to wash away the salt. Her fingers returned to the guitar and started playing chords she wasn't even paying attention to. Whatever song she might be drawing from her instrument, it came from her subconscious. Her conscious mind was otherwise occupied.

"You're a crazy girl," she said aloud, and then she smiled. Talking to herself sort of proved the point, didn't it? Her mother had always been a little crazy, and now Donika knew she shared the trait.

Her hunger didn't come only from her stomach. Her whole body felt ravenous. Her skin tingled with the memory of Josh's hands— on her belly, her breasts, the small of her back, the soft insides of her thighs—and of his kisses, which touched nearly all of the places his hands had gone.

She squeezed her legs together and trembled at the thought of stripping off her clothes, of running through the woods, and then Josh, his body outlined in moonlight, catching up to her. She'd felt, in those moments when she raced along the rutted path and he pursued her, as though she could spread her arms and take wing . . . as though she could have flown, and taken Josh with her.

Touching him, kissing him, that had been a little like flying.

"God," she whispered to herself. "What's wrong with you?"

Her fingers fumbled on the strings and she stopped playing, a sly smile touching her lips. Nothing was wrong with her. It all felt so amazingly good. How could anything be wrong with that?

But that was a lie. There was one thing wrong.

Her hunger. She yearned for Josh so badly that it gnawed at her insides. She wondered if her mother had seen it in her eyes this morning, had sensed it, had *smelled* it on her.

Donika needed to have his hands on her again, to taste his lips and the salty sweat on his fingers and his neck. She felt as though she couldn't get enough of him. She wanted him completely, yearned to consume him, and the only way to do that was to do the one thing she promised herself she would not do.

She had to have him inside her.

Only that could satisfy her hunger.

Her certainty thrilled and terrified her all at once.

With the smell of cinnamon filling the kitchen, her mother leaned back in her chair, hands over her stomach as though she had some voluminous belly.

"I don't think I ever eat again."

Donika smiled, but it felt forced. They had followed the same recipes they had always used, brought over from Albania with her mother years ago, passed down for generations. Somehow, though, the food had tasted bland. Even the cinnamon had seemed stale in her mouth. The smell of dessert had been tantalizing, but its taste had not delivered on that promise. She had eaten as much as she did mainly because she hadn't wanted to hurt her mother's feelings. And the hunger remained.

How she could still feel hungry after such a meal—particularly when nothing seemed to taste good to her—Donika didn't know. She chalked it up to hormones. Today was her sixteenth birthday. According to her mother, she had become a woman all of sudden, like flipping a switch. She had never believed it really worked that way, but given the way she felt, maybe it did. Maybe that was exactly how it worked. She always craved chocolate right before she got her period—could have eaten gallons of ice cream if she'd given in—so this might be similar.

Or maybe it's love. The thought skittered across her mind. She'd heard of people not being able to eat when they were in love. It occurred to her that this could be another symptom.

She tasted the idea on the back of her tongue. Did she love Josh? Maybe.

She hungered for him, certainly. Longed for him. Could that be love? No. Donika had seen enough movies and read enough books to know that desire and love might not be mutually exclusive, but they weren't the same thing either.

But desire like this? It hurts. It burns.

"—you listening to me, 'Nika?"

"What?" she asked, blinking.

Her mother studied her, concern etched upon her face. "You okay? You feel sick?"

"No. Sorry, Ma. Just tired, I guess."

A lame excuse. She expected her mother to call her on it, maybe to make some insinuating comment about her walk in the woods the night before, about how maybe if she wasn't always out talking to boys and running around with her friends, she wouldn't be so tired. Her mother didn't let her do very much, and she'd been hanging around the house all day playing guitar, and then cooking, but logic never stopped her mother from suspicion or judgement.

But Qendressa didn't say anything like that.

"You like dinner, though, right?" she asked, and just then it seemed the most important question in the world to her. "Your sixteenth birthday the sweetest. You should be happy today. Celebrate."

Donika felt such love for her mother, then. Sometimes she became so angry and frustrated with the woman's old world traditions, but always she knew that beneath all of that lay nothing but adoration and worry, a mother's constant companions. She thought she understood fairly well for a fifteen-year-old girl.

Sixteen, she reminded herself. *Sixteen, today.*

"I love you, Ma."

They both seemed surprised she'd said it out loud. It had never been common to speak of love, though they both felt it all the time.

Her mother smiled, took a long, shuddering breath, and then began to cry. Donika stared at her in confusion. Qendressa turned her face away to hide her tears and raised a hand to forestall any questions.

After a moment, she wiped her eyes. "You all grown, now, 'Nika. Walk with me. Tonight, I tell you the story of how you were born."

"What do you mean, how I was born?"

Her mother smiled and slid her chair back. It squeaked on the kitchen floor. "Walk with me," she said as she stood. "In the woods. How you like. And maybe you learn why you like it so much."

Donika got up, dropping her napkin on the table. Bewildered, she tried to make sense of her mother's words and behaviour, doing her best to push away the hunger inside her and to not think about the fact that Josh had said he'd be out on the corner later, waiting for her if she could manage to get out tonight.

Her mother took her hand. "Come."

Together they left the house. The screen door slammed shut behind them as if in emphasis, the house happy to have them gone. The porch steps creaked underfoot. When her mother led her across the driveway toward the path, Donika hesitated a moment. The woods were hers. She might see other people in there, but something about going into the forest with her mother troubled her. Much as Donika loved her, she didn't want to share.

"Ma," she said, hesitating.

"It won't take long," Qendressa said. "But you need to know the story. Should have told you long time ago. I am selfish."

Donika shook her head. What the hell was her mother talking about?

They walked into the trees. The summer sun had fallen low on the horizon. Soon dusk would arrive. For now, wan daylight still filtered through the thick trees, slanted and pale, shadows long.

"My mother, she knew things," Qendressa began. Her grip on Donika's hand tightened. "How to make two people love. How to heal sickness in body and heart. How to keep spirits away."

Donika tried not to smile. This was what their big talk was about? Old World superstition?

"She was a witch?"

Her mother scowled. "Witch. Stupid word. She was smart. Clever woman. She used herbs and oils—"

"So she was the village wise woman, or whatever," Donika said, and it wasn't a question this time. She thought it was kind of adorable the way her mother said herbs—with a hard 'H,' like the man's name. But this talk of potions and evil spirits made her impatient, too. "I get that she taught you all of that stuff, but how can you still believe it after living in America so long?"

Her mother stopped and pulled her hand away. "Will you be quiet and listen?"

The anguish in her mother's voice stopped her cold. Donika had never heard her mother speak that way. The daylight had waned further and now the slices of sky that could be seen through the thatch of branches had grown a deeper blue. Not dusk yet, but soon. It seemed to be coming on fast.

"I'll listen," she said.

Her mother nodded, then turned and continued along the path. Donika watched the ground, stepped over roots and rocks. The woods were strangely quiet as dusk approached, with the night birds and nocturnal animals not yet active and the other beasts of the forest already making their beds for the evening.

"She knew things, my mother. And so she taught me these things, just as I teach you to cook the old way. When I married, I made a good wife. Even then, I made money as a seamstress, just like now. But always my husband knew that one day the people in our town would start to come to me with their troubles the way they came to my mother. The ones who believed in superstitions."

Donika couldn't help but hear the admonishment in those words. Her mother wanted her to know she wasn't the only one who still believed in such things.

"There were spirits there, in the hills and the forest. Always, there were spirits, some of them good and some terrible. Other things, too. Believe if you want, or don't believe. But still I will tell you.

"I loved my husband. He had strong hands, but always gentle with me. Some people, they acted strange around my mother and me, but not him. He was so kind, and smiled always, and when he laughed, all the women in our town wanted to take him home. But it was me he loved. We talked all the time about babies, about having a little boy look just like him, or a little girl with my eyes.

"And then he dies. Such a stupid death. Fixing the roof, he slips and falls and breaks his neck. No herbs or oils could raise the dead. He was gone, Donika. Always his face lit up when he talked of babies and now he was dead and the worst part was there wouldn't be any babies."

The patches of sky visible up through the branches had turned indigo. The dusk had come on, and full darkness was only a heartbeat away. It had happened almost without Donika realizing, and now she heard rustling in the underbrush and in the branches above. A light breeze caressed her bare arms and legs and only then did she realize how warm she'd been.

She halted on the path and stared at her mother, eyes narrowed. "What are you talking about, Ma? What the hell are you . . . you had *me*."

Qendressa slid her hands into the pockets of her skirt as though fighting the urge to reach out and take her daughter's hand. Her features were lost in the gathering darkness.

"No, 'Nika. You came later."

"How could I—"

"Hush now," her mother said. "Just hush. You want to know. You need to know. So hush."

Something shifted in the branches right above them and an owl hooted softly, sadly. Her mother glanced up sharply and scanned the trees as though the mournful cry of that nightbird presented some threat.

Donika shook her head, more confused than ever. "Ma?"

Qendressa narrowed her eyes and took a step away from her daughter, casting herself in shadows again. "You know the word *shtriga*?"

"No."

"No." Her mother sighed, and the sound was enough to break Donika's heart. "I was so much like you, 'Nika. Still very young, though already I was a widow. So many questions in my head. I walked in the forest always, cold and grieving and alone. I knew I had to have a baby, to be a mother. I would never love another, but a child I could love. I could have what my husband and I dreamed of . . . even if part of it is *only* a dream.

"One night I am in the forest, walking and dreaming, and I hear voices. Some men and some women. I hear a laugh, and I do not like the way it sounds, that laugh. So I walk quietly, slowly, and go through the trees, following the voices. I walked in the forest so much that I learned to make almost no noise at all. From the trees, I see them, two women and three men, all with no clothes. I felt ashamed to spy on them like that. I would have gone, but could not look away.

"They looked up at the sky and reached up to their mouths and they slipped off their skins, like they were only jackets. Inside were shtriga. They looked like owls, but they were not. I could not breathe and just watched, praying not to be seen. They flew away. I stood there until I could not hear the wings anymore and then I could breathe again."

Qendressa paused. Donika realized that she had been holding her breath, just the way her mother had described. As the story unfolded, she had pictured it all in her mind, so simple to imagine because of all of the hours she had spent walking these woods by herself and because, just last night, she and Josh had been naked beneath the trees and the night sky. But this . . . her imagination could only go so far.

"Ma, you must have been dreaming. You said you were dreaming, right? You fell asleep. That couldn't have been real."

Her mother approached her, stepping into the moonlight, and Donika saw the tears streaking her face. Sorrow weighed on her and made her look like an old woman.

"No?" Qendressa said.

Somewhere in the trees, an owl hooted. Donika flinched and looked up, searching the branches, just as her mother had done. A second owl replied, sharing the sad song.

"Even when they were gone, I could not go away. I should have run. I did not know when they would be back for their skins, the shtriga, but I knew that they *would* be back. The shtriga went 'round the town and through the forest and they hunted the lustful and licentious. They had the scent of those whose lust was strongest, and the shtriga drank their blood to sate their own hungers."

"Sounds like a vampire," Donika said.

Qendressa frowned, shaking her head. "No, 'Nika. Vampires are make-believe. The shtriga are real. But the power they have, it has rules. The shtriga must come back to its skin by morning.

"My mother had told me many stories of them. How they grow. How to stop them. And I dreamed of a baby, 'Nika. It hurt my heart, I wanted it so much.

"I knew I only had till morning, and maybe not even that long. I ran into the clearing and I took the skin of one of the women, with her beautiful black hair. I carried it home, hurrying and falling, and I locked the door behind me. I took my scissors and sat at my work table and I cut the skin of the shtriga. I cut away large pieces and later I burned them.

"And then I started to sew. With the shtriga's black hair for my thread, I patched the skin back together, only now it was not the skin of a grown woman, but the skin of a baby girl."

Donika shivered and hugged herself, staring at her mother's eyes shining in the moonlight, tears glistening on her face.

"No," the girl said.

When her mother spoke again, her voice had fallen to the

whisper of confession.

"I sat and waited in the corner of the room, in a chair that my husband had loved so much. A little before dawn, the shtriga comes looking for her skin. I left the window open and the owl flew in and landed on my work table. It spread its wings and ducked its head down to pick at the skin it had left behind. The owl pushed itself into the skin.

"When the sun rose, a baby girl lay on my work table and she cried, so sad, so lonely. I took her in my arms and rocked her and I sang to her an old song that my mother loved, and my baby loved it, too. She didn't cry anymore."

Qendressa bit her lip and gazed forlornly at her daughter. Through her tears, she began to sing that same old song, a lullaby that Donika knew so well. Her mother had been singing it to her all her life.

"I don't believe you."

But then the owls began to cry their mournful song again, hooting softly, not only one or two but four or five of them now. Donika saw the fear in her mother's eyes as the woman searched the trees. Qendressa put out a hand to her.

"Come, 'Nika. We go home."

Donika stared at her.

"I don't believe you," she said again.

But she could taste the salt of her own tears and feel them warm upon her cheeks. She backed away from her mother's outstretched hand, shaking her head. Denials rose up in her heart and mind but somehow would not reach her lips.

She knew. The hunger churned in her gut, gnawing at her, and she knew.

"Why did you tell me?"

Qendressa sobbed. "Because you are not my baby anymore, 'Nika. You sixteen. Sixteen years since that night. I know the stories. You are shtriga now."

Donika felt something break inside her. She spun on one heel and ran. Low branches whipped at her face and she raised her arms to protect herself. She stumbled over roots and rocks that she'd always avoided before. The owls hooted above her and now she could hear their wings flapping as they moved through the trees, keeping pace.

In her life, she had never felt so cold. No matter how fast she ran, no matter how her pulse quickened, she could not get warm. Her sobs were words, denials that felt as hollow as her own stomach. The hunger clutched at her belly and a yearning burned in her. Desire.

Josh. She summoned an image of him in her mind and focused on it. They could run together. He would hold her. He could touch her, and maybe, for a little while, the madness and hunger would fade.

A numbness came over her, but Donika began to get control of herself. She still wept, but silently now. Her feet were surer on the path. She saw the stone wall to one side and the firepit ahead and the memory of last night gave her something to hold on to.

Soon, she found herself at the end of the path, stepping out into the backyard of the bitter old couple. An owl hooted, back in the woods, and she hurried away from the trees, wanting to leave the forest behind for the first time in her life.

She strode across the back lawn unnoticed. A dog barked nearby, the angry yip of a canine scenting the presence of an enemy. Donika made her way between houses, but as she came in sight of the corner where Josh would be waiting, she paused.

Hidden in the night-black shadows of those homes, she watched him. Josh sat on the curb, smoking a cigarette, content to be by himself. He waited for her, and didn't mind. In the golden glow of a nearby streetlamp, he was beautiful to her. They would run through the dark woods together once again, but this time she would give herself to him.

Desire clawed at her insides. She ran her tongue out to wet her lips. She could almost taste the salt of his skin, and the urge to do so, to taste him, tugged at her.

A smile touched her lips and she almost called out.

Donika's smile faded.

No, she thought. *It isn't love. Desire isn't love. Hunger isn't.*

She understood hunger now. Donika fled silently back into the woods, where she belonged. The owls cried and flew with her. Loneliness clutched at her until she realized that she wasn't alone at all. She had never been alone.

The woods received her with love. She could never go back to her mother's house. Not now.

She hurtled along the path and then left the trail, breaking off into rough terrain. She raced through the woods, leaped fallen branches, and exulted in the night wind whispering around her. Her tears continued to fall but they were no longer merely tears of sorrow. Her mind whirled in a storm of emotions, but beneath them all, the hunger remained.

Surrendering to the forest and the night, she stripped her clothes off as she ran, paying no attention to where she left them. The moonlight and the breeze caressed her naked flesh and now the warmth returned to her at last. She felt herself burning with want. With need. And then she could feel her skin hanging on her the same way that clothes did and she reached up to the edges of her mouth and pulled it wide like a hood, slipping it back over her head.

Donika slid from her skin and, at last, took flight, returning to the night sky after sixteen very long years. Reborn.

She flew through the trees, thinking again of the boy she desired, thinking that maybe he would be inside her tonight after all, and they would both get what they wanted.

Her mouth opened in a low, mournful cry. It was a tune she'd always known, a night song that had been in her heart all along.

THE HISS OF ESCAPING AIR

Courtney Davis crossed Montana Avenue on strappy, five-hundred-dollar heels, her sheer dress cascading around her upper thighs with every swing of her hips. Enormous black sunglasses hid most of her face even as they drew attention to her identity, and her blonde hair fell in shoulder-length waves that perfectly framed her features.

The world knew her business—thanks to TMZ and the tabloids, they knew every detail of her divorce proceedings, and had seen her in positions not meant for public inspection—but they could not possibly know of her crime.

A car honked at her and she fought the instinct to give the driver the finger, just in case someone should film her doing so. Then she remembered why she had chosen Santa Monica for this meeting in the first place—no paparazzi. Montana Avenue was trendy as hell, but the celebrities generally hung out elsewhere. The shops and boutiques and restaurants here were for the wives of wealthy men, the producers and studio heads and lawyers who raked in all the real Hollywood cash.

In a few short years, Courtney had gone from waitress to actress to sexy screen star to celebrity, and then her manager had taken her up to a meeting at the home of James Massarsky, to discuss a part, and she'd become a Hollywood wife. In his thirty years in the industry, Massarsky had gone from mailroom to major talent agent to studio boss to independent producer. Part of his appeal, to Courtney, was that his initial rise mirrored her own. But James had been around longer, and in that time he'd earned his reputation as a bastard and as a brilliant businessman, picking up seven Oscars and three wives along the way. He was a man who got what he wanted, and after their first meeting, what he wanted was Courtney Davis.

She hurried across the street, her heels clicking on the pavement.

She hopped onto the sidewalk, pretending to be oblivious to the handful of people who shot her the "hey, isn't that—" stare that so many of the semi-famous endured in L.A. People dined on outdoor patios, but she passed those by without looking inside, just as she did the little dress shop and the new Kismetix cosmetics store. The women she knew who shopped and lunched and lingered in Santa Monica were not her real friends, but other Hollywood wives—and she could ignore them if she wanted to.

That was good. Courtney wasn't in the mood to talk.

You're a fool, she told herself, as she avoided the water dripping from the edge of an awning. It had rained this morning, but the sky had turned perfectly blue afterward. The sun shone its warmth down upon her, and she shook her head with the moment of her epiphany.

You could've met this guy anywhere. Burbank. Sherman Oaks. Hell, she could've arranged for her accomplice to meet her up in Santa Barbara at some roadside bar, like in an old-time mystery novel. Somewhere with a million times less chance that someone she knew would see her, and know she'd been here.

When she had made arrangements for this meeting, she had been tempted to suggest drinks at the Ivy in Beverly Hills. She'd have felt at home there, with friends around her. But the Ivy was more than just a see-and-be-seen sort of place. It was Paparazzi Central. Photos and videos would be inevitable, and she didn't want that.

Montana Avenue wasn't much better, really. Her chances of being seen by someone, of word getting back to James, were high. But in the end, though she hoped to delay it as long as possible, she had decided it wouldn't matter much if her soon-to-be ex-husband found out about today's rendezvous. He would likely think what anyone seeing her in some clandestine coziness in a Santa Monica restaurant would think—that she was having an affair.

If only it were that simple.

At the corner, she turned off Montana onto a narrow side street, where trendy crumbled away like all Hollywood façades. She paused there, in the shade of a tree that grew up out of the sidewalk, and stared at the patio outside Lemongrass, the little bistro halfway down the block.

There were other reasons for her wanting this meeting to take place somewhere familiar. Outside of her Los Angeles, the places she hung out, the trendy clubs and shopping districts and the studio lots, the rest of the world seemed brittle and unreal, the dry husk of an empty beehive, no more substantial than dust and cobwebs. Ever since the day she had arrived in L.A., shitbox car loaded up with all her earthly belongings, Wisconsin license plate revealing the almost absurd truth about her small-town-girl past and her sickeningly trite Hollywood dreams . . . ever since then, she had known that this place was what she had lived for. She needed to be a part of this world.

Hollywood had a vibrant urgency that made it matter. The rest of the world was the façade. Whatever happened to her—celebrity, divorce, scandal—it only mattered here. Courtney Davis no longer believed she really existed outside this place.

She understood the shallowness of this thinking, and had come to terms with it. The small town Wisconsin girl still lived inside of her. She tried to be a good person, to create a life full of love and kindness. But somehow that person co-existed with the all-night clubbing that had gone on before she married James Massarsky, and the bitterness that marriage had brought her.

So, yes, perhaps James would learn more quickly than she would like about her meeting today. But Courtney wondered, now, if that had been her plan, subconsciously, all along. Maybe she wanted James to find out, so that he would know who it was that had hurt him, and stolen from him.

Lemongrass must have had live music out on the patio, for she heard sweet, gentle guitar rising on the light breeze, accompanied by a rich, warm voice. The song was unfamiliar to her, but the singer had an aching sadness in his tone, and it settled around her heart and made her linger a few seconds longer under the tree.

"This is a little strange, don't you think?" Courtney asked.

Behind the wheel of the car, Don Peterson shrugged. "Nah. Guys like this, they think in 'old Hollywood' terms. Every one of them wishes they could have been Jack Warner and acts like the fucking Godfather. Massarsky is really the last of a dying breed, younger than the rest but with the same mindset. That's why he's an independent producer, now. There's only so long an agency or a studio is going to let themselves be run around by a guy whose life is a scorched-earth policy. That's what boards of directors are for. So now Massarsky works for himself."

"Jesus, Don," Courtney said. "That really makes me want to be in one of his movies. Thanks for the pep talk."

Her manager laughed. "Relax. This is the old Hollywood thing. The director wants you. The producers want you, even though they're bitching because you won't show your tits—"

"You know—"

He held up a hand even as he steered them in amongst the trees.

"I know, Courtney. This is me, remember? No nudity. I get it, and I respect it. That's your choice. Massarsky likes to meet people, look them in the eye and shake their hand. It's an old-school thing. Once you get his seal of approval—which Brad is one hundred percent sure you will—you'll never have to deal with him directly again. This isn't an audition. You'll talk. He'll try to impress you. You'll be impressed, or pretend to be. And we'll go. End of story. Don't be nervous."

She smiled. "I'm not nervous."

"You shouldn't be."

"I am."

"I know."

Don drove up winding roads that took them into hills higher than Courtney had ever known existed in L.A. She'd taken Coldwater Canyon many times, but this was different. Commuters drove that road. Up here, it was all private, a world apart from the buzz of life in the city.

A white wall sprang up to the right. In places she could see over it, down into valleys where massive, sprawling estates covered acres, with neighbours half a mile distant from each other. Soon they climbed a steep curve to find a gatehouse waiting at the top, complete with a uniformed guard, security cameras, and more fences. Don pulled up to the gatehouse as the guard leaned out.

"Courtney Davis and Donald Peterson to see James Massarsky."

The guard checked a clipboard, nodded without saying a word, and reached into the gatehouse. The gates swung slowly open. Don thanked the guard and drove through, and then they were travelling along a much narrower, even more winding road. Tall hedges lined the sides. There were wooden fences, stone walls, even warnings about electrified gates.

"Look at that," Don said.

He pointed to a small bit of exposed property on the left side of the road, where a trio of deer nibbled grass in amongst a few trees.

"That's so weird. What are they doing in here?" Courtney said, mostly to herself.

"I'm sure they're stocked, like fish in a private pond. The whole neighbourhood is fenced in. The deer are just more pretty things to look at."

Courtney said nothing more until they pulled into the long driveway of Massarsky's home, wondering how much of the man's life was defined by acquiring pretty things to look at. Massarsky had built his legend on too much alcohol and too many women, a childish temper, and a savant's eye for choosing film projects. But he had to have some serious smarts to have gotten to the top and surviving there for so long.

The stone driveway ended in a circle, off of which there were several individual parking spaces, each separated by a thin strip of perfectly manicured grass. Two slots had cars already in them, each pristine and elegant. Don parked in the last available slot, and even as they got out of the car and turned toward the house, the front door opened and James Massarsky stepped out.

Massarsky was fifty-six years old and moderately handsome in a tanned, relaxed, country club sort of way. His curly hair was thinning and he had a roundish belly that only added to his casual air. In a pale blue t-shirt and knee-length cargo shorts, all faded and rumpled, he didn't look like a Hollywood mogul. Of course, she hadn't met many, and none on his level.

"Hello," he said, smiling. "I saw you drive up. Sorry for the grubby look. I was out in the garden, checking on my tomatoes, and sort of lost track of time."

Courtney smiled. He grew tomatoes.

"I'm James Massarsky," he said, putting out his hand.

"Don Peterson," her manager said, shaking. "And this is Courtney Davis."

When he took her hand, James Massarsky gave her a paternal sort of smile. His grip was firm and welcoming.

"Hell, I know who you are," he said. "Thirty years in this business hasn't broken me of my love of movies, yet. You were fantastic is that Scorsese picture, Courtney. What I want to know is if that performance came from you, or from Marty's cameras and a great script."

Off guard, she gave him a small shrug. "I've wondered the same thing. But thanks, just in case."

Massarsky hadn't let go of her hand, and now he looked at her oddly and squeezed a bit tighter. Then he laughed softly and looked at Don.

"You've got quite an actress here," he said, obviously having already forgotten Don's name. "She's gonna take you far. Why don't we go in the den and we can talk about whether or not I'm going to be along for the ride."

"Sounds good," Don said.

Massarsky pointed them along a corridor and shut the door, which had been standing open. Wonderful breezes swept through the house and sunlight rushed in from the tall windows in every direction.

"Marta!" the producer called toward the back of the house.

"Yes, Mister?" a thickly accented woman's voice replied.

"Can we get some drinks in the den, please?" Massarsky said. He turned to his guests. "Want a soda? Juice? Something harder?"

"Juice would be great," Courtney said.

Don nodded. "For me, too."

Massarsky smiled. "Marta, three of those pomegranate juices, okay? We'll be back in the den. Don't forget the ice!" He glanced at them again. "You've gotta have the ice. Makes it sweeter, somehow."

Pomegranate juice. Courtney said nothing. Massarsky hadn't even asked if they liked pomegranate juice. She'd had it in martinis before, but never on its own, and knew it had a sharpness to it. It wouldn't have been her first choice, but there was no arguing with James Massarsky. He was the sort of man who was used to deciding what other people would like to drink.

The rest of the house—what she could see of it as they passed through—was bright and airy, a true Hollywood palace of the sort that she had only ever seen in movies or on television or in magazine layouts. But as they made their way back into the den, they passed into dark corners of the man's home, a kind of living museum of Massarsky's history in the industry. Bookshelves were lined with leather-bound volumes of the scripts of every movie he had ever had a hand in, with no distinction between the classics and the crap. Photographs on the walls in the same hall showed Massarsky with a who's-who of Hollywood royalty, some in their prime, but many more recent. Jack Nicholson, Meryl Streep, Jodie

Foster, Will Smith, Steven Spielberg, and Clint Eastwood. There were photos with four American presidents and a handful of sports stars as well. Some of the photographs had clearly been cropped to remove non-famous faces. In several, the arms or hands of those who'd been removed still remained in the pictures. Courtney assumed that the attractive blondes who recurred in several of the photos were Massarsky's ex-wives.

The den itself was darkest of all. The blinds were open, but the room seemed to swallow sunlight. The brown leather furniture and rich wood of the shelves and tables and the mantelpiece over the fireplace embraced them all. As Don and Massarsky took seats on creaking leather, Courtney wandered a bit, examining some of the odd knick-knacks that sat on shelves along with more bound scripts and a lot of books that looked unread, spines unbroken.

"Go ahead and look around," Massarsky said, though she'd already begun. "There are all sorts of odd mementoes in this house. I'm a collector. I've acquired hundreds of bits of Hollywood history over the years, not to mention the folklore of the industry."

"Folklore?" Courtney asked.

Massarsky laughed. "You don't want to hear this."

She smiled. "I do."

"Some of it's gruesome stuff, some sensational in that old Hollywood gossip rag kind of way. You know, the costume Lauren Bacall was wearing the first time she and Bogart made love. It was on the set of *To Have or Have Not*. That sort of thing."

Courtney liked that he had said *made love* instead of *had sex,* or something even cruder. Massarsky was an old-fashioned sort of man, befitting his age, the sort who might be a barbarian in the presence of other men, but still knew how to act the gentleman.

She cocked her head curiously and picked up a small glass cube. Inside, three yellowed nuggets rattled. She turned toward him.

"Are these—?"

"Teeth? Yes. Bobby DeNiro had them knocked out during the

filming of *Raging Bull*. I bought them from Jim Feehan, the old-time boxer who trained DeNiro for that film. They're the real thing."

Don, who'd been keeping his mouth shut until now, probably wanting her to establish a rapport with Massarsky, couldn't stay quiet any longer.

"How can you be sure?" the manager asked.

Massarsky might have been offended, but he smiled. "I asked DeNiro."

"He didn't mind that you had them?" Courtney asked, amazed.

Massarsky spread out on the chair, relaxing, king of his castle. "Far from it. You want to know the truth? A lot of these things have legends around them, like they've got some kind of Hollywood magic. In the late seventies, I knew guys who claimed that in the Golden Age, there were real muses in this town, captured or brought to life or summoned, I don't know. But I'm talking real muses, like in Greek mythology. Writers and directors and studio bosses worshipped these women, and they got genius in return."

Courtney and Don both stared at him, unsure what to say.

The producer laughed. "I'm not saying I believed them. But when I say these guys believed, I'm totally serious. They bought into it, hook, line, and sinker. Anyway, a lot of the stuff I've collected has that kind of lore around it. But most of it is just weird and fascinating to me. The story behind DeNiro's teeth is this—after he had them knocked out, he went to his dentist, who brought in a doctor. Turned out the mercury in the fillings he had in those teeth had been poisoning him."

"So losing those teeth might've saved his life?" Don asked.

"I wouldn't go that far," Massarsky said. "Still, it's a great story."

At that point, Marta arrived with a tray bearing three tall glasses of pomegranate juice, each with a slice of strawberry on the rim and full of ice. Courtney was surprised there weren't little tropical umbrellas in there as well.

The woman vanished as quickly and quietly as she appeared.

"All right," Massarsky said, "more chitchat later. I'll even give you a tour if you want. Right now, let's talk about *this* movie. *Daughter of the Snows*. What appeals to you, Courtney? This isn't the sort of thing most people would expect from you."

She smiled as she came around the leather sofa and took a seat, purposely placing herself between Don and Massarsky, who sat in matching chairs at either end of the coffee table.

"That's exactly why I want it. It's not about being beautiful or witty, it's about pain and survival. It's the kind of film where what's going on in the actor's eyes is at least as important as the words coming out of her mouth."

Caught sipping his pomegranate juice, Massarsky paused and regarded her carefully, without any trace of a smile. The mask of easy confidence had slipped, and she saw the man beneath, shrewd and intrigued and more than a little bit lonely.

"You actually meant that," he said.

Courtney nodded. "Of course."

Don Peterson's presence in the room was completely forgotten. The two of them looked at one another for several long seconds, and then Massarsky's smile returned.

On the patio outside Lemongrass, the guitarist launched into another song Courtney didn't know, a sweet, slightly upbeat love song he introduced as "Everything Under the Sun." She left the shade of the tree on the corner of Montana and continued down the side street, staying on the opposite sidewalk from Lemongrass. With every step, more of the outdoor dining area became visible, and through the five sets of open French doors she could see many of the tables inside as well.

Just inside the doors, off the patio, a thin, fortyish man she knew as Wilkie sat with his back to the street. From this angle she could only make out part of his profile and his thick tangle of black hair, but it couldn't be anyone else. He sat alone at a table for two, and opposite him, a red balloon had been tied to the back of the empty chair. It danced a bit with the breeze coming off the patio, and she felt her chest tighten. If it came loose somehow, it might be carried out the open doors by the wind, might float off into the sky, the ultimate children's tragedy, and yet perhaps far more than that.

Wilkie seemed unafraid.

But why should he be afraid? After all, it was only a balloon.

When they returned home from three weeks in the Mediterranean, the honeymoon she had always dreamed of, Massarsky—now "James" to her—showed his new wife the last, most precious items in his strange collection. They were all bits of Hollywood history, oddities with charming or gruesome tales behind them, and her husband had become the curator of his own little museum, in a room he called the library, to which only he had the key.

"Finally," he said, turning with a ringmaster's flourish, passing through shafts of light coming through the tall windows, dust eddying in air so infrequently disturbed. "The crown jewel."

James pulled a gold, braided cord and a small curtain drew aside, as though to reveal some tiny stage upon which puppets might perform. But this was no puppet theatre. Behind the little curtain was a rectangular glass case thirty inches high and twelve wide, within which rested a single, red balloon, its string hanging beneath it and coiling at the bottom of the case.

Courtney arched an eyebrow, chuckled a bit, and reached out for her husband's arm. "A balloon?"

He looked at her, this man who had made her so happy, who believed in her so thoroughly, and his eyes sparkled with mischief.

"Not just any balloon. I'm going to assume you've never seen the film, *The Red Balloon*. Mostly, I'm assuming so because, as far as I know, only a few hundred people in the world have ever seen it in its completed form. While he was shooting *Cimarron*, the director

Anthony Mann got a script from Leigh Brackett, who had adapted *The Big Sleep* in '46 and then done damned little until *Rio Bravo* in '59. Glenn Ford was starring in *Cimarron*, and Mann convinced him to star in *The Red Balloon*. They did the picture for MGM in 1960, but it was never released. Somebody—I've heard a lot of names, from Jack Warner to David Selznick to Bob Hope, believe it or not—bought the film from MGM and put it in a vault somewhere. It's never been released. Ford went straight into making *Pocketful of Miracles*, basically as an apology from MGM."

Courtney waited a moment before urging him on. "And? Why did whoever it was not want the movie released?"

James Massarsky smiled. "Brackett's script—and Mann's movie—was about a Chicago mobster who was obsessed with a red balloon. The balloon never lost its air, never went flat, and the mob boss believed that as long as he had the balloon in his possession, that he would never be sick or injured, that he wouldn't grow old, and that it might even keep him alive forever. But he had to keep it safe, because if it popped or deflated, he would die. Supposedly, Brackett heard the story from some people she knew who were actually connected to the Chicago mob. The movie ended with the balloon being stolen, and the mob boss dying, but the narrative left it open for the audience to decide if it was all just coincidence, or the truth."

Courtney processed that a moment, then laughed, shaking her head. "You think someone kept that movie from being released because the story was true?" She looked at the glass case. "And you think that's the real thing, right there?"

James brushed her blonde hair from her eyes, leaned in, and kissed her. Then he shrugged, that manic, almost sprite-like mischief still in his eyes. "I've had this thing nearly two years, and it's still inflated. In that time, I haven't had so much as a sneeze. You're the audience, sweetheart. You be the judge. Either way, it's a great story."

"What'd this guy do to you, anyway?"

Courtney thought of all the things she could have said, the way her life and her career and her self-esteem had been disassembled, all of the humiliating examples of her ruination that she could have listed. Instead, she met Wilkie's gaze firmly with her own.

"He broke me."

They sat just inside Lemongrass, half the table in shadow and half bright with sunshine that streamed in through the open French doors. The breeze off the patio warmed her, and the cute, slightly scruffy guitar player continued to play songs that were unfamiliar and yet fun and thoroughly agreeable. On another occasion, drinks with a handsome stranger under such circumstances would have been a pleasure. But Wilkie was a thief, not a date, and Courtney didn't like the way he looked at her.

"You don't look broken to me," he said.

She stiffened, hackles rising. "You don't know me. And who asked you? When Alison gave me your number, she said you were professional and discreet."

Wilkie played with the salt and pepper shakers on the table, a lopsided grin spreading across his face. He picked up his beer—Stella on tap—and took a long sip, watching her over the rim of the glass. When he set it down, he wiped his mouth, staring at her.

"Your friend there, Alison? She doesn't know me very well. I did a job for her once, and I guess I got it done, or she wouldn't have sent you to me. As for the job you asked me to do . . ." he pointed to the red balloon, tied to the back of her chair. "It's right there."

Courtney had ordered a pomegranate martini, aware of the slight irony, if irony was even the word. Symmetry, then? Perhaps. She had taken a few sips from the drink but otherwise it sat untouched in front of her on the table. At first she had wondered if this was indeed the red balloon from her husband's collection, and how she would be able to tell. But the string was just that—a real string, like on a kite, and grey with age—not a thin ribbon like people used these days. Beyond that, she just knew.

The red balloon wasn't something she could have brought up in their divorce proceedings. There were loads of material things that she had asked for in the settlement, from furniture to art to the house in Maine, but if she'd tried to get any part of his personal collection, her lawyer had told her such claims would be next to impossible to justify. But James had *hurt* her, and Courtney wanted to hurt him back.

This was the way.

She took a deep breath, suddenly tired of Wilkie. Why was she sitting here having a drink with this man? Distracted, wanting to be away from here, to be done with him, she reached into her clutch and pulled out a folded envelope, sliding it across the table.

"The rest of your fee," she said. "Feel free to count it."

Wilkie smiled. He had a weathered, surf-bum look about him, but his eyes glittered with intelligence. "No need. I trust you. So, our business is concluded? All done, right?"

"All done," Courtney agreed as she slid back her chair.

"Then you got what you wanted. The balloon's yours. But I've gotta ask . . . why? I know I said 'no questions asked,' so you don't have to answer, but what's so important about a damn balloon that you'd run the risk of hiring someone to break in and take it?"

She hesitated—it wasn't like she owed the guy an explanation—but the genuine curiosity in his eyes got to her. Glancing around the restaurant, wary of being overhead, she gave a slow nod.

"All right. You want the story?"

"I do. It's a weird job, you have to admit."

Courtney smiled thinly. "You don't know the half of it."

And she told him.

Wilkie sat and listened with a bemused expression, frowning now and then until at last she had finished and he cocked his head to one side and gave her an indulgent smile.

"You do realize how nutty that all sounds?"

She paused, playing her own words back in her head. Of course she knew how it sounded. She slid sideways in her chair and set about picking at the loose knot he'd used to tie the balloon string to the chair.

"So this movie," Wilkie went on, undeterred by her silence. "Have you seen it? Did your ex have a copy?"

"Not that I know of. I always assumed he just knew the story about the mobster. He told me only a few hundred people had ever seen the movie and he never claimed to be one of them. The screenwriter, Brackett, probably heard the story in a bar. Just because she wrote the script doesn't mean she believed it."

As Courtney managed to free the balloon from its knot, wrapping the string around one finger, she noticed that Wilkie had begun to stare at it.

"It's just another Hollywood fable," she said. "There are a thousand of them."

Wilkie leaned back in his chair. "True enough. But according to your ex's story, somebody believed it enough to pay a fortune to get MGM to shelve the movie, put it in a vault and never let it out. Whoever did that, they sure as hell believed. And your husband believes it, doesn't he?"

"Completely."

"What about you?" Wilkie asked. "Do you believe it?"

"Of course not," Courtney said automatically.

Wilkie gave her a lopsided grin and leaned forward, studying her. "Bullshit. Look at the way you're holding onto that string. Maybe you wanted that thing just to deprive an asshole of his favourite toy, but you're an actress, too. A Hollywood girl, past her prime—"

"Fuck you, Wilkie," she muttered. "I don't have to—"

"—you can't tell me that a little part of you didn't want it because you think it's going to keep your tits from sagging." He scoffed, shaking his head. "Jesus, immortality from a goddamn balloon."

Courtney slid her chair back, its feet scraping the floor. Several people turned to look but she ignored them, glaring at the thief.

"I don't know if I believe it or not, but I'll tell you this much," she said. "I was with James for nearly five years and in that time I never saw him so much as sneeze. He never had a fever or a bruise, never went to a doctor, never cut himself, never had to take medication for anything. *Anything.*"

As she stood, Wilkie did the same.

"Y'know what?" he said. "I'm going to do you the biggest favour of your life, no charge."

Courtney rolled her eyes and started to turn away. As she did, Wilkie reached out and grabbed hold of the balloon string, tugging it toward him even as he snatched up a fork from the table. She understood his intention instantly, cried out and grabbed his wrist, trying to break his grip on the balloon string. As he struggled against her, she bumped the table, toppling her martini glass, which shattered on the floor even as Wilkie used the fork to puncture the wattled rubber of the balloon's neck.

"No!" Courtney shouted, lunging at him.

Wilkie wrested himself free of her and let go of the balloon string. Courtney slipped and fell to the floor, her left hand slamming down onto shards of her broken martini glass. She cried out in pain and jerked her hand back, still clutching the balloon string in her right.

"Rich people," Wilkie muttered, dropping the fork on the table as he hurried from the restaurant.

Courtney knelt on the floor, shaking as she stared at the large, curved shard of pomegranate-stained glass that stuck up from her palm. She blinked in surprise as she realized that there was no blood. A frown creased her forehead and she could hardly breathe. In disbelief, she plucked the glass from her palm with her right hand, balloon string still twined about her fingers.

The slice left behind by the glass shard closed as she slid it from the wound, flesh sealing itself back up like water flowing in to fill a void. Staring at her unmarred palm, she blinked with the realization that the low hiss she heard came from the balloon. The chatter of voices and clatter of dishes and glasses and silver and the rich, mellow music from the patio seemed to vanish, leaving only this new sound. This deadly sound.

Her body went numb. She felt the colour drain from her face as she staggered to her feet. The hiss of escaping air filled her ears and at last she reacted, grasping the balloon's neck, pinching off the tiny puncture, stopping the leak.

Heart thundering in her chest, she stared at the balloon. It had not lost very much air, was still far from wilting. Could she patch the hole somehow? Maybe.

Courtney glanced around. Most of the patrons studiously ignored her, some whispering, perhaps assuming they'd just witnessed some kind of lovers' quarrel. Only one person, a man sitting by himself, perhaps waiting for someone to join him, studied her curiously. A busboy came toward the table with a dustpan and brush and began to attend to the broken glass. A waitress appeared and started toward her, and Courtney fled, picking up her little clutch bag and exiting through the open French doors, walking amongst the patio crowd. The drinks had already been paid for, so nobody would come rushing after her.

Her heels clicked on the sidewalk as she hurried to the corner of Montana Avenue. Her pulse throbbed in her temples and tears burned at the corners of her eyes. *Oh, my God. Ohmygod.*

She faltered, the strength going out of her as she leaned against the wall outside a hideously trendy boutique. Her fingers hurt from pinching the balloon so tightly between them. She held it in front of her eyes, staring at it, studying it. Did it look a bit flaccid now?

Her lower lip trembled.

Slowly, she moved it up to her ear, and realized that she could still hear the hiss, a slow, quiet seeping sound that was present despite her best efforts, her tightest grip.

Courtney bolted. Eyes wild, she ran along Montana Avenue, past

Kismetix and half a dozen other shops. Perfectly made-up wives and daughters arm in arm, chins in the air, stared at her and made way as she rushed along, desperate to be rid of the balloon.

It had been true all along. She had wanted to hurt James, to deprive him of his prize, and now she had taken possession of it. It *belonged* to her. That meant she would reap the benefits, and suffer the consequences. The ground seemed to tilt underneath her and she whirled in a circle, a scream bubbling up the inside of her throat.

No, no, please no. Not me.

A tan, middle-aged brunette stepped out of Jamba Juice, right next door, and held the door for her little boy, who was busily sipping away at the straw in his drink. Inspiration seized her. Skin prickling with fear, breathless, wild with desperation, Courtney strode over to them and dropped into a crouch right in front of the boy.

"Hey, little buddy. Want a balloon?" she said, thrusting it toward him.

On instinct, the boy reached his free hand out for the dirty string.

"Thanks, but I don't know if—" the mother began.

But the boy had already tightened his fist around the string. Elated, heart unclenching, Courtney let go of the balloon's punctured throat and stepped back. The hiss seemed loud to her, but the mother and son didn't seem to notice. The woman cast an odd look at Courtney, and a slightly distasteful glance at the dirty string in her son's hand, and then thanked her, just to be polite, as she guided her boy a little farther along the sidewalk.

Courtney fled, walking as fast as she could without breaking into a run. Her heart seemed to pound against the inside of her chest and her face still felt flush, but the rush of terror began to subside. *Fucking James.* Never mind Wilkie; the thief hadn't understood what he was doing. But James . . . without even realizing it, he had nearly killed her.

Killed. She froze, catching her breath, raised a hand to her eyes. Jesus, what had she done?

Courtney turned and saw that the mother and son had stopped in front of Kismetix. The woman knelt in front of her boy, their Jamba Juices on the sidewalk, while she tied the dirty string of the balloon around his wrist so he wouldn't lose it. Already it sagged a bit in the air, but they didn't seem to have noticed.

The boy had dark hair, like his mother, and he grinned as he looked at her, cocking his head, making strange faces, just monkeying around the way little children did. He couldn't have been more than four.

What am I? Courtney thought.

"Wait!" she called, running after them.

The mother rose, she and the boy both holding their juices again, and turned to see what the fuss was about. Courtney raced up to them and the woman gripped her son's wrist, taking a protective step in front of him.

"What's wrong—" the mother began.

"I'm sorry. It was a mistake. You have to give it back," Courtney said, the words streaming out too fast, frantic, a jumble. "Please, I'm sorry, I know it's weird, but I shouldn't have given that to him. It's not for him."

The woman scowled. "Excuse me? What the hell are you trying to do? That is so completely not cool."

"I know, and I'm—"

"Just go away," the mother said. She turned her back on Courtney, and marched the little boy along beside her. "Come on, Justin."

"No, listen," Courtney began, grabbing the mother's shoulder and trying to turn her around.

The woman spun, slapping her hand away. "Don't put your hands on me, you psycho. Back off, right now. If you wanted the stupid balloon, you shouldn't have given it away, but you did. My boy is three years old. You can't be all nice and give him something like that and then take it back. Go and buy a new one!"

The little boy tugged on his mother's blouse. "It's okay, Mumma, she can have it."

Courtney's breath caught in her throat and she reached out.

"Forget it," the mother said. "It's the principle of the thing. What's fair is fair."

By now other people had slowed to watch the spectacle unfolding on the sidewalk. Someone had a cell phone out, no doubt getting video of the confrontation. It would be online in minutes, but Courtney barely registered the whispers and the looks of disgust and disapproval from the onlookers.

She lunged for the balloon with one hand, reaching for the boy's wrist with the other.

The mother swore in disbelief and threw her Jamba Juice at Courtney. The plastic cup and straw bounced off of her, bright green slush splashing Courtney's clothes and neck and face. As she reached up to wipe the stuff from her eyes, the woman shoved her hard, and Courtney fell backward, sprawling onto the sidewalk.

"No, please, you don't understand," she pleaded.

"You don't put your hands on my son, you crazy bitch," the woman said, but already her voice was retreating.

Courtney jumped up, calling out, still wiping at her eyes. She blinked to clear her vision, but more people had gathered on the sidewalk. Several of them whispered her name. A man and two women came out of Kismetix to stare.

"Out of the way. Please!" she cried, trying to push through them, but the people wouldn't move.

Someone spoke to her from the crowd, then, a quiet voice, telling her calmly that the police had been called, that she needed to go. Numb and hollow inside, she could only stare over the heads of the people gathered around her. Stare at the red balloon, bobbing happily in the air, wilting even as it receded into the distance. The balloon vanished around a corner as the mother and son walked out of sight.

As kind hands turned her around and got her walking away from the crowd, it occurred to her that she had gotten what she wanted. She had taken away James's most precious possession. She had hurt him.

I win, she thought, her mind and heart brittle. *I get to live.*

Then the tears came, in great, wracking sobs.

I get to live.

ACKNOWLEDGEMENTS

Enormous thanks are due to Brett Savory and Sandra Kasturi at CZP for their patience, good humour, and the loving attention they give to all of their books, as well as all of the original editors of the stories appearing herein. Gratitude always to my agent, Howard Morhaim, my manager, Peter Donaldson, and to Allie Costa and Lynne Hansen, who make a pretty amazing support team. Special thanks to Neil Gaiman for his kind words and advice regarding the final story in this collection.

ABOUT THE AUTHOR

Christopher Golden is the *New York Times* bestselling, Bram Stoker Award-winning author of such novels as *Of Saints and Shadows*, *The Myth Hunters*, *The Boys Are Back in Town*, *Strangewood*, and the upcoming *Snowblind* and *Tin Men*. He has also written books for teens and young adults, including the Body of Evidence series, *Poison Ink*, *Soulless*, and *The Secret Journeys of Jack London*, co-authored with Tim Lebbon. His current work-in-progress is a graphic novel trilogy collaboration with Charlaine Harris entitled *Cemetery Girl*.

A lifelong fan of the "team-up," Golden frequently collaborates with other writers on books, comics, and scripts. He has co-written three illustrated novels with Mike Mignola, the first of which, *Baltimore, or, The Steadfast Tin Soldier and the Vampire*, was the launching pad for the Eisner Award-nominated comic book series, *Baltimore*. As an editor, he has worked on the short story anthologies *The New Dead*, *The Monster's Corner*, and *Dark Duets*, among others, and has also written and co-written comic books, video games, screenplays, and a network television pilot.

Golden was born and raised in Massachusetts, where he still lives with his family. His original novels have been published in more than fourteen languages in countries around the world. Please visit him at www.christophergolden.com.

PUBLICATION HISTORY

"All Aboard," "Under Cover of Night," and "Breathe My Name" were first published as part of the Bram Stoker Award-winning collection *Five Strokes to Midnight*, edited by Gary A. Braunbeck and Hank Schwaeble.

"Put On a Happy Face" first appeared in *Blood Lite 3*, edited by Kevin J. Anderson.

"The Art of the Deal" first appeared in *Lords of the Razor*, edited by Joe R. Lansdale.

"Quiet Bullets" first appeared in *Son of Retro Pulp Tales*, edited by Joe R. Lansdale and Keith Lansdale.

"Thin Walls" first appeared in *Death's Excellent Vacation*, edited by Charlaine Harris and Toni L. P. Kelner.

"Mechanisms" first appeared in *Hellbound Hearts*, edited by Paul Kane and Marie O'Regan.

"The Secret Backs of Things" was first published online at *Horror World* by editor Nanci Kalanta.

"Nesting" first appeared online in *Horror Literature Quarterly*.

"The Mournful Cry of Owls" first appeared in *Many Bloody Returns*, edited by Charlaine Harris and Toni L. P. Kelner.

The original text of "The Hiss of Escaping Air" was published by Peter Crowther at PS Publishing as a limited edition chapbook to coincide with FantasyCon 2008 in the UK. It has been revised considerably for its appearance in this volume.

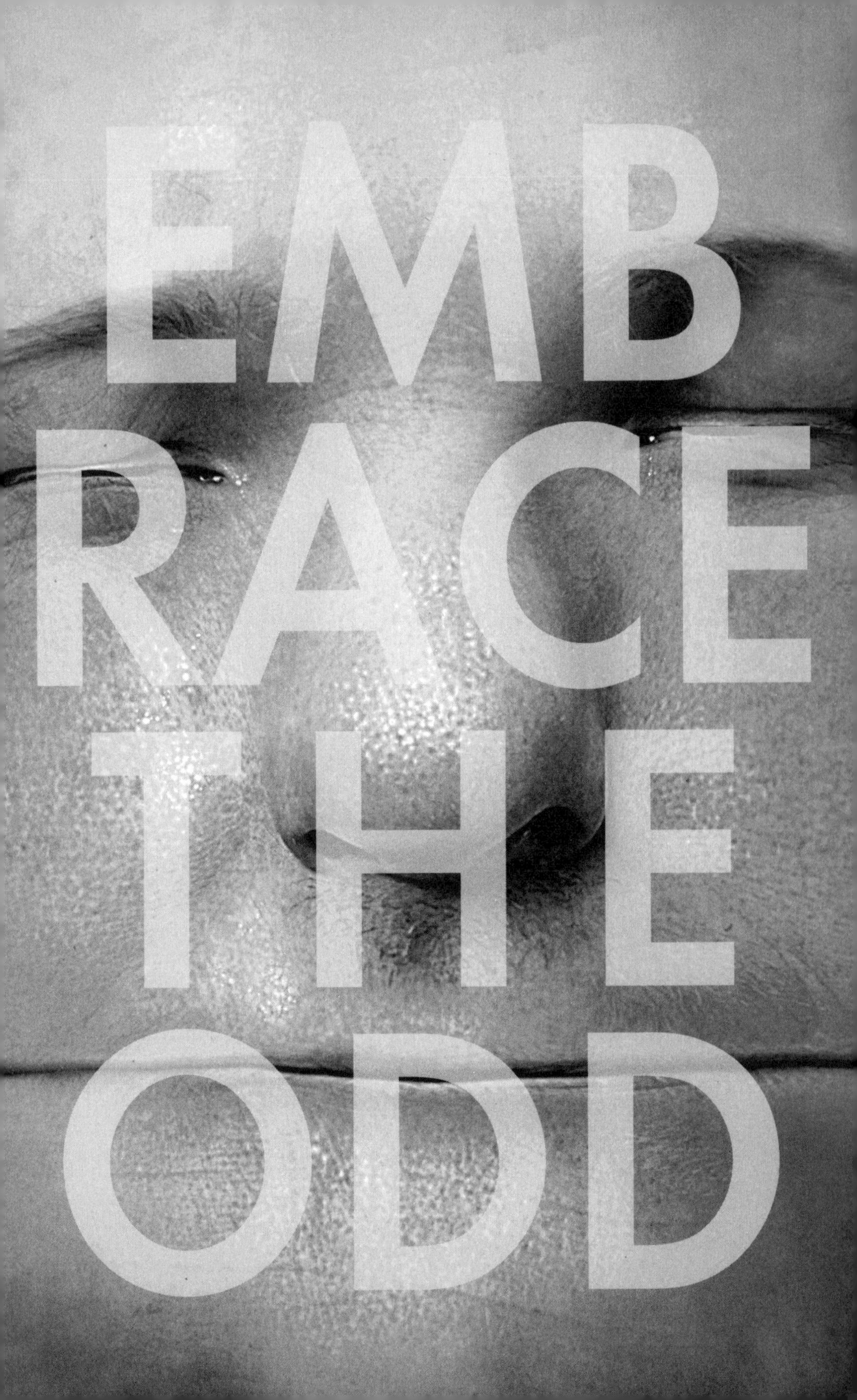
EMB
RACE
THE
ODD

THE INNER CITY
KAREN HEULER

Anything is possible: people breed dogs with humans to create a servant class; beneath one great city lies another city, running it surreptitiously; an employee finds that her hair has been stolen by someone intent on getting her job; strange fish fall from trees and birds talk too much; a boy tries to figure out what he can get when the Rapture leaves good stuff behind. Everything is familiar; everything is different. Behind it all, is there some strange kind of design or merely just the chance to adapt? In Karen Heuler's stories, characters cope with the strange without thinking it's strange, sometimes invested in what's going on, sometimes trapped by it, but always finding their own way in.

AVAILABLE NOW
978-1-927469-33-0

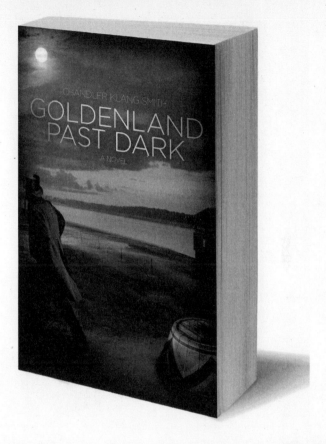

THE WARRIOR WHO CARRIED LIFE
GEOFF RYMAN

Only men are allowed into the wells of vision. But Cara's mother defies this edict and is killed, but not before returning with a vision of terrible and wonderful things that are to come . . . and all because of five-year-old Cara. Years later, evil destroys the rest of Cara's family. In a rage, Cara uses magic to transform herself into a male warrior. But she finds that to defeat her enemies, she must break the cycle of violence, not continue it. As Cara's mother's vision of destiny is fulfilled, the wonderful follows the terrible, and a quest for revenge becomes a quest for eternal life.

AVAILABLE NOW
978-1-927469-38-5

ZOMBIE VERSUS FAIRY FEATURING ALBINOS
JAMES MARSHALL

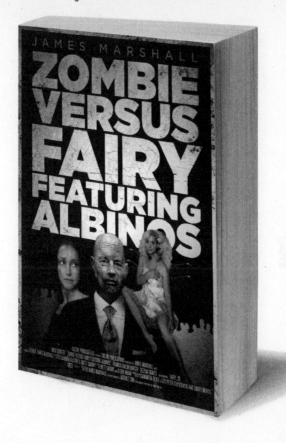

In a PERFECT world where everyone DESTROYS everything and eats HUMAN FLESH, one ZOMBIE has had enough: BUCK BURGER. When he rebels at the natural DISORDER, his marriage starts DETERIORATING and a doctor prescribes him an ANTI-DEPRESSANT. Buck meets a beautiful GREEN-HAIRED pharmacist fairy named FAIRY_26 and quickly becomes a pawn in a COLD WAR between zombies and SUPERNATURAL CREATURES. Does sixteen-year-old SPIRITUAL LEADER and pirate GUY BOY MAN make an appearance? Of course! Are there MIND-CONTROLLING ALBINOS? Obviously! Is there hot ZOMBIE-ON-FAIRY action? Maybe! WHY AREN'T YOU READING THIS YET?

AVAILABLE NOW
978-1-77148-141-0

THE *MONA LISA SACRIFICE*
BOOK ONE OF THE BOOK OF CROSS
PETER ROMAN

For thousands of years, Cross has wandered the earth, a mortal soul trapped in the undying body left behind by Christ. But now he must play the part of reluctant hero, as an angel comes to him for help finding the Mona Lisa—the real Mona Lisa that inspired the painting. Cross's quest takes him into a secret world within our own, populated by characters just as strange and wondrous as he is. He's haunted by memories of Penelope, the only woman he truly loved, and he wants to avenge her death at the hands of his ancient enemy, Judas. The angel promises to deliver Judas to Cross, but nothing is ever what it seems, and when a group of renegade angels looking for a new holy war show up, things truly go to hell.

AVAILABLE NOW
978-1-77148-145-8

THE 'GEISTERS
DAVID NICKLE

When Ann LeSage was a little girl, she had an invisible friend—a poltergeist, that spoke to her with flying knives and howling winds. She called it the Insect. And with a little professional help, she contained it. But the nightmare never truly ended. As Ann grew from girl into young woman, the Insect grew with her, becoming a thing of murder. Now, as she embarks on a new life married to successful young lawyer Michael Voors, Ann believes that she finally has the Insect under control. But there are others vying to take that control away from her. They may not know exactly what they're dealing with, but they know they want it. They are the 'Geisters. And in pursuing their own perverse dream, they risk spawning the most terrible nightmare of all.

AVAILABLE NOW
978-1-77148-143-4

IMAGINARIUM 2013
THE BEST CANADIAN SPECULATIVE WRITING
EDITED BY SANDRA KASTURI & SAMANTHA BEIKO

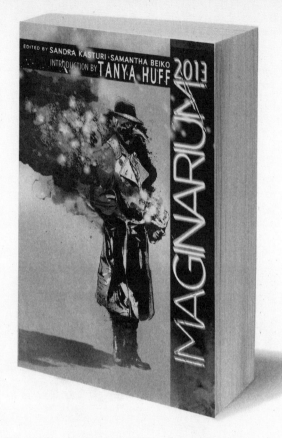

INTRODUCTION BY TANYA HUFF
COVER ART BY GMB CHOMICHUK

A yearly anthology from ChiZine Publications, gathering the best Canadian fiction and poetry in the speculative genres (SF, fantasy, horror, magic realism) published in the previous year. *Imaginarium 2012* (edited by Sandra Kasturi and Halli Villegas, with a provocative introduction by Steven Erikson) was nominated for a Prix Aurora Award.

AVAILABLE JULY 2013
978-1-77148-149-6

CELESTIAL INVENTORIES
STEVE RASNIC TEM

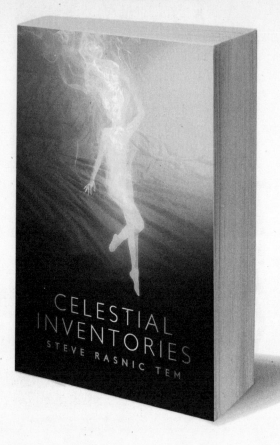

Celestial Inventories features twenty-two stories collected from rare chapbooks, anthologies, and obscure magazines, along with a new story written specifically for this volume. All represent the slipstream segment of Steve Rasnic Tem's large body of tales: imaginative, difficult-to-pigeonhole works of the fantastic crossing conventional boundaries between science fiction, fantasy, horror, literary fiction, bizarro, magic realism, and the new weird. Several of these stories have previously appeared in Best of the Year compilations and have been the recipients of major F & SF nominations and awards.

AVAILABLE AUGUST 2013
978-1-77148-165-6

THE DELPHI ROOM
MELIA MCCLURE

Is it possible to find love after you've died and gone to Hell?
For oddball misfits Velvet and Brinkley, the answer just might
be yes. After Velvet hangs herself and winds up trapped in a
bedroom she believes is Hell, she comes in contact with Brinkley,
the man trapped next door. Through mirrors that hang in each
of their rooms, these disturbed cinemaphiles watch the past
of the other unfold—the dark past that has led to their present
circumstances. As their bond grows and they struggle to figure
out the tragic puzzles of their lives and deaths, Velvet and
Brinkley are in for more surprises. By turns quirky, harrowing,
funny and surreal, *The Delphi Room* explores the nature of
reality and the possibilities of love.

AVAILABLE SEPTEMBER 2013
978-1-77148-185-4

CHIZINEPUB.COM CZP

WIKIWORLD
PAUL DI FILIPPO

Wikiworld contains a wild assortment of Di Filippo's best and most recent work. The title story, a radical envisioning of near-future sociopolitical modes, received accolades from both Cory Doctorow and Warren Ellis. In addition, there are alternate history adventures such as "Yes We Have No Bananas" (which critic Gary Wolfe called "a new kind of science fiction"); homages to icons such as Stanislaw Lem ("The New Cyberiad"); collaborations with Rudy Rucker and Damien Broderick; and a posthuman odyssey ("Waves and Smart Magma").

AVAILABLE SEPTEMBER 2013
978-1-77148-155-7

MORE FROM CHIZINE